HEART OF THE STEAL

Heart of the Steal #1

AVON GALE & ROAN PARRISH

PHILTRE PRESS

Edited by Julia Ganis, JuliaEdits.com
Cover design by Natasha Snow
First edition, July 2017

ISBN: 978-0-9989671-3-4
Print Edition

For people falling in love despite the odds.

CHAPTER 1

Will

I'D NEVER UNDERSTOOD the appeal of parties. That my twin sister was a party planner and therefore I was currently obliged to attend this one, well…at least there was free top-shelf whiskey.

I sipped my drink as Charlotte made her way over to me. I braced for her usual "Stop scowling, Will," though no doubt she'd say it with a smile. Party-mode Charlotte was as smooth as the expensive bourbon I was currently enjoying.

"Have you tried the mini asparagus quiches?" Charlotte asked instead, linking her arm with mine. "They have Gruyère and dill and are to *die* for."

"I did. They're delicious." Trying the appetizers had given me something to do besides talk to strangers.

She smiled, surveying the crowd with a satisfied look. "It's going well, don't you think?"

"Of course." I raised my glass. "This is as good as the quiches." Better, as far as I was concerned, but I didn't say it. My sister was proud of her hors d'oeuvres. It would've been too hot for whiskey and quiche, if the central air weren't keeping the worst of the D.C. summer heat outside where it belonged. I couldn't say the same for my own apartment.

"It better be. Oakley paid for premium booze." Her eyes darted around the room, cataloguing everything at once. We might have been opposites with regard to extroversion and introversion, but we were both detail-oriented, observant, and appreciated the aesthetic. Of course, I took one look at the well-appointed house with the cathedral ceilings and the fifty-or-so well-dressed rich people and it just made me tired. My sister, on the other hand, looked triumphant.

"So you're pleased?" My sister's event planning company was her pride and joy, and it wasn't easy to make an impression in D.C. Everything here ran on favors and networking. Charlie had been thrilled to get the Oakley contract, even if the guy was a bit of a sleazeball. Oakley had an impressive art collection though, which was the carrot Charlie had dangled to entice me to attend. That, and the premium bourbon and delicious appetizers. Hors d'oeuvres. Whatever.

"Very." She snagged my glass and finished off the whiskey, then glanced at me, as if I was going to say anything. I'd need more than a sip to do her job, and I could always get another one. She pressed the glass back in my hand, and then her eyes went wide. She nudged me and said in a low voice, "My target for the evening has arrived."

I raised my eyebrows. "Fox Fêtes is a cover for assassins? You know I'm going to have to call in that tip."

She laughed. "No, my white whale is here."

I stared at her. "Uh."

"Your literary references need work, Will." She nodded toward a tall man in the center of the room, who I could only see from the back. "Do you know who that is?"

I resisted pointing out my sister was the one with all the

friends, and followed her gaze. All I saw was silver hair in a braid, and I had no idea to whom it belonged. "No, but I'm sure you'll tell me, Captain Ahab."

"That's Amory Vaughn. He's a philanthropist, and he's in charge of the Vaughn Foundation. When I saw his name on the guest list, I knew tonight had to be *perfect*. I checked around, and he isn't loyal to any one party planning company. But I think he should be. Specifically, to mine."

"Ah." I had no idea who he was or what the Vaughn Foundation did, but he must be rich. Who else had foundations named after them? "Have you spoken to him yet?"

"No, I'm still in the plotting stages. First I want the party to speak for me." She glanced at me. "You should introduce yourself though. I hear he's an avid supporter of the arts."

I waited.

"And might just be bisexual like me," she added with a meaningful wink.

Charlotte overestimated my ability to pick up men, considering I'd been single since my only long-term relationship had ended more than ten years ago.

"He's a bit old for me, isn't he?" I said, eyeing that silver-white hair. I might not have been the best at picking up men, but at thirty-four and gainfully employed I didn't think I was quite at the stage where she needed to find me a sugar daddy either. "Are you trying to hook me up with someone who'll drop dead in a few years to help out your business's cash flow?"

"Now that you mention it…" Charlotte winked at me again. "No, he's not that much older than you, I don't think. It's just the hair. See?"

Her white whale had finally turned around, so I got a look at the rest of him. She was right—he looked like he was in his late thirties or early forties. Even from across the room I could tell he had features that were more striking than handsome. I had no intention of trying to lure in a man for the sake of my sister's business, but if I was going to try…he certainly wouldn't be a bad choice.

Of course, it was only hypothetical. "You're a lot more charming than me, Charlie. Maybe you should do the seducing."

"Ew, don't ever say that word." She gave a theatrical shudder. "Also I'm not fucking people to get contracts."

"You'd let me do it though?"

"Yup." She grinned back at me, a less subdued version of my own smile. "I have absolutely no problem with that. Anyway, like I said, he's into art—even that modern art stuff you like."

I liked all kinds of art, including some modern, and old grad school habits died hard, but I'd given up talking about it to Charlie since she was about as interested in art as I was in party planning. "I do want to go see Oakley's collection." Even if I suspected his desire to collect art wasn't motivated by sheer appreciation. Keith Oakley was not the kind of man who had art because he appreciated it. He was the kind of man who had art because it appreciated.

"Excuse me, Charlotte?" One of the catering staff appeared with a table linen crisis and Charlie went off to handle it, allowing me to slip back into my habitual observation. And fine, maybe now I was observing Amory Vaughn more than anyone or anything else at the party.

He was wearing a gray suit that perfectly complemented

his fair skin and hair, and if the effect was any indication it probably cost more than all the top-shelf liquor at this party. At some point my stare must have turned a bit too obvious, because Vaughn turned like he felt my eyes on him and met my gaze steadily. He was too far away to make out his eye color, but I could tell they were pale. Strange that a man who was so...*colorless*...would be the most vibrant thing in the room.

I didn't know much about Keith Oakley—hell, I wasn't even sure exactly what a hedge fund was—but I had a feeling we wouldn't get along. And his guest list didn't seem much more likely to be new-friend material. But Amory Vaughn...I couldn't stop looking at him, even after he'd caught me. And after our eyes met this time, he didn't look away. He held my gaze and the corner of his mouth quirked up, as if he knew I was checking him out. I thought about letting my eyes deliberately wander up and down his body, and see what happened. Thought about, but didn't do it. I was bad at flirting.

He did it to me though. And then he *winked*.

If I *were* good at flirting, I suppose I would have winked back. Since I apparently hadn't gotten any better at it since the last time I'd tried, I just took another sip of whiskey and watched him turn his attention to a woman who'd approached him. I also decided that while I was enjoying watching him, and while the mild flirtation had gotten my blood heated, standing in one spot was making me look like a serial killer. Or a museum docent. Since I was neither, I scanned the room for a less obvious observation spot, and got a refill on my way there.

It was easy to keep track of Amory Vaughn. He was

easily the tallest man in the room. It was more than that though. He had a presence about him—and a crowd, which made sense if he gave away money. While I couldn't follow what he was saying, I caught enough to hear that he had a southern drawl that was pure old money. That I then started thinking about that voice speaking in my ear while in bed was…stupid, since I had zero luck with men and had only had a few one-night stands. But hot. It was also hot.

He saw me watching him again, even from my new vantage point. Our eyes met a few more times, and I couldn't ignore the pleasant tingle of awareness that went through me when it happened. My face felt flushed from more than the whiskey, and if there was ever a time I'd had such a strong physical reaction to a man I'd never even *spoken to*, I couldn't recall it. I savored the feeling, but it also reminded me how long it'd been since I'd heard anyone's voice in my ear in bed that wasn't porn through a set of headphones.

I wanted another whiskey, though I knew I shouldn't have one. The buzz I already had probably explained why I was making eyes at a stranger in a party full of hedge fund managers and investors and…whoever these people were. I was still considering the pros and cons of another drink when I noticed that Mr. Tall, Fair, and Charming was making his way across the room…to me. Looking at me with an expression that clearly said I was the destination he had in mind.

My heart thudded in my chest, and my mouth went dry. I managed to slide my empty glass onto the tray of a passing server before I completely panicked. Staring at an attractive man across the room was one thing. But my mind was blurred by whiskey and a long day of work, and I didn't have the usual mental faculties I would need to navigate a conversation with a stranger. A hot stranger. A confident, stranger whose eyes were locked on mine with a single-mindedness that suggested he had no anxiety whatsoever about casual conversation.

Maybe those drinks were a good thing, Drunk Will encouraged slyly. Drunk Will very often sounded like Charlotte.

It was not a good thing. Knowing me, I'd open my mouth and "I wasn't looking at you" would come out. No, I'd rather keep my one-night stand a hypothetical than ruin it with the stark reality of my terrible flirting skills.

With that conviction, instead of letting the hot man I'd been staring at approach me, I made my getaway downstairs to Oakley's art collection. With no booze, no food, and no schmoozing, it was a much-needed respite. I still felt flushed and too hot, but at least the air was cooler and I was alone with nothing but the muffled sound of the party above me. Most of Oakley's artwork wasn't quite as interesting as the man I'd been subtly eye-fucking, but it was safer. It wouldn't try and talk to me.

I found myself in front of a J.D. Staunton oil painting called *Sunset Down*. Unlike the rest of Oakley's mediocre collection, it was gorgeous, vibrant oranges and reds and yellows blending one into the other. There was a thin line of blue-black at the very bottom of the painting, like the darkness of night lurked just beneath the horizon to swallow the light of the sunset.

"I overheard our esteemed host saying he purchased this painting because it coordinated splendidly with the rug."

The voice raised all the hairs on the back of my neck, and made me wonder if my panicked running off had been read as an invitation.

Maybe it was, said Drunk Will.

Amory Vaughn moved to stand beside me, but his eyes were not on the artwork. I finally turned, reminded myself I was not so out of touch with humanity that I couldn't have a conversation—especially about something I loved—and said, "That doesn't surprise me. He has it lit all wrong too." I gestured. "It's a sunset, and he's lit it like it's the middle of the day."

"And why is that, do you imagine?"

I had to force myself not to shiver at the sound of his voice. I'd always had a thing for voices. It was why I watched porn with earphones. I liked to hear the sounds, the gasps, and the dirty talk, even if it was sometimes absurd.

I glanced around at the other paintings. It was a respectable collection, but nothing was as valuable or interesting as the Staunton. "It's the most expensive, so it gets the spotlight." I glanced at him, trying to think of something to say. "What do you see?" I asked, eventually. When nervous, I fell into familiar habits. Asking questions was definitely familiar.

"Are you asking me about the rug or the painting?" he asked. His eyes were a clear, pale gray, adding to the unusual effect of his hair and his suit.

"The painting," I answered.

He smiled, like I'd missed a joke or he'd been teasing and didn't expect me to answer. If Charlotte could hear my attempt at flirting, she'd weep. Her white whale—and that coveted contract—was about to take a deep-sea dive.

"I think it's lovely." He wasn't looking at the painting. "Reminds me a bit of Turner's colors, only bolder."

Turner was my favorite painter, and I'd written my master's thesis on him. I loved how he rendered the violence inherent in natural disasters with such striking delicacy. I could have talked about that at length if I wasn't fighting my body's reaction to this stranger's scent and the caress of that silky voice. "It's harder to convey subtlety in oils," I said. "And I think the point of the painting is the honesty of it."

"Not something one often finds in D.C.," he murmured, and I gave a genuine laugh. "Are you an investor?" he asked.

I blinked, confused, and then shook my head. "You mean in hedge funds? I don't even really know what those are."

He smiled, and my stomach gave an entirely unwelcome flutter. "I meant in art."

"Oh, no," I assured him. "Just an appreciator. You?"

"Oh, I am definitely an appreciator," he said, his voice a purr. He held his hand out. "I'm Vaughn."

"Will," I said, and reached out to shake his hand. The second our skin touched, I felt my cock start to harden. I knew it'd been a while, but Jesus.

"So, Will, what brings you here?"

"My sister's the event planner. Charlotte Fox." Might as well throw that in there in case I didn't manage to harpoon her whale. I spread my arms out and smiled. "So I'm just here for the good whiskey, the free food, and moral support. You?"

"The asparagus quiche was delicious. Please convey my compliments to your sister. And I suppose you could say I *am* an investor, of a sort. I'm the head of my family's philanthropic foundation, and that means I attend quite a few parties. Most of them are exceptionally dull." He moved closer, and my heart rate kicked up another notch. "I'm finding this one unexpectedly enjoyable, however."

"That because of the art collection?" I asked. Warmth curled in my stomach and spread through me, like the sunset from the Staunton had slipped directly into my veins. He smelled good, Vaughn. I caught eucalyptus and amber, along with something woodsy and natural, like pine. It made my mouth water.

"The Staunton is lovely, but I've seen better." He reached out slowly, eyes still on mine, and drew a single long finger down the lapel of my suit jacket. It was one of the hottest things any man had ever done to me, dressed or undressed; in bed or out. I shivered, and my breath caught in a sharp inhalation. I could see how much he liked my reaction. There was something sly and challenging in his expression before he leaned down and kissed me.

His mouth was hot and his hands were suddenly on my shoulders, giving me a little push until my shoulders hit the wall. I slid a hand around the back of Vaughn's head, fingers caressing the strands of braided hair. I slid my other hand down his chest as we kissed, feeling lean muscle, strong but sinewy. I rested my hand on his stomach as we kissed, as if I could measure the space between us, and I made a sound as we broke apart to breathe.

I did not make out with strangers at parties. I couldn't even really blame the whiskey either. Vaughn was overwhelming, as bold as that goddamn Staunton, and so attractive that the second his mouth met mine I knew I wasn't going to push him away. Vaughn dropped one of his hands and began to boldly rub me through my pants while his mouth did wicked things to my neck.

"You—" I didn't know what to say, so I just pulled him back in and kissed him again. He nipped at my bottom lip with sharp teeth, and I widened my legs as his hands began to work at my belt. There was a momentary pause that I took as him asking for permission, and I gave it with a rough jerk of my head and a choked groan.

Vaughn made short work of my pants and slid his hand inside. His grip was tight and the right kind of rough, his mouth beneath my ear as he jacked me.

"That's it," he whispered in a filthy drawl. "Fuck my hand, come on." He lightly sucked at the skin beneath my ear. "I can feel you're getting close. You are, aren't you?"

It didn't take me long, my senses heightened by the inherent danger of public sex and the suddenness of the encounter. I grabbed at his arm hard and wondered what the fuck I was supposed to do if I came all over myself, but I was far too turned on to even consider stopping him. As if he read my mind through my gesture, he kissed the edge of my ear and said, "I've got this."

It should have been cheesy, but as it was followed up by Vaughn going to his knees in one smooth motion and taking my cock in his mouth, I just gasped incoherently as he swallowed around me, and threw my forearm up against my mouth to muffle my shout as I came down his throat.

The intense orgasm left me shaking and worn out, and I leaned back against the wall and fought to catch my breath and stay on my feet. I vaguely felt Vaughn tucking my spent cock back in my pants and fixing my clothes, and he honest-to-god patted me on the chest as he pulled away. I watched him through half-lowered eyes as he ran a hand over his hair, though I didn't think I'd mussed him at all. He looked as put-together as he had that first moment I'd laid eyes on him.

"Um," I said, graceless and still brain-dead from the orgasm. I made a vague motion that was half wave and half obscene gesture, indicating that I'd return the favor as soon as my legs stopped shaking.

"I'm afraid we're about to have company," he said, and I heard voices and steps approaching. "Unfortunately," he added, and while he looked every inch the cool, calm, and collected ravisher, there was a bit of a flush to his fair skin and his strange, pale eyes now burned with heat.

I smoothed my hands down my own suit, sure that I somehow had *I just got sucked off by a stranger* written all over me. "It was, ah. A pleasure to meet you, Vaughn." I was right back to awkward, apparently.

Vaughn just leaned in and kissed me on the cheek. "The pleasure was all mine, William."

The gallery was slowly filling up with people, and I caught a glimpse of my sister grinning at me from across the room. Two people came up to Vaughn, one of whom was Keith Oakley.

"I heard you're something of an art collector yourself, Vaughn. Did you see my Staunton?" Keith asked. "It's my newest acquisition."

"I did indeed. It's quite something," said Vaughn, and I found myself turning away to hide my smile.

The longer I stood there though, the more I began to fret over what I'd done. I kept glancing at Vaughn, who went right back to socializing like he hadn't just blown me in between million-dollar paintings. He was apparently a popular guy, because most people who came down to the gallery wanted to talk to him about something. I gradually moved away, uncomfortable with the crowd, with wondering if I'd just made a colossal fool of myself, if I was making more than I should've out of a brief moment of pleasure.

I thought about going to Vaughn, giving him my number. Seeing if he wanted to go to an actual museum sometime. Together. On a date. We'd gotten along, and clearly the physical attraction was mutual. Why not? I so rarely met men I connected with, much less had such an intense reaction to—wasn't it at least worth exploring? I was never going to be anything but lonely if I didn't take these kinds of opportunities when they presented themselves.

Instead, I thought about that ominous stripe of black on the Staunton, the night sky waiting to swallow the bold bright lights of a dying day. And I left without saying thank you to my host, or goodbye to my sister, and without giving Amory Vaughn my number. I told myself it was better this way, but I didn't really believe it.

I was in a morose mood when I went back to my apartment in Arlington, though not so morose that I didn't spend some quality time thinking about Vaughn. It had been one of the hottest sexual encounters of my life—all right, probably *the* hottest sexual encounter of my life. But after I'd gotten off thinking about it, when I was lying in my bed covered in sweat with a sticky hand…I felt the pang of loss, knowing that was all it could ever be.

Vaughn might be a Staunton, but I was most certainly a Turner. Bold just wasn't my style.

✧   ✧   ✧

I WOKE UP late the next day, and got ready to go for a run.

But when I opened my door, I found something in the hallway—a very large something—propped up on the wall adjacent to my door.

It was a painting. More specifically, I saw when I opened the crate, it was the Staunton, *Sunset Down*, which was supposed to be hanging in Keith Oakley's gallery.

There was a note taped on the wall above the painting. Hands shaking, I leaned in to read it, knowing better than to touch anything with my bare hands.

I trust you have better lighting.

Underneath was an invitation to what I assumed was his home on Saturday, along with a postscript that said, *The Hugo Boss from last night will suffice. For now.*

I stared at the Staunton and the note, so many warring reactions roiling in my stomach that the thought of a run dissipated to nothing. Shock, anger, and there, just behind my ribcage, a trickle of disappointment.

This morning I'd thought that if nothing else, my unexpected amorous encounter might possibly lead to my sister getting that contract she wanted so badly. And maybe it *would* lead to more. She'd get her Moby, and I'd get my Dick.

Now I had to arrest Amory Vaughn.

CHAPTER 2

Vaughn

THE TREES WERE on fire. The setting sun painted red, yellow, orange, purple in the sky, tipping the edges of the oaks' leaves and firs' needles black against its blaze. The air around my Falls Church home was sweet with lilacs, the smoke from my pipe, and the subtle scent of Arpège from Valerie, who sat next to me at the picnic table strewn with half-eaten wedding cake samples. The taste of sugar was bright on my tongue, even through the smoke and the bourbon.

Maybe a little too much bourbon, if I were being honest. Because though I should have been thoroughly occupied by my best friend on the last evening before her wedding, instead, the leaves weren't the only thing that sunset had set on fire. The swirl of color, so like the Staunton painting that had been the highlight of Keith Oakley's party two nights before, had set my mind ablaze with *him*.

William Fox.

The one who had at first seemed like an ordinary man with unremarkable brown hair and an ill-fitting suit, and had, with a few passionate words, captured my imagination.

He'd introduced himself as "Will." Just Will. I smiled at

the memory of him giving himself to me as easily as his name promised. But if Will was what he gave the world, then I would think of him as William. William Fox. It suited him, with his wary amber eyes and the slinky way he'd moved under my hands. In my mouth. His fingers in my hair, mine wrapped around his hard heat, and then his hips as I swallowed him, clean salt and the musk that was just William Fox.

I cleared my throat as my mouth flooded with saliva at the memory, and spread my legs wider to accommodate my response to the memory of dropping to my knees at the sensibly shod feet of the handsome stranger, and tried to return to the present before Valerie could call me on being distracted.

I swiped a finger through the lavender frosting between layers of green tea cake and licked it off thoughtfully. What was matter-of-fact William Fox's favorite kind of cake? Probably vanilla. And if you teased him about it he probably responded with a logical and well-reasoned explanation of how high-quality vanilla was a complex and delicious flavor, cultural associations notwithstanding. I snorted at the thought.

"This could have been us, you know," Valerie said, voice wistful with bourbon and memories.

"It would have been lovely for the month it lasted," I said. And I meant it. "Before we killed each other, that is." I meant that too.

"Yes, I know." Val sighed with the same combination of resignation and relief she'd always shown about the end of our romantic relationship. "So, do you think you'll ever do this?"

"What, eat wedding cake samples procured under false pretenses on the night before my wedding to the man of my dreams?"

Her swat caught me on the shoulder. "Yes."

"Well, I'm not quite the cake fan you are, truth be told."

Cookies. I was suddenly sure that William Fox was more of a cookie man than a cake one. Chocolate chip cookies, or perhaps ice cream. Mint chocolate chip.

"Very ha," Val said, elegant nostrils flaring. But her gaze was discerning, despite the bourbon.

The truth was that I *had* thought about a wedding to the man of my dreams. I wasn't sure why it had always been a man, given that I swung both ways. Maybe it was the tendency of the wedding industry to be shown from the perspective of women who were assumed to be straight.

But, yes, I had imagined a wedding in the sprawling backyard of the Falls Church house, the lush foliage that surrounded the grounds insulating the festivities from the outside world, the sun filtering through the leaves, turning them to stained glass and dappling the ground below. I had imagined the clean air shot through with laughter and music and conversation, with the smells of food and commingling perfume, cologne, and aftershave. Imagined being magnetized to another man no matter how far apart on the grounds we drifted, the connection between us thrumming like a plucked harp string, vibrating us back together again.

I had, in short, imagined the wedding that was going to happen tomorrow. Because if I couldn't have it for myself, at least I could host it for my best friend.

I cleared my throat. It felt like the lavender frosting had gotten stuck somewhere halfway swallowed and I threw back another sip of bourbon to burn it down.

"I suppose time will tell," I said. I took Val's hand before she could press the matter. "I'm so happy for you." I clinked my glass with hers. "And heaven save Dallas if he treats you like anything less than a queen."

"He wouldn't dare," she said. For all that she wasn't afraid to ask for exactly what she wanted, Valerie was generous and down to earth, and if people treated her like a queen it was only because they were pleased to serve at her behest.

She sipped her bourbon, head tilted back to look at the sky, ash blonde hair hanging over the back of her seat. The stars were always visible here, except on the foggiest of nights, and for as long as I could remember that had given me comfort—the sense of being connected to a place in the universe. A fixed point where I could watch the angle of the stars change with the seasons.

I had a loft in D.C. as well, a modern loft gleaming with stainless steel appliances and polished poured cement floors and countertops, but the Falls Church house felt like home. It wasn't just the stars or the beauty of the leaves changing in the autumn and the flowers blooming in the spring. It was the history. My family's home had played host to generations of Vaughns, and when I was here I felt connected to something larger than myself. It was what made my work feel worthwhile, remembering that the work of generations of my family had produced the wealth that I now divested myself of to help others create things for themselves and their own families' futures.

So what if I was forty-two and that if things kept going the way they had been then my family name and the dollar signs attached to it would be the only things I left behind? So what if the things that brought me the greatest thrills weren't things I could ever take credit for—well, the less said about those the better.

I told myself I was just melancholy at the thought of my best friend getting married, even if it didn't change anything between us. Melancholy that I'd be hosting with no one I'd like to invite as a plus-one.

Melancholy enough that I'd been reckless. After sharing a few minutes of conversation with William Fox, I'd imagined dancing with him under the canopy of trees, clinking champagne with him in the flutes that Grandmother had bought in France. And after sharing a few minutes of...other things, I'd imagined taking him upstairs after the wedding was over, stripping him out of whatever horrible suit he'd surely wear, and bending him over the window ledge in the master bedroom so we could look out at the detritus the party had left behind as we came together.

I'd been reckless and I'd left William Fox a rather...aggressive invitation to the wedding. One that would either impress him mightily, or send him running in the other direction.

But he'd been so adorably out of sorts about Oakley's mercenary approach to art collecting. So grumpily offended by his treatment of it. And so deliciously oblivious to my flirting or to his own appeal that I'd wanted to give him *something*. I'd wanted to give him something that no one else could.

"Where did these cake samples come from, anyway?" Val asked, jolting me to attention. She was managing to eat bites of cake without choking while still looking up at the stars.

"From Crumb Coat, an aggressively modern up-and-coming bakery in the square that specializes in these kind of unusual flavor combinations." I gestured to the jewel-bright slices of cake on the table. "I knew your mother would punish you for the rest of time if you actually chose any of them for your wedding cake, but I thought you'd like them."

"Yes, Mother would have a conniption, and yes, they're delicious. I especially liked the rose cake with lemon frosting. Oh, and the pretzel with salted caramel, dear *god*. Mmmm, and what is this one? I love this one."

"Blueberry streusel with currant cream cheese frosting. I'll order a cake from them for one of the next parties to offset the cost of all these free samples," I said.

Val's eyes looked a little misty when she turned them to me and smiled. Yes, a bit too much bourbon for sure. "Thank you for all this. The wedding. The arrangements. For officiating. Just…thank you for everything."

She grabbed my hand and twined our fingers together like she'd done a thousand times over the years. Her engagement ring cut into my finger, a reminder of what tomorrow would bring.

"I hope one day you'll get to plan something for yourself, instead of always for everyone else," she said, her words ever so slightly slurred.

And I knew she meant to be kind, but it stung just a little, a tiny barb working its way under my skin and sitting there uncomfortably for a long time after.

IT WAS PERFECT. The late summer weather was cooperatively mild, Val and Dallas Fairbanks were gorgeous, the guests were enthusiastic, and the food and alcohol were flowing liberally. The white fabric of the tent looked sharp against the perfectly even green grass outside. I didn't even mind sacrificing the grass beneath the tent to Val's insistence on flooring so that high heels wouldn't sink into the ground while dancing. Lines of potted ferns gently encouraged guests from the large tent to the smaller one that housed the food and the bar. A few children turned cartwheels on the soft grass near the tree line, and a few more lounged apathetically in the sun, tired from a game of tag.

The ceremony and my speech had gone off without a hitch and now I could relax a bit until the next person needed me. Only one thing hadn't gone to plan: William Fox hadn't accepted my invitation.

I'd run through all the possibilities I could think of. One of his neighbors had gotten curious about the box outside his door and taken it for themselves, so he'd never seen it. The note had fallen off the wall and stuck to someone's shoe, so he hadn't gotten it. He was some kind of aggressive home-body and hadn't even opened his apartment door since the party three days ago. He'd been horrified that I would liberate the Staunton from Oakley's possession, and planned to rip me a new one if he ever saw me again. He'd called the police in outrage to report me as a thief and they were just backlogged, but would show up any day. Or perhaps he simply hadn't been interested in me. And how was *that* the possibility that hurt worst?

I was caught in a thoroughly boring conversation about overseas tax law, and had finally given up any hope that my plus-one might materialize when I glanced up to see the man himself picking his way carefully along the path from the driveway.

William Fox, in the flesh. And in that same damned suit, ill-fitting, and too heavy for the weather. I excused myself and made my way toward him, fizzing with excitement, even if Mr. Fox was apparently *not* a punctual date.

When I got close, I smiled and raised a hand, suddenly feeling…was that *nerves*? I couldn't remember the last time I'd been nervous about anything. But when he turned toward me, he didn't smile back. I thought I saw a flicker of something like regret in his eyes as he looked me up and down, then his face fixed in a stern mask of professional distance.

"Mr. Vaughn. Could I have a word with you…in private?"

"Mister is it, now?" I flirted, hoping that he was just nervous around a lot of new people. But my stomach gave an uncomfortable twinge.

"It is essential that I speak with you." He sounded stilted and adjusted his jacket awkwardly.

"Something tells me that your presence here does not indicate an acceptance of my invitation."

His expression turned grim.

"Well then," I said, falling back on manners. "I'm afraid that I have host duties at the moment. But please do stick around. Have a drink, enjoy the food. Valerie has exquisite taste."

His eyes narrowed but he just said, "I'm willing to give you time, but I'm not leaving here until I speak to you."

"Suits me just fine, William." I turned back to the party, disappointment buzzing under my skin. I could feel William's presence just over my right shoulder. Gesturing him toward an empty chair, I told him to make himself at home, and walked toward Valerie.

I was thrown. Not just disappointed but a bit embarrassed. As if I'd committed a faux pas in front of someone I respected.

When I got to Val, I glanced over to find that William hadn't moved—hadn't even sat down at the mostly empty table I'd brought him to. "Val, do me a favor."

"Anything, sugar."

I filled a plate with succulent barbequed pork, truffled bacon macaroni and cheese, and several of the miniature blue corn muffins, and handed it to her. "Take this over to that man with my compliments?"

"The handsome one in the horrible suit?"

"That's the one. His name is Will."

Even if this turned out to be the last time I saw him, it felt essential that no one called him William except me.

Val took the plate with narrowed eyes, but clearly saw that I'd said all I was going to on the matter. Her smile said that she'd play along but wouldn't forget that I owed her an explanation. She wasn't a fan of secrets, Val. Another reason we'd never have worked out in the long run.

When I next saw Val, she was dancing with Dallas, their hands entwined and their cheeks pressed together, so I didn't intrude to ask how William had received the food. Val looked peaceful, and I was full of love for her. She'd found someone who appreciated her and made her happy. What would it be like to have someone accept everything about you? I scanned the thinning crowd and found William in conversation with one of the bartenders, though he didn't seem to be drinking. He didn't strike me as the particularly accepting sort.

About an hour later, Valerie and Dallas left, off to their home in Newport for a pre-honeymoon weekend, and the crowd dispersed. I found William examining my dahlias around the side of the house, sitting back on his heels in the mulch outside the flowerbed.

"Do I need to have a word with my gardener?"

"What?" William's nose wrinkled adorably when he was confused.

"Generally, if I find people staring into my flowerbeds at parties, then either the punch has been altered or I'm in need of a word with my gardener."

"Uh, no, I was just…looking."

Looking could have referred to anything from *Snooping* to *So bored of this party I preferred to pull weeds.*

William straightened, brushing the dirt off his hands, and followed me inside. The staff was still cleaning up so I took him to the study and poured myself a brandy from the decanter on the sideboard. William shook his head when I held it up to him. I took a sip of brandy mostly because its warm, mellow golden taste was almost the color of Will's eyes.

I stepped close to him and noticed a spot of barbeque sauce at the corner of his mouth. If I kissed him right now, I would taste brown sugar, tomato, and smoke on his lips along with that dark earthy flavor that was his alone.

"So, William. You came. But something tells me the sentiment behind my invitation has gone rather astray."

"Then you admit that you left the Staunton painting and a note outside my apartment," he said flatly, and my eyes narrowed.

"Have I miscalculated your interest?"

William looked like he couldn't decide whether to laugh or yell. It was smoldering.

"You have miscalculated my profession," he responded. We were standing close enough to kiss, and when he reached a hand into his jacket, my breath caught. I wanted to help him strip it off and kiss that spot of barbeque sauce off his perfect mouth.

But he didn't take his jacket off. He slipped his hand out holding something from his pocket. A badge.

An FBI badge.

I was lightheaded. I spent three beats of my heart wondering what the medical diagnosis would be for dying of sheer irony. I spent the next three mourning the story that I'd apparently been writing in my head. The story of how William and I might someday stand where Val and Dallas had stood today, looking into each other's eyes and pledging ourselves to one another. Silly.

And then I locked it down. I drained my face of any expression and painted a new one on: vague concern. This expression said, *Why on earth would an FBI agent want to talk to little old me?*

CHAPTER 3

Will

VAUGHN WAS GOOD, I'd give him that. The briefest flicker of surprise, maybe unease, and then the same quiet, disinterested expression I'd seen on his face when Oakley came up to him at the party and asked about the Staunton. That he was giving it to *me* made me angry, and it shouldn't have. He *should* have been distancing himself from me. He *should* have been doing everything a criminal does when the law eventually catches up with them.

Because that's what he was. Despite his gorgeous historic home, despite the way he looked in a suit, despite the drop in my stomach when I'd shown up and thought *this isn't his wedding, is it?*, Amory Vaughn was a criminal. A thief who'd stolen a valuable painting and delivered it, with a note, to the home of an FBI agent.

Not just any FBI agent either. "My name, Mr. Vaughn, is Special Agent Will Fox. I'm with the FBI's Art Crimes Division. So you can, I'm sure, see the predicament here."

Only there shouldn't be one. I should be arresting him. I should have done it the second I showed up, not eaten his food and given him the time to see to his guests.

"The Art Crimes Division," Vaughn said, sounding

spectacularly unconcerned. "So you're more than just an appreciator of art, then. You're a defender."

I stared at him, weighing my words as carefully as I always did. As carefully as I should have the night of Oakley's party. "It's my duty to recover stolen works of art and see that the perpetrators are punished to the fullest extent of the law."

"I heard once that art is often reported stolen for the insurance money," Vaughn said conversationally, as if we were having this discussion over drinks.

"People steal for a lot of reasons," I said stiffly. "And they're all illegal."

Vaughn cocked his head and regarded me with those pale eyes. The night we'd met they'd been warm, teasing. They were neither at the moment. His gaze was steady and cool, calculating. I could see him trying to get out of this, and for reasons I didn't want to think about, my cock twitched. I wanted so very badly to ask him how he'd managed to steal it.

"And has Mr. Oakley reported his painting missing? How do you know it's not because he's a terrible investor of other people's money and needs a quick infusion of cash?"

I laughed. I couldn't help it. But I was still annoyed he'd gotten the sound out of me at all. "Mr. Vaughn, please. Do you think this is my first day on the job?"

He gave me a slow once-over, just like he'd done at the party. My reaction was the same, only tinged with anger instead of awkwardness. Maybe more than tinged. The anger and the overwhelming attraction for this man that I couldn't deny combined to make my blood heat.

"I would imagine it isn't, William."

"It's Agent Fox," I corrected. No one ever called me William, even my parents. In the back of my mind I heard his voice, warm and drowsy and thrumming with sexual promise. *The pleasure was all mine, William.* "Keith Oakley is out of town, and his finances are not your concern, Mr. Vaughn. His painting, on the other hand…"

"So you're here to, what, arrest me?" Vaughn smiled at me in obvious challenge. The son of a bitch was enjoying this. "I don't see any cuffs."

"I'm a federal agent. What you've done is a serious crime, Mr. Vaughn, and it would be a good idea for you to remember that."

"Would it?" Vaughn didn't look in the least bit worried, but I wasn't buying it. I'd seen that momentary flash of surprise when I'd shown my badge.

The only thing that had kept me from arresting Vaughn was the fact that Keith Oakley hadn't *technically* reported the painting as stolen yet. According to his assistant, he was out of town for the next two weeks. But it was a technicality and I knew it; all I needed was probable cause, and I had that in spades.

"It would," I said. I glanced around the elegant, well-appointed study and my eyes touched on the paintings displayed on the walls. They weren't the kind I normally enjoyed: stuffy portraits of old-fashioned, wealthy white men on horses and the like. Less art than narcissism. I glanced back at Vaughn.

There was a hint of amusement in his voice when he said, "These paintings are all portraits of my esteemed ancestors, I assure you, William. I'm happy to put you in touch with Miranda at the Virginia Historical Society if you'd like to review their provenance."

"What I'd like?" I glared at him, my feelings about being duped by someone I'd felt a genuine connection with momentarily overtaking my professionalism. "What I'd *like*, Vaughn, is to not be here at all. What I'd *like* is for you to stop trying to play me and realize that I am holding all the cards, and you are facing a charge of grand theft larceny."

"William, William," he tsked, shaking his head. "You don't admit you're holding all the cards if you want to win the game."

Anger sluiced through me, and I took a step forward. I was not a threatening man, though I was trained to be one if I needed to. "This isn't a game, Vaughn."

He didn't move away. It was a strange reversal of the night we'd met, when he'd moved so boldly into my personal space. "Of course it is," he said softly, a hint of something strange flickering across his striking features. "If you don't want to be here," he continued, "then you're free to leave."

"That's the thing," I said, ignoring how good he smelled, that sharp citrus-and-woodsy smell mixed with the fresh outdoors. "The person who can't leave isn't me."

"Am I making a run for it? Resisting arrest?"

He reached up, and I reacted on instinct, grabbing his wrist. "Don't touch me."

"No?" Vaughn didn't move, but his fair skin flushed, and his eyes began to thaw like melted ice. "You seemed to like my touching you a great deal the night we met. When I kissed you. When I shoved my hand in your pants and stroked your hard cock until you were writhing against the wall."

Goddamn it. My breathing came faster, and I still held Vaughn's wrist. We were standing too close together, and I couldn't seem to push him away even though I knew I should. He was a few inches taller than I was, but lanky. I had muscle on my side, and years of training...and yet I did nothing but stand there.

Vaughn was relentless. "When I played with your dick and you fucked my hand until you were so turned on you would have done *anything*. When I swallowed your gorgeous cock, on my knees in public, and you came down my throat so hard you almost screamed for me."

Two things happened at once. I pulled him closer without meaning to, and he moved to press himself against me. I was hard, and I could feel the unmistakable evidence of his arousal against my thigh. But I wasn't turned on as much as I was angry—or maybe that was why I was turned on.

I forced him backward, toward the large desk beneath the windows. Night had fallen, but I could see the glimmering fairy lights from the tent, twinkling like stars beyond the dark glass. "Let me explain something to you, Amory. I'm very good at my job, and no matter how good you are at sucking cock, it won't stop me from doing it if I need to."

This time when he reached for me, I didn't stop him. He tilted my chin up, which was both infuriating and erotic. "Then arrest me, Agent Fox. Go on." He was practically purring.

"Amory Vaughn," I started, trapping him against the desk, my body on fire with want and my heart pulsing like I'd just run a marathon, "you're—"

Infuriating. Attractive. And I want you so goddamn bad.

"I'm what, William?" He was breathing fast too, his chest

rising and falling rapidly, his eyes hot. He leaned back with absolute insolence, palms flat on the desk, deceptively at ease.

Under arrest. I couldn't say it. Instead, I made a frustrated sound and grabbed him by the back of the neck, pulled him close and kissed him. The kiss said everything I couldn't—*How dare you be what I want and what I can't have? How dare you play with me like you know you'll get away with it just because of who you are? How dare I want to let you just because you feel so good against me?*—and I found myself reaching down to rub the bulge in his pants as we kissed.

Vaughn shuddered hard and groaned into my mouth, his hands coming up to grab my shoulders. He pulled away and tried to say something, but I wouldn't let him. I chased his mouth with my own, biting hard on his lower lip as I struggled to get his belt free, his pants undone.

"Put your hands on the desk and don't fucking move them," I growled against his mouth, and before he could say anything, I dropped to my knees in front of him.

I didn't know why I was doing this, only that the haze of lust and anger—both at Vaughn and myself—was too much for me to fight. I yanked his pants down hard, glaring up at him in case he thought to argue, and took his cock in my hand, giving it several rough strokes.

I slid my mouth over his erection and started sucking him, fast and hard and deep, using my hand as I did it. It was the messiest blowjob I'd ever given. There was no finesse, no teasing, no drawing it out. There was just me, on my knees, sucking Vaughn's cock and ignoring the painful throb of my own, my tongue working the underside of his shaft.

Vaughn groaned when I swallowed around him, one of

his hands coming up to slide into my hair and hold me still. His hips moved, and I grabbed them, shoving him back. I pulled off his dick and glared hotly up at him, my breathing fucked up and my eyes narrowed. "I said, put your hands on the desk and keep them there." My voice sounded…well, like I'd been choking on cock. Rough and angry, just how I felt.

Vaughn's head was thrown back, and he was panting harshly. When he glanced down at me, he seemed to be considering the pros and cons of doing what I'd said. In the end, getting off won out and he did as instructed.

"Fuck, William," he moaned, as I went back to deep-throating him. I wanted him to come *and* I wanted it to never end. He tasted as good as he smelled, and the reason I didn't want his hands in my hair to help him fuck my throat is because I knew just how much I would like it.

I reached down and rubbed my free hand over my own erection, sparks of pleasure flaring at the touch. I forced myself to stop and redoubled my efforts to get Vaughn off. It didn't take long before I felt him tense, felt his cock throb before he came in my mouth. I swallowed the same way I'd sucked him off, like I was trying to prove something.

When it was over, I stood up and pressed the back of my hand to my mouth. Vaughn was leaning against the desk, flushed and panting, his pants undone and his softening cock glistening wet. I wanted to fuck him more than I'd ever wanted anything in my life. But I turned away to regain my composure, the reality of what I'd done the only thing that was capable of cooling my ardor. When I finally had myself under a modicum of control, I turned around.

Vaughn had tucked himself back into his pants and was

watching me with an expression halfway between pleased and anticipatory. Good.

"Keith Oakley," I began, and had to clear my throat. He smiled. I ignored it. "Keith Oakley is on vacation for the next two weeks. My sister, Charlotte, still has the security code and a house key she was to return to him when he's back from vacation. I'll see to it the Staunton is back where it should be."

His eyes widened a bit, and I could tell he hadn't expected that. "Is that so?"

"I said I had all the cards. You're the one who thought he knew what they were." I strode over to him and pressed myself up against that lean, muscular body. I inhaled his scent, let myself remember it, and gave in to the temptation to reach out and tangle my fingers in the ponytail that secured his long hair. I pulled, not gently, and gave him a harsh, punishing kiss. "Now we're even."

And then I left.

✦   ✦   ✦

I SHOULDN'T HAVE been surprised when he called me a few days later, but I was. Surprised, and annoyed that the sound of his honeyed drawl in my ear was as delicious as I'd known it would be. I'd thought our encounter in his office would be the end of this…whatever it was. Association.

As soon as I'd left Vaughn's house in Falls Church I'd returned the Staunton to Oakley's house. If I'd been caught, it would have been the end of my career, and I reminded myself of that fact with every step I took into his opulent house. But no one was home, Charlie's security code took care of any alarms, and the Staunton was back where it belonged: unappreciated and terribly lit.

"Mr. Vaughn." I put an emphasis on the *mister.* "Is there something I can do for you?"

"Oh, William," he said, and laughed. "I thought you'd make it a little harder than *that.*"

I couldn't quite believe he was a real person. I'd never met anyone in my life who spoke the way he did. I dealt with wealthy people regularly as part of my job, but none of them could turn a phrase like Vaughn. From anyone else, his manner would probably seem affected. Somehow, he made it work. He *really* made it work, damn him.

Of course, at the moment all he was doing was setting my teeth on edge. "How did you get this number?"

"The FBI directory, and a very helpful operator. It's not exactly a state secret, you know. You *are* a public official, and I am the public."

I snorted. Hardly. "And why is it you're calling me, exactly?"

"Why, to thank you, of course," he said smoothly. "For your assistance in that tricky little matter that might have caused me no end of inconvenience."

Tricky little matter, indeed. I was still horrified at what I'd done. Not so much the blowjob as the non-arrest that came after it. Even if there was no way in hell I could have arrested a suspect after sucking him off.

Which is why you did it.

That voice, unfortunately, was not Drunk Will. It was Sensible Will. Too bad he hadn't been around earlier. "You don't need to thank me."

"Don't be silly, of course I do. Will you have dinner with me, so that I may do so properly?"

My mouth dropped open, which until that moment, I'd always thought was hyperbolic. "You must be kidding."

He made a soft tsk sound. "Of course not; that would be incredibly rude. How about Friday?"

Was this... How could he... "You're not asking me on a *date*, are you?"

"It would appear I am," Vaughn said. "So, Friday? Or would another day work for your schedule?" His voice turned teasing. "I'm flexible."

I had to resist the urge to slam the receiver against the desk. I took two slow, deep breaths and said, "Let me see if I can make this very, very clear to you, Mr. Vaughn. We're done. Don't call me again."

Hopefully the dial tone would do better at conveying what he was so determined not to hear.

Apparently it didn't. Because not two hours later, I got a very enthusiastic phone call from Charlotte, eager to tell me that she'd just landed an exclusive contract—with the Vaughn Foundation.

"This is huge, Will," my sister enthused, while I seethed quietly in my chair. "*Huge.* If I rock this—and I will—then I'm going to make a name for myself and ah, this is it! This is totally the break I was waiting for. Did you end up talking to him at the party?"

Oh, did I ever. "Briefly."

"What'd you think of him?"

The memory of Vaughn on his knees, his mouth on my cock, assailed me. I searched wildly for something to say that wasn't in relation to cocksucking and said, "That he looked like Lucius Malfoy."

She snorted. "Actually, he kinda does. But he's raising

money for the Willowbrook College art department, so I'd say he's more a philanthropist than evil wizard."

I wasn't so sure about that.

CHAPTER 4

Vaughn

I WAS IN a perilous mood and I had been for two weeks. Ever since I met the first person in a very long time who'd sparked my desire, my fascination. Ever since he'd turned out to be an FBI agent who tried to arrest me. Ever since I'd made every effort under the sun to convince him to go out with me anyway, and had every call, email, and letter rebuffed. Rejection wasn't something I was accustomed to, but that didn't mean I couldn't take it. No, this wasn't about my pride, and it wasn't about winning.

This was about how, FBI agent or no, I couldn't get William Fox out of my head.

As such, I was anything but pleased about the fact that I was due at an obligatory Willowbrook College donor lunch.

Even on a good day, I would have been in no mood to make polite conversation with the particular brand of pompous windbag such lunches inevitably elicited. Trustees of the university who believed their money entitled them to puppeteer programming, deans of the university who cared far more about the reputation of the school than about the students who attended it, and the professors the deans thought would make the best impression on donors:

dinosaurs holding tight to the prestige of academia as they collected student evaluations in a garbage can until they could convince themselves to retire and finish the books they'd been boring junior faculty with stories of for decades.

Today, I was positively fighting a scowl.

I must have complained a bit too vociferously as Natalie briefed me on the attendees, because she rolled her eyes at me and gave me the lecture that had become standard over the last six months since I'd hired her: that this was part of the business of being a Vaughn; that these people were more likely to donate to the foundation's causes in the future if they rubbed elbows with me in other venues; that—and this one was a new addition and indicated that she'd apparently gotten more comfortable with me—I myself was a straight, middle-aged white man with a lot of money, so I should know better than anyone that those categories didn't necessarily mean someone couldn't be interesting.

It was delivered with an eye roll and a bit of a sideways smile that I supposed was intended to soften the blow. I was certainly white, and though I bristled at forty-two being categorized as middle-aged, I couldn't argue with her math. But there was one part of her comment I absolutely couldn't let stand. In fact, I was surprised she didn't know, since I made no secret of it whatsoever.

"Natalie. My dear," I said. "While I take your point about books and covers and judging, let me be very clear about one thing. I'm about as straight as a corkscrew."

I chucked her lightly under the chin and then swept from the room as her mouth dropped open, deciding I'd let her process that with one of the other staff members while I was gone. Flush with the rare joy of delivering a perfect exit line, I decided that since I was early I'd stop and get a cappuccino, maybe walk along the wooded paths that cut through the campus, in an attempt to lower my blood pressure before the donor lunch.

Before I got to the stairwell though, Natalie had run after me, tapping me on the shoulder. When I turned around, she was grinning, but didn't say anything. I raised an eyebrow at her expectantly but she just kept smiling and put her hands on her hips.

"You should go look at the art show," she said finally. And for all that she was about twenty-five and a foot shorter than me, she said it like she was used to being obeyed. And wasn't that just a little bit delightful?

"Oh? Why, pray tell."

"Because you love art. And even though you act like you're not interested in this lunch—okay, fine," she corrected when I glared at her. "Even though you don't want to go to the lunch, you *do* care about the money being raised because you actually care about the students and their work. And seeing the people your money is helping is the best way to deal with those asshats at lunch. You'll have seen what you're supporting so they won't matter as much. Besides, it'll give you something interesting to think about while they're all yammering."

"Why the sudden interest in my emotional well-being, hmm?"

"It's not *sudden*, first of all—it's like twenty-five percent of what you hired me for." I snorted at that. "And...ya know..." She looked at the floor where the scuffed toe of her green ballet flat stood out against the richly polished ashwood flooring I'd put in three years before. "We kind of…play for the same team." Her voice ran out on the last word, but her meaning was clear.

"Ah, I see. You play for the white, middle-aged, bisexual, billionaire, brandy enthusiast team as well?"

"Uhhh." Natalie was black, very much not middle-aged, and I strongly suspected that she was neither a billionaire nor a brandy enthusiast. "Not…exactly?"

I took pity on her and patted her on the shoulder. The last thing I'd wanted to do was make her uncomfortable.

"All right, from one team member to another, I'll go look at the student art. Thank you for the suggestion." I inclined my head to her solemnly, then winked and got in the elevator, leaving her smiling and just a little bit exasperated.

It was how I so often left them.

At the studio space, I was immediately glad I'd taken Natalie's advice because there was a lot of fascinating work here. Chalk up one point for team queer at the Vaughn Foundation. I made a mental note to give Natalie a raise. Then I made an immediate follow-up note to wait long enough that it didn't appear I'd given her a raise because she'd outed herself to me. One really couldn't be too careful about these things.

There were the standard computer-edited self-portraits rendered ethereal by lighting; violent sculptures made of garbage and nails and loathing; abstract color field paintings; attention-seeking photos of partial nudity.

But there were also a set of hoops holding stunning embroideries of trees, rendered in brilliant colored thread, leaves perfectly formed, roots reaching off the canvas to hang in jagged threads. There was a digital piece that layered skeletons of different animals with insects, the jut of bone stark against the filmy stretch of wings. In a pen and ink drawing, a loping wolf was paired with a portrait of a man who looked directly off the paper, one eye drooping with palsy, his lips drawn back over teeth as fanged as the wolf's. He looked about the age to be the artist's father.

The piece I couldn't look away from was a large painting hung well below eye level. The background was chaotic and swirling but the figure was rendered in meticulous brushstrokes, all purples, mauves, amethysts, and pinks, as if a rose-colored filter had been slipped over the eye. The canvas was square, and the painting was of a young man with his hands outstretched, open palms cupped to receive something, empty, waiting. The perspective was masterful, the hands reaching toward the viewer intrusive because of their scale. They made the piece feel like you owed it something. The floor beneath the painting was strewn with money, condoms, twisted tubes empty of paint, and crumpled pieces of paper, one of which, when I bent close enough to read it, seemed to be an acceptance letter for James Novack—which was the name of the artist on the tag next to the piece—into the MFA program at Yale.

The painting was called *Oliver* and I knew what I would be buying from the show when it opened.

It was a good thing I'd momentarily buoyed myself with the gallery's offerings, because the company at lunch was as excruciating as I'd predicted, and the food even more so. How did you ruin rolls? I pushed overdone roast beef and underdone green beans around on my plate as my mind wandered to the current object of my fascination.

The fact that the FBI unit William Fox worked for was

Art Crimes and that I had, not long after swallowing Will's come, stolen the Staunton painting out from under Oakley's (comparatively flaccid) security system was…well, it was half romantic gesture, half calling card, and half indulgence. And, yes, as the president of the Vaughn Foundation, and something of a math whiz if I let loose the reins of modesty, I *did* realize that added up to one and a half wholes. But that's how you succeeded as the head of a major philanthropic institution: by understanding that abundance begets abundance.

The problem with a calling card, though, was that convention dictated you leave a new one every time. And though William had followed up on mine—and what a follow-up it turned out to be—he'd staunchly refused to come calling again. In fact, he'd told me to get lost in no uncertain terms.

If I wanted to see him again, then, I would need to contrive a way to make it happen.

I'd already set one ball in motion by reaching out to Fox's sister, Charlotte, an event planner, and hiring her for the Vaughn Foundation's upcoming gala. But something *also* told me that William wasn't much for subtlety, and it would take more than what could be written off as a coincidence to set the game afoot.

I was adjusting the overstarched napkin in my lap to hide the erection burgeoning from thoughts of William and games when I was jolted back to the dingy reality of the faculty dining room by a truly inelegant snort from the buffoon sitting next to me.

It was Curtis Loel, a dean of the university and, I happened to know, an absolute cad. (Loel would do well to note that the staff at a country club never fail to notice the activities of the patrons, and that this information is accessible to anyone with the money or the charm to elicit it.) Loel was agreeing with Artie Vikander, the dean of something I hadn't bothered noting when he introduced himself, that student art shows were a pro forma waste of time.

"It's for the parents, really. The college-age version of sticking their kids' scribbles on the fridge," Vikander said.

"Yes, only these scribbles cost their parents about two hundred grand," Loel drawled, his sneer practically audible.

"Some of this year's work is rather good—" This was Margaret Chun, the Dean of Students who was slightly less loathsome than the rest, and therefore was interrupted immediately.

"Good, not good, who cares?" Loel gestured carelessly, a forkful of dry roast beef plunking to the ground. "The point is that none of it will sell. Maybe—*maybe*—if one of the kids' parents is feeling charitable, they'll buy something."

"Which, in a way, is worse," Vikander chimed in. "Because that sets them up to think that it's possible in the future."

Loel nodded sagely, spreading butter thickly on one of the tasteless rolls.

"It's a good experience for them to at least go through the motions of setting their work up for display," Chun said, speaking lightning fast, as if she knew it'd be a miracle for her to get a full sentence in if she didn't rush.

"Look, the point is," Loel said, crumbs stuck to the butter glistening on his lips, "that it's not about the art at all. None of these kids are going to have careers in art. Maybe a few of them will pack up their Honda Civics and move to

New York City and try to make a go of it, but they won't make it. Because no one cares about art anymore. And the ones who do only care about art that's already established. These kids aren't visionaries. No one is ever going to pay the kind of money for—for little Jamie's painting of a dust bunny representing his inner emptiness that I paid for the Saska hanging in my living room!"

He finished with a flourish, looking around the table. Vikander nodded once in emphatic agreement, Chun examined her plate carefully, and the other two deans, who hadn't even tried to squeeze their way into the conversation, smiled faintly and exchanged uncomfortable looks.

"Why are you here, then?" I asked, looking between Loel and Vikander. They'd been alternately kissing my ass and trying to impress me during the whole lunch. Now they both drew back in almost comical synchrony.

"I beg your pardon?" Loel said, finding his tongue first.

I kept my voice as lazy and friendly as ever. "If you don't believe in the mission of the art department, or in the students who attend the university, or in their potential future success, then why on earth are you wasting your time at a lunch that is in service of raising funds to support their futures?"

Loel bristled all over again. "Well, I...naturally, I...it's my job to...of course I wouldn't...that is—"

"We would never suggest," Vikander jumped in, "that the students have no futures, merely that...ah, that..."

I took a sip of water out of the red wine goblet it was served in (of all the ridiculous pretensions), and waited, expressionless, as if I had all the time in the world to allow the end of either of their sentences to coalesce.

After what felt like an eternity of silence, during which a muscle in Vikander's eye began to twitch and Loel turned redder and redder, one of the younger professors cleared his throat awkwardly.

"Will you be at the show, then, gentlemen?" he asked innocently. Everyone at the table nodded tightly, and he turned to me.

"Oh, I wouldn't miss it for the world," I told him. And I winked at Loel, a plan already beginning to take form.

A plan that would attract William Fox and punish Curtis Loel in one fell swoop.

✧   ✧   ✧

IT WAS A truth universally recognized that a man living alone in an affluent area felt invulnerable enough to consider the hiding of a spare house key more convenient than it was unsafe. Curtis Loel was a man living alone in such an area, and his spare key was hidden in a rather hideous ceramic frog lurking beside the coiled-up garden hose, next to the mudroom entrance off his back garden.

The Saska was beautiful—haunting blues and grays that made me feel like I would be sucked into it if I stood too close—and I revised my impression of Loel slightly when I saw that it *was* alarmed. I had bet sixty/forty against. It was always nice to have a little surprise with one's larceny. Loel had the alarm hooked into his electrical system though, so a simple flip of the breaker took care of that.

I swaddled the painting in bubble wrap and slid it into the garment bag I'd brought with me. I was in and out in about eight minutes. I even waved hello to a woman jogging by in expensive exercise gear as I walked a few streets away to where I'd parked my car, taking care to hold the garment bag as if it held the weight of a suit and not a multi-million dollar painting.

✧　✧　✧

THE FIRST TIME, I was twenty-one. It was in London, at a Vaughn Foundation party and I was there with my mother. It was the year before she died. The whole weekend had been a fog of London-gray autumn, and I'd gone where I was told to go and done what I was told to do, like a robot. A ghost. I was only there to shadow my mother, see how a Vaughn did things. Learn my place. As if I didn't already know it. When these people looked at me all they saw were dollar signs. I had no utility beyond my money and my last name.

If I were being honest, I'd always felt that way. As if my path had been laid long before I was born, and my only job now was not to trip as I put one handsomely-shod foot in front of the other.

My parents were kind people, but I knew they viewed their work as noblesse oblige rather than a project of passion. They didn't have a lot of that in their lives, period, and they didn't much value it in others. When I'd turned eighteen and legally become a board member of the Vaughn Foundation, I'd asked my parents for a small allocation of funds within the VF to work on a project of my own. I'd wanted to sponsor an afterschool arts program for queer youth. My mother, who made all the decisions regarding new funding, said it was a nice idea but not something VF was interested in. We needed to stay on brand, she explained, and queer youth were not a part of the Vaughn Foundation's brand.

Even though I had been one of them. *Thanks, Mother.*

I'd always known I was attracted to both men and women. It was finding out that this wasn't the case for everyone that had surprised me. And, of course, the realization that my catholic preferences weren't shared by everyone was swiftly followed by the understanding that they weren't approved of by everyone either. Not that I cared. If there was one thing being a white man with money was good for, it was looking people dead in the eye and knowing that I didn't *have* to care about their prejudices against me.

But, unfortunately, others weren't so privileged in the fuck-off-forever category, hence my desire to use the Vaughn money to help them tell people to fuck off. And when my mother said no, I quietly took half of the percentage of the trust fund I'd come into when I turned eighteen, and simply started my own. Without the Vaughn name. In fact, I wasn't sure anyone knew the charity was associated with me at all, except the woman I hired to run it.

At the party in London, I was…all right, I was mopey, and self-pitying, and paying more attention to the rather remarkable ass and posture of one of the tuxedoed waiters passing hors d'oeuvres. I decided he had to have been a dancer, and I followed him, first with my eyes, then around the curtain that divided the reception area from the rest of the hosts' home. The waiter was going back into the kitchen, and I decided to poke around a bit. Distract myself.

I wandered into the bedroom mostly out of petulance. I figured I'd rifle the medicine cabinet and see which of our hosts were maintaining their sense of poise only with prescription help.

And there it was, hanging between the vanity and the door. A small painting—too small for the space, really. Only about two feet by two feet. It wasn't famous. It wasn't flashy. It was just beautifully framed and professionally lit.

And I had to take it off the wall. It wasn't even that I wanted to own it. I just wanted to...be in charge of it. I hardly even thought about what I was doing. I just reached up and lifted it off the wall. Had I considered it, I'd have thought perhaps it was alarmed, but I didn't.

Once I held it in my hand, it was transformed. On the wall, it had been art. Untouchable, distant, separated from me by more than space. Now, it was just an object. Now, it was something I had power over. I felt a rush like nothing I'd ever known rip through me. I was buzzing with excitement, everything gone sharp and clean and new.

I could have hung it right back up and walked away, considered it like a snort of cocaine or a shot of espresso, but I didn't. I looked at it for a long time—at its beautiful brushwork and the tiny overpaint in the upper right hand corner that I could see when I tilted it to the side. Just a small bump where the cloud had originally extended farther to the right. Then I shrugged out of my jacket, draped it over my arm, and walked back to the party, carrying the painting in my hand, hidden from sight but pricking me with jolts of excitement, like the snap of a rubber band or the prick of a tack.

I'd be lying if I said that I didn't...abscond with anything else over the years. Opportunities presented themselves. Objects fell into my path, almost as if they wanted to leave with me. I procured a great deal of art through perfectly legal means as well, building a collection that meant something to me; one that wasn't based on investment, but purely on pleasure.

And that's how it was over time. Sometimes I'd go years without obtaining. Other years, I...wouldn't.

It wasn't a compulsion. I could stop any time I wanted, and I never stole from museums or from people who would consider it a true loss. Unless, of course, they deserved it.

Did I consider myself a kind of Robin Hood? No. Because I did it for myself.

Except that suddenly, after years without even a whiff of the impulse that often caught me in its fist, I had done it again.

And I had done it for Agent Will Fox. Not *for* him, precisely, but to get his attention. And oh, how I'd wanted his attention. I'd wanted everything about him.

When you'd been doing it as long as I had, you learned things. Like who was the type of person who alarmed their artwork, or their home. Who was the type of person who would even notice that something was missing. And who was the type of asshole so secure in his dominion over his own little world that he considered it unassailable.

I would've bet my own art collection that Keith Oakley belonged to the latter category, and I would have kept it. I'd sidled up to a woman standing in front of a Maritza Jean painting in the front hallway. If anything were alarmed, this painting would be, situated so close to the door. I'd bent as if to pick up something I'd dropped and bumped into her just enough that she had to take a step backward to steady herself. On the painting.

"Goodness, I'm so sorry," I'd said, shaking my head at my own clumsiness. "Please excuse me. I swear, I'm a menace at parties."

I'd given her the look that made most women of a certain age smile back, and I'd caught her elbow, surreptitiously lifting the edge of the painting off the wall with my other hand as I steadied her. Nothing. No alarm, no sudden rush of a security guard, no sound of the door automatically locking.

"No harm done," she'd said, smiling.

"Well"—I'd gestured to the painting, which was now slightly askew—"I almost pulled this down on top of us for good measure."

She'd laughed and I'd laughed—silly, silly Vaughn—and I'd taken her elbow and gotten her another drink. She was a lovely woman; couldn't have stumbled upon a nicer one to figure out the Staunton was likely equally unprotected.

Three hours later, I'd graciously offered my assistance to the harried caterer's assistant, and, under the cover of a garment bag, relieved Keith Oakley of what should never have been his.

It didn't feel so much like theft as it did an opening gambit. My way of knocking on the door of the first man in ages who had tied me up in knots and saying, *Your move.*

CHAPTER 5

Will

ELIZABETH RICE, THE deputy director, was about fifteen years older than me and had never once used my first name. She was kind, but excruciatingly professional in the way that let you know she cared about your career and didn't much want to go grab drinks after work.

She greeted me with a smile and waved at me to have a seat in front of her desk. "I have a case for you that I think you'll find interesting," she said, pushing a folder over at me. "Do you know who Curtis Loel is?"

I squinted at the name on the folder, but it wasn't familiar. "Doesn't ring a bell. But he's local?" I recognized the address, in a neighborhood I could never afford.

"Yes. A dean at Willowbrook College," she said, and I opened the folder. There was a photograph of Mr. Loel, a sixtyish-year-old man with a stare that suggested he had no sense of humor. "He reported a Saska stolen from his residence."

My eyebrows went up at the thought of anyone making enough money in academia to afford a Saska. I studied the documents in the folder, which also included a photograph of the painting, *Stormfront*.

My immediate thought was that it was insurance fraud, but according to the file, there was no sign of financial distress that would prompt someone to file an insurance claim. I closed the folder, already eager to get to work on this new case. It would take my mind off things that I had no business thinking about, especially at work.

"The police file is on its way over," she said. "There was no sign of forced entry, and Loel doesn't have a security camera anywhere on his property. Nothing else of value was taken from the home."

That definitely sounded like insurance fraud, but time would tell. I went back to my office and made some phone calls, went over the police report that was faxed over and made some initial notes before phoning Curtis Loel and agreeing to meet him at his home later that afternoon.

"It's absolutely inconceivable to me how this happened," Loel said for the sixth time, setting my teeth on edge as I made a survey of the room that was now minus a Saska. He was, understandably, more upset about the ease with which someone had broken into his home than the aesthetic lack caused by the painting's absence. "I heard nothing. Nothing!"

Well, thieves did tend to be quiet.

The police report had been thorough and I saw nothing to challenge their findings that there'd been no forced entry. Someone had simply walked in, taken the painting, and walked out. I completed my examination of the room and we went to the kitchen, which looked as if no one had ever used it. There was a door that led to a covered back porch, and another that led to the garage. Upon further examination, I noticed there was yet another door that led from the garage outside. It was unlocked, and I noted it even though Loel couldn't recall if it'd been that way for any length of time. There hadn't been prints found at the scene, but in my opinion, it would have been the easiest way to leave with the painting.

"Can you tell me anyone who might have a reason to take your painting?" I asked.

"The obvious answer is money," Loel said. "Isn't it always?"

He had a point there.

"I never thought about someone stealing a painting off my wall," he said, shaking his head. "It seems like something from a movie. Who's usually responsible for things like this?"

"The culprits behind most valuable art thefts are generally involved in some way with organized crime," I pointed out. "They occasionally hire your more common thief to steal art, but you almost always find something else missing in that case—jewelry, silver, other valuables. As long as whatever syndicate it is gets their art, they don't much care about what else is stolen. Are you positive nothing else of value is missing?"

"Nothing is missing," he said. "Just the Saska."

"And you can't think of anyone who might have a grudge against you? Perhaps at the university?" I asked politely.

"I'm the dean of an art department," he said wryly. "I'd like to think even if some of the professors took issue with me and my administration, they'd leave the art alone and go for my Rolex collection."

I gave a brief smile and asked him to go over his schedule for the last few weeks. He'd noticed the Saska was missing a few days ago, but that didn't mean it hadn't been missing *before* that.

Most of his schedule sounded like typical academia minutia, including a donor lunch the week before and an upcoming art show.

"Any possibility there's a student with an axe to grind who might want to steal your painting?" I asked.

"I can't think of any off the top of my head, Agent Fox. I do have events here for donors, and students are usually in attendance. But only the ones I can trust will behave themselves around donors."

"Have you had any of those events recently?"

"Not terribly, but I'm happy to send you the guest list from the last few. I'll have our contact in the development office email it to you." He snapped his fingers. "You should come to the art show tomorrow night. It's something of a big deal for the students—important donors, that kind of thing. Any of the students who've been to my home will be there, and others besides."

The others, who I took it were the ones he *didn't* trust to be around the bigwig donors at his house. I closed my notebook and rose from the stool where I'd been sitting. "All right. I'll do that, thank you."

It wasn't until I was in my office later, transcribing the notes, that I realized where I'd heard of the Willowbrook College art department recently.

The gala my sister was planning—what had she said it was for? To raise money for an endowment for the Willowbrook art department, on behalf of the Vaughn Foundation.

Following a hunch, I called Loel immediately. "You said you had a donor lunch the other day. Would you mind telling me who that was with?"

He listed off some of the attending staff from the college, and then said, "There was only one donor present, as he's a fairly major prospect and we like to give them all of our attention. His name is Amory Vaughn. He's the president of the Vaughn Foundation, and they—"

"Thank you," I interrupted. "I know who Amory Vaughn is. I'll be in touch."

Son of a *bitch*.

CHAPTER 6

Vaughn

I T WAS ELEVEN, the night before the public opening of the student art show. Late enough that I'd be unlikely to run into any faculty, but early enough that no one would remember someone who was clearly not a student wandering around in the middle of the night. I parked in a seldom-used lot and took the Saska in its garment bag with me to the art building, and in through the side door that I'd taped the lock on earlier when the building was open. I peeled the tape off as I entered and let the door shut with a soft *snick*.

In the dark, the sculptures and installations that dotted the hallways were startling, sinister, and the piles of wood, metal, broken mirrors, empty frames, and other detritus hazardous. I made my way to the gallery. There would be no alarms; not inside the building, not for student work. I had been hoping for a spare nail left in the wall—a painting mounted and then moved—on which I could hang the Saska, but no such luck. I'd brought one with me, but I'd rather not risk the noise of hammering it in.

Along the wall outside the gallery were student studios, and I tried the knobs, hoping to find one unlocked. On the fifth knob I tried, I found it, and inside was the easel I was looking for, appropriately paint-flecked and wobbly. It would work just as well to set the Saska up on the easel as to hang it on the wall; maybe even better. I tucked it under my arm and headed back to the gallery. As I followed the line of studios back around to the gallery entrance though, I noticed a gleam of light coming from the gap underneath the studio door directly across from the gallery entrance, and froze.

There was no other way into the gallery from this direction, nor any way out of the building. I stood for a few heartbeats, waiting. Then absent humming came from the studio and I cursed the industriousness—or night owl schedules—of the young. If the student had just arrived and was in for a lengthy work session, there was nothing for it. I either had to walk past his door, or stand here and wait until he left. And I hated to wait.

If he was working and humming, hopefully he was engrossed and listening to music on headphones. I could probably walk right past him and he wouldn't notice. One thing I'd learned long ago was that when people were in a place they shouldn't be, or at times they shouldn't be there, they were far too concerned with feeling out of place themselves to register that you were also out of place. Chances were that even if he saw me he'd assume I had every right to be here. An adult wearing a suit presented enough of an authority figure to most people that they'd look the other way.

I waited another minute, maybe two, and when the humming continued, I walked slowly, softly, toward the gallery door. Just as I passed the occupied studio—as if I'd awakened it by looking—the door swung open, revealing a paint-speckled young man wearing headphones and holding an iPhone.

We both froze, midstep, like bandits in a cartoon. He was likely more startled than I was, eyes going wide at the sight of me. Then his gaze went to the easel under my arm and his eyes narrowed. He yanked off his headphones and settled into a languid, cocksure stance.

"What are you doing with Martin's easel?"

"Borrowing it," I replied, infusing my voice with the elixir of entitlement and uncaring that said I had every right to be wherever I wanted and to do whatever I was doing and it would behoove anyone I met to remember that.

"Borrowing it for what?" the young man said suspiciously.

"It is in service of a good cause, I assure you."

I took a step farther into the hallway so I could see past him into his studio. And when I did, I lost any concern I had that he might prove a trouble.

"And what are you working on, my young Beltracchi?"

"Huh? Just a painting for school."

He crossed his arms and jutted his chin, leaning against the doorframe. It was a lazy, unconcerned pose. But it was a calculated one that had the bonus of blocking the doorway. I should know. I'd cultivated a similar one myself over the years.

I pointed at the canvas on his easel.

"Has Willowbrook begun assigning forgeries as part of their curriculum, then?"

The panic that flickered over the boy's face was schooled to neutrality almost immediately, but I'd seen it.

"Not sure what you're talking about," he said. "Who are you, anyway?"

"Just an art appreciator. May I?"

I brushed past him. On the easel stood a decidedly not-bad-at-all forgery of *Percival Rising*, an early Meredith Palmer.

"I'm impressed," I said. The boy was now fidgeting beside me, mouth open on a denial or an explanation, but I cut him off, pointing to another painting leaning against the wall. "You did *Oliver*, for the student show."

"Uh, yeah."

"It's the best piece in the gallery."

"Thanks." He looked reluctantly pleased.

Turning back to the Palmer forgery, I leaned in close. The brushwork was good, the style meticulous. But...

"Have you ever seen this painting, or only reproductions?"

I could see him trying to find an answer that didn't give anything away, and I waved him off.

"You've never seen it. Palmer edges her green with scarlet on the palette, then she uses a fan brush to feather it in. You can't see it in the reproductions, but on the canvas, these greens all have the barest thread of scarlet running through them. It lifts the tone of the whole piece. Gives it an energy, a sense of movement."

His eyes were wide.

"Nice to meet you, James Novack," I said, and turned to leave.

"Wait! What are you doing here? Who are you?"

I paused in the doorway. He looked very, very young, blond hair in a careless swoop, eyes unshadowed.

"I propose a gentleman's agreement. I won't mention your...extracurricular pursuits, and you won't mention my presence here after hours. Deal?"

I held out my hand to him, and he shook it. Then he narrowed his eyes at me and leaned in, clearly intrigued.

"But what *are* you doing here?"

I held up the easel and the garment bag, and winked at him.

"Oh, you'll know it when you see it. I assure you. Good night, James."

CHAPTER 7

Will

I DIDN'T ATTEND things like student art shows much anymore, but I did generally enjoy them. I'd never been gifted at making art, as much as I loved it, and the yearly show at the University of Maryland was always a favorite activity of mine when I was in school. Willowbrook's show was clearly a much bigger deal than the show at U of M had ever been. It was opening night and a prime opportunity to show off for donors and parents alike.

I arrived early and took a look at all the paintings, impressed at the quality and the passion of the students. I was struck by a painting of a young man with hands open and waiting, the floor in front of it strewn with bits of what appeared to be trash. It was an interesting approach to draw the viewer into the work itself, and not the sort of thing one would necessarily hang on their wall in their living room and brag about owning, but I found the stark emotion of the piece to be incredibly moving. It was active in a way that made me think of Futurism, and I was impressed as hell by the talent and thought that went into it.

Still, my favorite was a simpler, much more subtle work. Watercolor was one of my favorite media—I appreciated the delicacy and the light touch involved, as well as the way the colors could blend to become bolder, sharper—and this one was masterful. There was a wash of slate through which I could just make out the textured material of the canvas, that gave the impression of hills and valleys. It was overlaid with greens, violets, and yellows in seemingly random distribution. The tag said *Rain on the Mountainside*, and I gave a delighted laugh, because that's exactly what it looked like to me.

I glanced at the price tag, wondering if perhaps I could splurge and buy this piece. It wasn't the price of, say, a Saska, but it wasn't cheap. And it shouldn't be. It was the sort of piece that came together so beautifully, so perfectly, that it looked deceptively simple. It would look lovely in my bedroom, on the wall opposite my bed. Buying it would mean sacrificing a weekend climbing trip or some new gear I'd had my eye on.

As I pondered my financial situation and the painting, I caught a familiar scent that made my entire body tighten with awareness. I didn't even need to look to know exactly who'd materialized next to me.

"I should have known you'd like this one, William."

"It's Agent Fox," I corrected, steeling myself to look over at Vaughn. He looked as wonderful as he always seemed to, his blue suit flawlessly cut, the color perfectly complementing his striking coloring. His hair wasn't braided, but was worn in a low ponytail, making me think again of Lucius Malfoy. Evil wizard, indeed. "And I'm not sure why you think you are in any way qualified to know what my taste is."

"You liked the Staunton," Vaughn said, sounding

charming as ever. His nearness, his scent, the memory of his hands on me and his voice in my ear...*fuck*. This was not the time to remember how powerfully attracted to him I was.

"This is nothing like the Staunton," I said stubbornly. I narrowed my eyes at him. "You don't seem surprised to see me."

"My delight far outstrips my surprise," Vaughn drawled, and it was so unexpected that I felt myself smile before I realized I'd done it.

Only the slightest distance separated us. Somehow, that was more of a tease than feeling the heat of his body; it was as if the mere closeness was enough to scorch my skin. I would not take a step away from him and give him the satisfaction of knowing he was affecting me. Hell, I barely wanted to admit it to myself.

"So what brings you here, William? Is your role merely as a patron of the arts, or has some absolute scoundrel absconded with a piece of student work? If the latter, I'm gratified to learn that the FBI devotes such exquisite resources to up-and-coming artists."

"I'm afraid my reasons for being here are confidential," I sniffed. "And what about you? Figuring out whose work is going to be worth stealing in a few years?"

He *grinned* at me. "My, William, what a thing to say. No, I'm fundraising for the Willowbrook art department. I'm surprised your charming sister didn't mention it, seeing as how her company is planning the gala."

I pitched my voice low, and finally closed the distance between us. "I'm only going to say this once, Amory. I don't know what the *fuck* you think you're doing or what kind of games you seem so fucking determined to play with me, but you *will not* involve my sister. Is that understood?"

I might not have been physically imposing, but I knew how to pitch my voice and hold my body to make me seem like a threat. Vaughn, however, seemed the opposite of intimidated. His eyes caught mine and held, and the tension between us crackled and sparked in a way that made me as furious as it did hard.

"It's not your *sister* I find interesting. Delightful and competent, I assure you. But not as...*intriguing* as her twin. You are twins, yes?"

I opened my mouth to say something—I didn't know what—when someone called for me. My conversation with Vaughn had distracted me so completely that I hadn't noticed the small space fill up with people. Now Curtis Loel was marching toward me like a man on his way to war, his face flushed and his mouth set. He barely looked at Vaughn.

"Mr. Loel," I said, politely.

"Agent Fox," Loel said, like my name was a curse. "I'm hoping you're here to work, not socialize. My Saska isn't going to find itself."

Wow. I fixed him with the flat stare that said I had no sense of humor and didn't respond to barbs. "I can assure you that I'm doing my job, Mr. Loel. If there's anyone here you'd particularly recommend I speak to, I hope you will let me know."

"If I knew who it was, I could have taken care of it my-self," he snapped.

When people said this, I always wanted to ask them why they thought suggesting vigilante justice to a federal agent was a good idea.

Loel must have finally noticed who was standing next to

me, because his entire demeanor changed. He smiled, greeted Vaughn with a handshake, and said he hoped Vaughn would enjoy the show. After a pointed look at me, he walked quickly away.

"So you know him," I said to Vaughn.

"Again, I'm raising money for a Willowbrook capital campaign," was Vaughn's answer.

"I have no idea what that means."

"It means the Willowbrook art department is in need of new facilities, and I've committed to raise enough money to see that they get them."

"Are you and Loel friends?"

Vaughn smiled at me. He knew what I was doing. "I wouldn't say we were, no."

Did you take his painting? I didn't ask. I doubted he'd tell me anyway. "Loel told me you had lunch with him the other day."

"I did, yes," said Vaughn. "Development officers like to introduce the money to the faculty and administration. Tedious, and often involving an affront to my culinary sensibilities, but necessary."

Vaughn clearly cared about the finer things, but I didn't *think* terrible food could be enough to make him steal a painting. I was thinking about how to question him that might actually get me anywhere when the whole feel of the room changed.

Whispers began, then voices steadily rose. Students drew phones from their pockets and tapped away intently, some with wide eyes, others with hands cupped over their mouths. I tracked them with my eyes, looking for the threat, the air gone suddenly electric. But they moved like a murmuration, swirling around an invisible center, and I couldn't make it out.

Finally, I saw what they were circling around. It was an easel, though only visible to me from the back. It didn't seem out of place in an art show, but the shocked looks on the faces of the crowd insisted it was making an impression. Was I about to witness a student get screamed at by a dean for a lewd nude, or an offensive send-up of a professor? A part of me kind of hoped so.

I walked toward it, vaguely aware of Vaughn trailing after me. Standing next to the easel was a thin boy with a cocky grin and a lot of tousled blond hair. He tipped his chin up at Vaughn flirtatiously.

"What a *generous* contribution to the arts from our most supportive benefactor," the young man said, and then coughed "*Douchebag.*"

I followed his hand to the easel. There sat—

Loel's missing Saska.

Next to it on the easel was a small plaque that read, "*Lost and Found: An Installation,* courtesy of Dean Curtis J. Loel."

The price was twenty-five dollars.

All around the gallery, people were taking pictures and their fingers flew over their phones.

A shout came from behind me and I turned to see Loel barreling toward me. "That's it! That's my painting!"

"Of course it is, sir," the boy said. "It says so right here. What an *amazing* gesture." He blinked innocently up at Loel.

"*Novack,*" Loel hissed. "I should have known you'd have something to do with this."

The boy—Novack—raised his palms. "Sir? Something to

do with what? I'll say, though, I would *absolutely* like to purchase the installation for twenty-five dollars. The easel is part of it, right?" He turned to Vaughn, eyes dancing with delight. "I don't suppose you could spot me a twenty, could you, daddy?"

He treated Vaughn to an X-rated wink and I turned just in time to see the amusement on Vaughn's face as he slid his hands into his pockets.

"I want that painting fingerprinted," Loel hissed into my ear. "I want whoever did this to me *found immediately,* Agent Fox, do you hear me?"

Around us, cameras flashed and other students got in on the game.

"But Dean Loel," one girl said, clearly filming as she spoke, "It says right there that the installation is courtesy of you."

Loel squirmed, only his desire to avoid scandal and humiliation keeping his fury at bay. He grimaced at the crowd and glared at me, and eventually the students trailed away, laughing among themselves.

I took down the names of people to interview—students who worked on the show, venue personnel, professors in attendance, the Novack boy—as I waited for the forensics department to show up and dust for prints. But I knew they wouldn't find any. Once again, a painting had vanished and reappeared. Once again, money had nothing to do with it. It didn't take an FBI agent to see the similarities. But once again, I doubted there would be anything I could do about it.

I sighed, finding a quiet place to call the deputy director and fill her in on the details as I waited for the forensics team. It was going to be a long night. Several times I found myself scanning the room looking for Vaughn, even though it annoyed me to admit that was what I was doing. A few times our eyes would meet, across the room, and the pull between us was a tangible thing....a tangible thing I was more determined than ever to ignore.

CHAPTER 8

Vaughn

I WAS STILL in my office, though I should have left an hour before if I wanted to miss the traffic getting back to Falls Church. Now I might as well just stay in my D.C. apartment for the night and head home for the weekend in the morning.

Natalie called a cheery goodbye and wished me a happy weekend. I wondered what I would have been like at her age if I hadn't been Amory Vaughn. Would I have left work on Friday afternoon with nothing more pressing than what bar to go to, or who to go home with on my mind? I shook my head. I was being a grouch, not to mention showing my age.

My parents had died not long before I was Natalie's age, so I'd been learning the ins and outs of the Vaughn Foundation, with the eyes of every board member on me, waiting for me to prove that it would be a mistake to leave the family holdings in my hands. I'd been learning how to live alone in the home I'd grown up in, every sound and movement seeming to echo in the emptiness they'd left behind. I hadn't been out at bars. I hadn't been out at all. Only Valerie had ever come to see me. Valerie and an endless parade of lawyers, investors, development officers, and financial planners.

With a sigh, I turned back to the Excel spreadsheet that had my eyes crossing, grumbling as I increased the magnification to two hundred percent, cells and numerals swimming on my computer screen. I'd spend one more hour attempting to make sense of this data and then I'd order sushi and sake to be delivered to my apartment so it'd be there by the time I arrived. I would eat, take a bath, and watch the DVRed episodes of *Antiques Roadshow* that I would deny enjoying to my dying breath. I held the pleasant evening up like a carrot for finishing the spreadsheet.

I'd just sunk back into it when my intercom buzzed.

"There's a Mr. Fo—er, Agent Fox to see you, sir," Margery said, and I smiled, imagining Will correcting her about his title. I added "stickler for protocol" to the ever-expanding list of things I was learning about *Agent* William Fox.

"Send him on up, Margery, thank you."

This was progressing just as I had hoped. Calling cards, after all, could go both ways. It was a lesson that young James Novack, for one, hadn't needed to be taught. The night of the art show opening, after I'd left William beset by Loel and waiting for a forensics team, my phone had chimed with a text from an unknown number. It had said *Nice one. – Beltracchi.*

How did you get this number? I'd replied, wondering if I should add pocket-picking, hacking, or wheedling to Novack's growing résumé.

He'd responded with a winky face, and I'd found myself smiling in return. Ah, the next generation. I'd saved the number in my contacts, just in case.

I shook out my suit coat from where it hung inside my

office door, and slid it back on, smoothing my white shirt more snugly into my trousers, and checking that my vest was buttoned properly. I checked the mirror. The fresco suit and vest were just a hair paler than navy, with a light blue stripe that looked silvery-gray, just like my hair. My crisp white shirt still looked fresh, even at five thirty on a Friday afternoon and I made a mental note to ask Darnell, my personal assistant, what brand of starch the dry cleaner had used, and to instruct them never to use anything else. The leather of my brown wing-tip oxfords and belt was buttery warm, the perfect complement to the blue suit. I nodded at myself in the mirror just as I heard the elevator ding.

The knock at my door was over-loud, aggressive.

"Come in," I called, walking back behind my desk rather than opening the door. Let him come to me.

The first thing that came through the door wasn't William though. It was a framed, stretched canvas. *Rain on the Mountainside*, the painting William had admired and I'd had delivered to his home. Will followed, looking distinctly rougher for a Friday afternoon than I did. I imagined he'd come straight from work and tried to reconstruct his journey, assuming he got off at five.

"William," I said, gesturing him inside. "What an unexpected pleasure."

He had been clutching the painting angrily, and now put it down, leaning it against the wall carefully, as if it were a baby he was dispensing with before getting in a fistfight. There was still the desk between us, and I came out from around it, drawn to the violence in him. The passion.

He stabbed an angry finger in the space between our chests. "You can't manipulate me, so stop trying!"

"How is it you think I've manipulated you?"

He shot me an exasperated look, then gestured between me and *Rain on the Mountainside*.

"The painting? That was a gift. I didn't steal it, I assure you. I bought it."

"Well, I don't want it."

"No?"

"I—*no*."

Liar. And not a very good one. Little practice, or little inclination? "That's too bad. Hmm, I wonder if the student artist who painted it will take it back," I mused, finger to my lips, watching him. He flinched.

"Damn you," he bit off, and I smiled. I liked watching William Fox off-kilter. I liked that very much.

"Well, I'll pay you for it, then." He rooted around in his bag, exasperated, finally coming up with a checkbook. He glared at me but took a step closer so he could bend over the desk to write the check. He was wearing a gray suit today, identical to the black one I'd seen him in before, and the notion of William trying on a suit, deciding that it looked good on him, and then buying it in two different colors filled me with an unexpected tenderness. Followed by a powerful urge to take him shopping with me and show him what would *actually* look good on him. Black and gray were all wrong for him. Too stark, too cold. With his rich brown hair, amber eyes, and honeyed skin, he should be wearing browns and blues, rusts and hunter greens.

I'd be lying if I didn't admit that my fingers itched to get this steel gray suit off him for reasons beyond the purely aesthetic too. Bent over my desk, the curve of his ass was on display and the powerful muscles of his thighs bunched in the cheap fabric. I wanted to strip away everything that was in the way of seeing how he was put together—his strong spine and muscular shoulders, the curve of his neck and the cut of his hips.

He thrust the check at me, brows drawn together. "Don't do it again."

I purposefully pressed my fingers into his as I took the check, and I didn't let him release it. "Do what, William? Buy you student artwork that you admired?"

"Don't-don't-don't…" He shook his head in frustration, his irritation clear. I could work with irritation. One strong emotion would do just as well as another. "Don't act like we're close. Like you know me. Like you know what things I like and who I am. Because you don't."

"But I'd like to. I'd like to know who you are inside and out. I wanted to see you again."

I'd banked on the same spark that had flared to life in my study after Val's wedding reigniting, if I could just get William close to me again.

I let go of the check then and it fluttered to the floor at our feet. Will glared at me, eyes wide, cheeks flushing. He stooped and snatched the check up, slapping it down on the desk and whirling back around to face me.

"You think that you can *do* anything, get *away* with anything, because you're rich and privileged and handsome," he spat out, though his lip twitched at "handsome," suggesting he hadn't meant to include it in his list of offenses. "But it doesn't work that way. Eventually, things catch up with you. Eventually, you make a mistake and give the game away. Eventually, you get caught. And I'm going to be there when you do."

He'd closed the distance between us and I could smell him: inexpensive aftershave and soap, and a hint of stale, after-work sweat clinging to his clothes. It was the smell I imagined was associated with the first kiss after a lover walked in the door. The kiss that said, *I'm so happy to be done with work and home, here, with you.* The kiss that said, *I'll go change and then we can start our evening together.* The kisses I'd thought about enough that they felt real, but never actually had.

"You're here now," I murmured, mostly to myself. I'd lost the thread of the conversation a bit, distracted by thinking about William coming home to…me. I wasn't sure where the thought had come from. I wasn't the coming-home-to type, or so I'd been told by enough lovers I assumed they must be onto something.

But William's eyes were narrowed and his color was high and his breath was audible. Either he was about to hit me, or—

The kiss hit me like a fist, and I had to grab him around the shoulders to keep from pitching backward under the onslaught. I allowed myself the briefest moment of victory that my plan had worked, and then I sank into the kiss. His mouth had the slightly sharp bite of coffee, but that gave way almost immediately to the warm caramel taste that was Will's alone. It was sugar and heat and richly turning leaves and I opened my mouth, desperate for more of it.

Will grabbed me and slid his hand up my back beneath my suit coat, trying to pull my shirt out of my pants without breaking the kiss and failing.

"God, of *course* you're wearing a fucking vest," he muttered, and his magnificent mouth was nearly a pout.

"Shall I take it off, William?"

He rolled his eyes and nodded impatiently. I took off my coat and unbuttoned my vest, keeping my eyes on his the whole time. Those wonderful amber eyes that were by turns suspicious and warm. Right now they were lit with the twin fires of arousal and anger, and I decided on the spot that an angry and turned-on William Fox was a great William Fox.

I shrugged out of my vest and he went for my shirt, pulling it up and over my head without unbuttoning it, swearing when the sleeves got caught at my wrists. I hadn't expected this. The way wanting something made him careless, indelicate.

Finally he pulled my shirt off and I made a mental note that I'd need at least two buttons sewn back on it later. Then Will came at me again and we were stripping each other thoughtlessly, wordlessly, our clothes mixing together on the floor of my office as Will shoved a pre-lubed condom into my hand and turned away from me, bracing himself on the edge of my desk and—Jesus—*offering* himself to me. Tilting his gorgeously muscled ass up to me, the gesture as aggressive an order of *Fuck me* as the words would have been.

I took a moment to sear the sight before me into my mind forever. William Fox, muscular arms rigid before him, shoulder blades spreading like wings, legs just wide enough apart for me to see the delicious darkness between them.

I must have waited a beat too long because Will looked over his shoulder at me. Glared, really. And for just a moment I saw the uncertainty in his eyes. Naked fear that maybe, just maybe, I didn't want him.

Which was absolutely unacceptable.

I groaned as I closed the distance between us in one step,

and ran a hand up his spine to his neck and into his thick hair, damp at the nape. I pressed one kiss there, where hair gave way to hot skin, another to the center of his spine, a third and a fourth to the dimples on either side of the cleft of his ass, lightly furred with soft, dark hair.

"You're exquisite, William. A work of art."

That, perhaps, was a slight miscalculation. While his eyes had softened at "exquisite," at "art," he snorted and dragged me forward to him, the message of speed clear.

"Well, you can't steal me," he said roughly. "And you can't buy me. So you better hope I'm not a work of art, or I doubt you'd know what to do with me."

I cursed myself for my clumsy speech, but smirked at Will. "I know exactly what I'm going to do with you," I said, pleased that my voice sounded as confident as ever.

"Oh yeah?" Will ground out, getting back into the spirit of things when I rubbed two fingers against his glorious hole.

"Oh yes." I kept rubbing him and bent to lick his ear. "I'm going to fuck you on my desk. And then I'm going to think about how you screamed for me every single time I sit at it."

I was so hard it hurt and I ground my erection against Will's naked ass to punctuate the sentiment. He groaned shakily as I pressed into him.

"On Monday morning," I said into his ear as I reached around and took him in hand. He cried out, knuckles white where he grabbed the desk. "I'm going to sit there and imagine you just like this. Legs spread, open and begging for me." I licked a stripe up the side of his throat.

"I'm not…begging…" Will gasped, and I smiled against his damp skin.

"No," I conceded. "No. Not yet."

I replaced my fingers with my cock, then and took his hips in my hands. I loved this moment. The moment just before penetration, when everything was still swirling arousal, yet to coalesce into the muscular pleasure of thrust and stroke, clench and slide. The moment when I was not yet as close as I knew I was about to be.

Only for once, I did feel that close. I held William's lean hips in my hands, and smelled his skin, and saw the scattered freckles on his shoulder blades, and I felt a rush of connection, as if I'd seen him this way before, though it was impossible. I dropped my head down, forehead against his spine, limned with sweat. Then I slid my hands down to cup his ass, giving him a squeeze for good measure, and spreading him wide for me. This time I paused to feel the tension running through William's frame, the gentle tremors of anticipation.

"Please," he whispered, every muscle tensed. "Come on."

"I told you you'd beg me," I growled, and I bit his earlobe—just a nip. Just a reminder of who was in charge. He groaned and I slid inside him in one powerful thrust that left me lightheaded and pulled a tremulous whine from Will.

I fucked him and he fucked back into me, his earlier anger and irritation channeled into pleasure-seeking. It was aggressive and messy and inelegant and so very much more than I had ever imagined it might be.

And I *had* imagined it.

When Will began to slide up the desk with the power of my thrusts, I wrapped my left arm around his chest, holding him up so I could continue pounding into him, and grabbed his heavy erection with my right hand, stroking it, then rolling his balls, which made him cry out and throw his head back in pleasure. He would've broken my nose if I'd been one second slower in reacting, but once his head was on my shoulder, I kissed his exposed throat just once, and then let slip the dogs of war.

I slammed into him and he shook around me, crying out my name in a voice that was nothing like what I'd heard from him but would live in my mind whenever he spoke, a relic stored away like something precious, even if I was the only one who knew it was there.

"Are you gonna come for me, William?" I asked, voice gone rough and low.

"Gonna...come," he gasped, and I could see just enough of his face to see his eyes were squeezed shut tight. "But not...for you," he added.

Stubborn, William. I would have laughed, had every molecule of my being not been in pursuit of my orgasm, hovering just on the other side of a few final thrusts.

I grunted, grabbed his dick, and jerked him, driving into him so hard he slammed into the desk. I felt him start to come, muscles gone tight, insides quivering on the edge, mouth opened in a silent scream. I reached down and pressed a finger to the tip of his dick, then gave him one final stroke, and his come spattered the side of my desk and ran down my fist as I unloaded inside him, pleasure shooting white-hot through me.

When I came to a few moments later, limbs still shaky, I had my cheek pressed to Will's sweaty back, my hand still curled protectively around his dick. I dropped a light kiss on his shoulder as he pulled away to stand.

He dressed in silence, seeming almost shy in the way he

wouldn't quite meet my gaze. I pulled my underwear and shirt back on, but left the rest. I had spare clothes in the closet.

William lingered at the door. I'd thought if I could just get him near me—or under me—that things could progress from there. But rather than wishing to take him out to a restaurant or a show, I found myself wishing he would come back to my apartment with me, order sushi—or whatever he wanted—and do this all again. In the time it took me to have the thought, though, Will had slid his shoes back on and grabbed the painting from its still-safe spot on the floor.

"I guess I'll…" He gestured to the door.

"Hey." I stepped close so that our chests were touching. Finally, he made eye contact. His amber eyes weren't hostile like they had been when he first showed up, but that wariness was back in place. "Hey," I repeated, "William. Have dinner with me."

He shook his head and looked down.

"All right. If not tonight, then when are you free?"

"I'm not going on a date with you."

It was measured, considered, final. "Why not?"

"Because." This time when he met my eyes they were cold with judgment. "You're a liar." And he pulled the door firmly shut behind him.

CHAPTER 9

Vaughn

THERE WAS ALWAYS the danger, with an early September gala, that the ballroom would end up looking like autumn had vomited. The party planner I'd used a few years ago had gone so overboard with decorative gourds that I was concerned for the structural integrity of the side tables, to say nothing of my guests' aesthetics.

But Charlotte Fox was as good at her job as her brother claimed to be at his. The décor was perfectly balanced between elegance and modernity—exactly the message I wished to send about the Vaughn Foundation and our pursuits. In the entryway were huge bouquets of pink, orange, red, and yellow cockscomb, their muscular stems, intricate folds, and fiery hues a dramatic welcome to the gala, evoking the turning leaves without being as literal as the decorative gourds.

The long banquet table was patterned with lines of sticks, each with a square of chocolate tied to it. Guests' names and table numbers were printed on the chocolate's paper wrapper, with a note that told guests they'd see what to do with it when they arrived at their tables.

The tables were draped with flannel tablecloths in subtle,

elegant plaids. Centerpieces were made up to look like tiny campfires, with pieces of wood and kindling cleverly arranged around enclosed burners that looked like flames. Each plate was a circle of wood, as if a log had been sliced like cookie dough, and piled on the plaid tablecloths were large, homemade marshmallows, each one branded with a familiar VF, and stacks of perfectly-formed hand-baked graham crackers, as well as more chocolate.

Already, guests were gathering at their tables, fitting the marshmallows onto the sticks they'd carried in from the foyer, and toasting them over the centerpieces' flames, sharing s'mores as gleefully as children. It was a masterful job of creating an immediate sense of community, fun, and anticipation, all from a stick and a snack. I had never seen as many smiles at a charity function before the bar was half tapped. I made a mental note to engage Charlotte Fox for every foreseeable event, even if I never saw her brother again.

And it seemed like that might be a very real possibility, given the way we'd last parted.

You're a liar.

Will's words echoed in my head, feeling as immediate now as they had when he speared me with them after we'd shared some of the hottest sex of my life. Of Will's too, I was willing to bet, if the way he'd clawed at my desk and begged me for more was any indication.

But apparently although he would fuck a liar, he wouldn't go out on a date with one.

It wasn't the way things usually went. In fact, over the years I'd gotten so used to partners who were after me because of my money or my family's position that I'd often defaulted to sex just to avoid the complications that came with dating. And, all right, the heartache that came with finding out that people you thought cared about you viewed you instead as a means to, well…means.

When Valerie and I had first transitioned from friends to lovers, we'd been twenty-four. I was fresh out of business school and she'd just gotten her first position at Holcum and Whitt. We'd known each other since we were children, always running around in the gardens of estates where our parents had taken us to parties, or playing hide-and-seek in the museum hallways during benefits.

It had just happened one day. We'd been down at the lake, lounging on the dock, and the sun had lit the droplets of water in her ash blonde hair like a halo. Her shoulders had been sunburnt from the day before and she was teasing me, pushing at my shoulder and rolling her eyes. And suddenly, for the first time, she was different. She wasn't my friend, Val, whom I'd known forever. She was beautiful, her very being changed suddenly.

It was the longest relationship I'd ever had. I was convinced that had been in part because we were already such good friends, and in part because for four months of it, Val had been in New York. We had been good together. A good team. But while we'd had a deep affection for one another, and were very sexually compatible, we weren't…in love. Certainly, we bickered enough that our friends joked we'd be married by Christmas, but our fights were the moments we were *most* passionate about our relationship. For the most part, we were invested in one another's happiness more than we were in our happiness together. And so, after a year and a half, we'd parted ways with a wistful sadness—regret for how perfect it would've been if we'd been able to translate a deep friendship into a lifelong romance and partnership. Alas, it wasn't meant to be. And we'd known it would have soured if we'd kept on past the expiration date. Her friendship was still precious to me, and I was so happy when she'd found Dallas Fairbanks.

Unfortunately, I'd never been as lucky again.

After Val, I'd dated widely and shallowly, as if I were making a point to anyone who was watching that I wasn't simply a prize to be won, or a meal ticket. But my next relationships all crashed and burned, or fizzled out—some in a few weeks and some a few months, but most never even lasted long enough to be considered relationships at all.

There was Terrence, the stockbroker who'd wanted me to fuck him on a bed strewn with hundred dollar bills. Millie, the lawyer who'd worked so much that we didn't actually see each other, merely texted back and forth to make and break dates for two months. Dhruv, a flight attendant who'd taken an interest in me during a brief period of frequent flights between D.C. and Houston, where he was based. Jonathan, whom I'd thought was a fundraiser and turned out to be a party promoter, with all the scare quotes the title implied, who was trawling for investors. And designer drugs. Sharon, who'd been sweet, but clearly had no interest in me sexually. Her mother, it turned out, had encouraged her to get involved with me, hoping we'd marry and help with her debts.

After Tucker, who thought I was looking to play sugar daddy in exchange for an escort to parties, I went into self-imposed dating hibernation for a few years. It wasn't as if it was something I actively enjoyed, after all. I liked people a great deal, but I was always more interested in figuring them out, like solving a puzzle. It was easy for me to be charming and ingratiating—after all, it wasn't just my job; it was basically my birthright. But it was no fun figuring people out when all they were after was money. That really *was* my job. And I didn't actually need to turn on the charm, since anyone who wanted my money wanted it in spite of my temperament.

No, one-night stands in neutral locations and platonic friends to accompany me to social engagements had served me just fine for years.

Until I'd met William Fox, who had somehow distinguished himself from all those one-night stands before the night was even over. And now, rather than me turning heel and leaving as soon as it was polite to do so, *he* was the one who had made it clear that he had no interest in our further acquaintance. No interest in getting to know me, though I was now more intrigued by him than anyone I could remember.

Because he was smart, and decent, and somehow still kind, even in his line of work. Because he wore terrible suits but still looked gorgeous, like a fine present in a wrapping of newsprint. Because he was ever so slightly awkward and terrible at flirting, or even being flirted with. Because his mouth and his scent and his body did things to me that no one's ever had before.

Because he upheld the law, and I flouted it. Oh, not just because of my extracurricular activities with regards to art. I'd simply never had to play by the rules. Growing up with the might of the Vaughn name and bank balance behind me had let me know from a very early age that there was no law you couldn't sidestep, no rule you couldn't bend. The world wasn't regulated, as we were meant to believe. That was just a convenient fiction we all perpetuated because the alternative was to acknowledge how very little we could depend on.

I could feel a fog of melancholy descending so I shook it off and made myself begin the rounds of greetings. Many of the partygoers were people I'd known much of my life, who'd been attending the annual galas since their inception. A few were even friends of my parents who'd known me since I was a boy.

A flash of red in my periphery had me turning to see James Novack, art forger extraordinaire, sweep into the hall with two friends. He wore black jeans and a bright red sweater, and when he caught my eye, he dipped his chin to me in greeting, flipping his tousled hair. Then he turned back to his friends and they found their places at one of the tables where students had been seated. As he sat down, he caught my eye again, and casually hooked a finger in the collar of his red sweater, and then he winked at me. Scarlet. He'd worn a sweater the color of the paint I'd told him Meredith Palmer edged her greens with. I had to give the little shit credit for a stylish play. He was proving to be very interesting indeed.

I signaled to Charlotte that she should start the appetizers circulating, and watched to see people's reactions to the food. Charlotte's caterer was one I hadn't used before and I hadn't had the time to sample the menu, instead giving her the go-ahead via text, but the trays coming out of the kitchen looked beautiful and people seemed impressed.

Butternut squash tartlets with fried sage leaves; a trio of bite-sized adult PB&Js—almond butter and blueberry jam, peanut butter and strawberry preserves, and cashew butter with fig spread; slices of roasted parsnip spread with white-bean puree; puff pastry parcels of smoked salmon, cream cheese, and capers; slices of perfectly pink roast beef dotted with spicy mustard and black garlic aioli; golden-brown balls of fried pumpkin risotto topped with a fluff of shaved asiago cheese. The platters emptied within minutes and I caught a glimpse of Charlotte walking briskly back toward the kitchen to signal the second wave.

I was considering sneaking into the kitchen myself, to sample the food before the whole night passed without me trying anything, but as I turned in that direction, I saw him.

William Fox. Standing at the entrance hall, his hands clasped behind his back completely spoiling the line of what was a far better-cut suit than anything I'd seen him in previously. It was a chocolate brown that made his coloring look warm and somehow more delicate than I'd noticed he was. I had no doubt Charlotte had picked it out for him, and probably the light blue shirt as well.

Suddenly self-conscious, I slid the paper with the points I needed to make during my speech into the pocket of my vest and ran a hand over my hair, which was queued back tightly. My dove gray Chittleborough and Morgan was tailored perfectly, from the Milanese buttonholes to the pick stitching. There was a slight sheen to the fabric, silk lending an airiness to the soft vicuña wool, that made my light eyes sparkle and my hair glimmer. I knew I looked perfect. So why didn't I feel it?

I'd hoped he might show up—had made it clear to Char-lotte that she should feel free to extend a plus-one of her choosing, knowing she would choose him. I thought again, as I had at Oakley's party and at Val's wedding, how out of place William looked in this world. But then, perhaps that was the lot of an FBI agent? Never quite of the milieu in which you spend your time. Always examining it from a detached distance. Always in service of it, or suspicious.

I wondered where in the world William Fox felt completely, totally comfortable. Absolutely himself. And damned if I didn't want to see what it was like to be there with him.

CHAPTER 10

Will

M Y SISTER HAD outdone herself.

When Charlotte first started Fox Fêtes, she used to rope me into helping at weekend gigs, and I'd actually liked that better than being a guest. At least I was doing something useful. But she'd long since found a competent and reliable core staff, and only required my assistance on an emergency basis. So, since then, I'd only attended parties like this as her plus-one. She liked to show off the results of her work, so I put on the only suit I owned that wasn't for work, and I showed up, every time. As I stood surveying the crowd gathering in the ballroom, I was charmed by her taste and proud of her success. There were a lot of happy people, and that should make for plenty of open pocket books.

I got a glimpse of my sister rushing around, and knew better than to try and bother her; we both afforded our careers single-minded focus. I didn't want to think about how closely our jobs were intertwining at this particular event, but it was difficult not to. Especially since I saw Vaughn almost immediately—he was hard to miss, with his height and that distinctive hair. And if I'd hoped the attraction would have abated since we'd last seen each other, the speed with which my eyes found him killed that hope.

I'd never seen a man wear a suit quite like Amory Vaughn, and this might have been my favorite so far—the light gray perfectly setting off his pale features and that silver-white hair. He was wearing a vest, which sent my mind back to that afternoon in his office for the thousandth time, when it had gotten in the way of me stripping him naked as fast as I'd wanted. I vaguely remembered popping buttons off his shirt as I was getting it off him. I'd nearly sent him an email offering to pay for the repairs, but realized it was a thinly-veiled excuse to speak to him and certainly did not convey the message of *We're through* that I'd made clear when I'd left.

My table was full of people I didn't know, and I was content to introduce myself as Charlotte's brother, answer curious questions about my job, and eat the outstanding food. Charlotte had a place at the table, but she only stopped by sporadically, far too involved with the proceedings to sit down and eat.

"Vaughn gave her a spot so that she'd enjoy herself," the woman who had introduced herself as Eliza Hayes, a fundraiser for a veterans' arts program, said with a fond smile. "He knows that no true event planner can rest until the party's over though."

"I don't think I've ever been to a party where the event planner is able to relax and enjoy herself," said her husband.

"Well, you know Vaughn," Eliza said with a wave of her hand. "He's got as many manners as millions. At the Pause For Paws fundraiser, I saw him have words with the host after he berated the caterer in front of everyone for not having enough appetizers." She laughed. "Of course, Vaughn did it quietly so none of us knew exactly what he said, but I'm sure it was politely withering."

I smiled at this story because I knew I was expected to, but the picture of Vaughn as a white knight was one that I desperately wanted to be true. The first course was served: a light mushroom gazpacho, dotted with truffle cream and brightened with a splash of fig vinegar. As people ate, I was subjected to a rousing conversation of what a generous and wonderful man our host was. I kept waiting for someone to say something negative or unkind. It was difficult to keep a clear picture in my mind of Vaughn as an amoral thief when faced with evidence that complicated the story.

I'd gone to get another drink when I ran into Charlie. She was smiling and her eyes were sparkling, so I assumed things were going as well on her end as they were for the guests. "Hey, Charlie."

"Will!" She grabbed me in an exuberant hug. "You wore the suit!"

Of course I'd worn the suit. I'd endured her taking me shopping for it, because she'd been convinced that if I wore any of my usual suits I'd make all of her guests nervous. "There's gonna be a ton of rich people there, Will," she'd told me. "They might think you're investigating them for fraud or something."

I had to admit the suit was the best I'd ever owned, and it'd had the price tag to prove it. But I didn't look like a federal agent, so mission accomplished. Of course, that meant I'd hardly get my money's worth out of it, because when was I going to wear a suit like this again if not to work?

"You look great," my sister enthused, and then a calculating look crossed her face. "In fact, hey, come with me."

"Charlie—"

It was no use. She was a force of nature, tugging me along with her through the crowd, and I knew exactly what was going to happen. Sure enough, we stopped when she'd found her target…the absolute last person I wanted to see.

"Mr. Vaughn," said my sister, all charm and professional friendliness, "I wanted to introduce you to my brother and my plus-one, Will."

I tried not to glare at her. She knew very well Vaughn and I had met before, though I'd played it off as having been a brief introduction at Oakley's. "We've met," I said, aware I sounded just as terse as my sister did friendly.

"Indeed we have," Vaughn said.

I tried not to hear his voice in my ear as he fucked me— telling me how he was going to think about making me beg when he was at work the next Monday—but failed. I wondered if he had.

"Nice to see you again, William."

I almost—*almost*—said, "It's Agent Fox." But this was a career coup for Charlie and I wouldn't ruin it for her. Still. He didn't get to win that easy. "You too, Amory."

His eyebrows raised a bit, and there was a sparkle in his pale eyes. "I hope you're enjoying yourself. Your sister has exceeded all of my expectations and ruined me for other event planners." Vaughn directed that charming smile at Charlie, and despite how easily I knew he could lie, there was nothing disingenuous in his voice at all.

Charlie fairly glowed from the praise. "I'm so glad you're happy," she said, beaming.

Vaughn lifted his glass to her. "More than. I confess I'm intrigued by what you might come up with next. We'll have to talk about my schedule in a week or so, when you're recovered from tonight."

Part of me wanted to punch Vaughn for ingratiating himself with the one person who was always on my side, and another part wanted to thank him for how happy he'd made Charlotte. Instead I just nodded politely and avoided shooting Charlotte a dirty look when she "suddenly" had to take care of something and left me there with Vaughn.

I steeled myself for whatever tactical maneuvering was about to take place, and was somewhat surprised when Vaughn simply smiled at me—not the genuine smile he'd given Charlotte, but one I'd seen him give strangers—and said politely, "If you'll excuse me, Agent Fox, I have a speech to give."

An unexpected rush of disappointment sluiced through me, and my feet felt like they'd sprouted roots that dug into the floor. Why was I reacting this way? Wasn't this what I'd wanted? For him to back off. But now that he was doing it, I found I didn't like it one bit. Jesus Christ, I needed to get out of here.

I was debating what you were supposed to say to someone who was going to give a speech—was it *Break a leg?*— when he said, "That is a wonderful color on you, by the way."

My eyes flew to his. That sounded almost…regretful.

"Thanks," I said, and then, "You look…well. You know. Very, uh. Put together."

And there, finally, was that genuine smile. Of course, it *would* be accompanied by laughter at my expense.

I scowled, and said, "Good luck with the speech," before turning on my heel and walking away. I hated how he fucked with my equilibrium, and for the first time I had to consider the mixed signals I was giving him. Threatening to arrest him one moment, bending over his desk the next.

I returned to the table just as Vaughn started to speak. The microphone amplified his deep, rich drawl, and hearing it in stereo was almost as good as hearing it low in my ear. I was hard under the table and completely unable to look away from him.

"I'd like to thank you all for coming this evening," he said, smiling. "I hope you are enjoying yourselves and that you will continue to do so. I'd like to thank Ms. Charlotte Fox, of Fox Fêtes, for making this such a lovely affair." He started clapping, and we all followed suit.

I wondered, probably uncharitably, if he'd be doing this if I weren't here. And the problem—the thing that was unbalancing me so completely—was that I believed he would. The simple truth of Vaughn's generosity, demonstrated here after I'd heard stories of it all night, made me take a bracing gulp of my whiskey as my resolve to end whatever this was between us waned dangerously.

"After dessert, we'll be having an auction to raise money for the Willowbrook capital campaign. Never fear, we've found someone more adept at these sorts of things than me. I've been told I talk far too slowly to be an effective auctioneer."

There was some good-natured laughter as Vaughn talked briefly about the items to be auctioned off, mostly expensive vacation homes.

"We certainly don't want anyone feeling left out, so please, do feel free to simply hold up your signifier"—he raised his paddle, fashioned in the shape of a cozy cabin, identical to the ones we all had at our tables—"if you'd like to donate without bidding after the auction. And thank you, again, for your generosity. The Vaughn Foundation prides itself on being supportive of the arts, and that includes the next generation of artists to come. We also have students from the Willowbrook art department here, who have generously donated some of their own work tonight. No doubt they are the rising stars in our midst, so take the opportunity to acquire their work before it's only available at Sotheby's."

Even though I was just another face in the crowd, I swear Vaughn's eyes met mine.

"You'll be getting great art at a steal, I assure you."

It should have made me mad. It should have reminded me of everything that Amory Vaughn was, beyond the money and the manners. It should have reminded me that I had been absolutely correct when I'd called him a liar.

Instead, I laughed. I couldn't help it.

It was the beginning of the end of my resistance, and I knew it.

The auction was hugely successful, and while I didn't participate—even the student art was out of my price range—it was more fun than I thought it would be. The auctioneer was a local celebrity who I didn't recognize but had the crowd excited, and I contributed a donation simply because I wanted the novelty of using my paddle. There was dancing after the auction, but I was far less inclined to participate in that. So I sat and drank my excellent whiskey while toasting marshmallows, and pretended I wasn't scanning the room for Vaughn.

Charlotte finally collapsed next to me, when the dancing

was in full swing and the last plate had been cleared. She looked exhausted but happy. "Ugh, this went so well, I can't believe it. I almost couldn't sleep the last three days. I kept dreaming something would go wrong."

"It didn't," I said, and toasted her with my glass. "So you can get a good night's sleep tonight, yeah?"

"Yeah." She gave a satisfied smile and leaned back in her seat. "I was mostly worried they wouldn't make the goal, you know? Like, how awful would that be? I'm hired for this event and it doesn't raise enough money."

"That would hardly be your fault," I said, but I wasn't surprised that she'd worried about it. We both had a tendency to take responsibility for things we shouldn't. "And besides, it raised the amount and then some."

She nodded. "Yup, and—" She glanced around, then leaned in and whispered. "Also, I'm not supposed to let this get out, but one of the Vaughn Foundation employees heard me talking to Forrest, the head caterer, about how I was nervous about them not raising the money. He said not to worry—that Mr. Vaughn didn't want it to be public knowledge, but he'd make sure of it. As in, if they didn't raise enough money, he'd just donate the rest himself. He's done it three or four times, apparently. Isn't that nice?"

It was nice. And I'd had enough whiskey that I could admit it.

"He's a nice man. Kinda weird. And you're right, he *does* sort of look like Lucius Malfoy." She giggled. "But it's great there are people like him in the world, you know?"

"Rich people who want to throw elaborate parties?"

Charlotte hit me lightly on the arm. "People who care enough about something to put their money where their mouth is," she said. "He's apparently a huge art lover, has this great art collection. And it was totally his idea to take the paintings that didn't sell at the student art show and auction them off for the scholarship, after he bought them all, *and* made the last-minute addition for the students to attend the party, even though I had to pay, like, super-high prices to add some more tables and linens, not to mention up the head count for food."

The students were the rowdy contingent on the dance floor keeping the party going, obviously fueled into soaking up every last minute by the free food and liquor. I couldn't say I blamed them. I'd been a student once too. It didn't surprise me Vaughn had bought the paintings he'd auctioned off, and I wondered what my lack of surprise meant.

Maybe it means you're well aware that he's more than just the liar you accused him of being.

I was still absolutely certain that Vaughn was behind the Oakley theft and the "prank" involving Curtis Loel's Saska. But he'd also raised a substantial amount of money for a capital campaign, given a bunch of unknown student artists money and exposure, and it wasn't as if this was the first time for any of it. I'd seen myself what his foundation had accomplished with him at the helm. He hadn't stolen Oakley's or Loel's art for personal gain, and while I couldn't condone what he'd done, that *did* make a difference.

I was still thinking about this when the lights rose, signaling that the party was over, and I shed my jacket to help Charlie pull the linens off the tables. They had to be bagged for cleaning before the rental company could remove the tables and chairs, and I knew this part was her least favorite.

She was a few tables away when Vaughn went over to her

and firmly insisted she stop and take a break. "I can take these off the tables just as easily as you can, Ms. Fox," he said. "You should eat something, since I'm fairly certain you haven't."

"I had dessert," my sister replied. "And, Mr. Vaughn, this is what you hired me for."

"I hired you to throw a wonderful party and you did," he said. "Now go sit, and let me finish this. I absolutely insist. And it's just Vaughn, please."

"Then you can call me just Charlotte," my sister said with a smile, and after another protest, she went to the kitchen. The sight of Vaughn, also stripped of his jacket, working alongside the staff, made up my mind. And maybe the whiskey helped. I doubted Vaughn would approach me again; not after the way I'd responded the last time. So if I wanted something to happen, it was up to me.

I bagged my linens, then walked over and held the bag open for Vaughn to deposit his. "I'd like to have a word, if I might."

He was surprised, I could tell, and he looked tired too. I wondered who he really was, Amory Vaughn. I wondered if he even knew anymore.

"I'm all ears, William," he said as he deposited the linens in the bag. Together, we moved to the next table.

"I said something to you that I want to apologize for," I said slowly. "The last time I saw you."

"You don't think I look put together?"

I blinked, until I realized he was referring to our brief conversation before his speech. "No, in your office. When I called you a liar."

"Ah." He studied me, pale eyes wary. He'd known what I

meant.

"That was…maybe a bit harsh of me," I said.

The linens had all been stripped and there was no one left in the ballroom but us, and the absence of the energy was strangely tangible.

"It's just, you have to understand the problem I have here. You're a thief—yes, fine, maybe you didn't do it for selfish reasons but you still did it, and don't you *dare* tell me that you didn't. But also don't tell me that you *did,* because as much as I want to know how the fuck you walked out of Oakley's house with that painting, I can't know that. I can't."

Vaughn opened his mouth, seemed to think better of it, and leaned back against the table. He crossed his arms, looking elegant and fuckable in that vest and his starched shirt, and I fought the urge to tear this one off him, as I had in his office.

"I don't get you," I said, finally. "I don't know who you are—the man who raises millions of dollars for charity, or the man who steals things, seemingly for fun. Even if the people you stole from *are* odious pricks," I muttered. I held up my hand, realizing I'd maybe had more to drink than I thought. "I'm not excusing your behavior. And I don't *understand* it."

"Well," he said, and now there was no smile, no hint of playfulness. "Maybe, just maybe, people aren't quite as black-and-white as you seem to think they are. Me included."

"There are things that are wrong, and things that are right, and those things are non-negotiable," I informed him. God, why was I so bad at flirting? "Did it ever occur to you that the things you do, stealing like that, it could end up costing you the chance do all of this?" I indicated the ballroom. I half expected an argument, or some flippant response, but he remained quiet, watching me. "I'm sorry I said that to you. I don't know what you are, not really, but I don't think 'liar' is a fair assessment." I took a deep breath. "And if you still wanted to go to dinner, you should ask me again because this time I'll probably say yes."

"Probably?" Vaughn frowned, but the tension in his shoulders had eased and I detected a hint of amusement in there. "I'm supposed to sacrifice my pride at being turned down for a *probably*?"

"Oh, take a risk, Amory."

Something flickered in his eyes that I couldn't read. At first I thought he was going to say no, or phrase it as a clever quip that I'd have to parry. But when he spoke, his voice was low and serious. "Have dinner with me, William."

And, god, the way he said my name. This time I said, "Yeah, okay. But you might not want to wear a shirt with so many buttons."

CHAPTER 11

Vaughn

TECHNICALLY, WILLIAM HAD agreed to dinner, but dinner wasn't what I had in mind anymore. Dinner wasn't nearly enough to impress Agent William Fox. To show him who I was. What we could—just maybe—be together.

I'd spent the days since he'd agreed mining everything I'd learned about him to plan our date. I wasn't under any illusion that I'd have a second chance if it didn't go well. In fact, I wasn't at all sure that he'd even go through with this one, since his assent had come on the heels of rather a lot of whiskey at the Vaughn Foundation gala.

I took a deep breath and glanced at the clock over the stove. If he was coming, he'd be here any minute. And wasn't there just something to be said for punctuality. At least I'd only be left in the agony of limbo for a few minutes before having to accept that he wasn't coming. Everything was clean and tidy—everything was always clean and tidy—but I moved through the kitchen and front room straightening the hang of a towel here and the angle of a book there.

I'd invited Will to the Falls Church house rather than to my apartment, though that was far closer to Will's apartment in the city. And though he'd been here before, the day of

Val's wedding, I wanted everything to look perfect for him. It was the part I could control. The roar of a motor came as I plucked one stray hair from my sleeve, and my heart gave an exuberant thud.

The William Fox I opened the door to was one I'd never seen before. Gone were the horrible suits he wore for work, and the lovely one he'd worn to the gala. Instead, he wore dark jeans, low hiking boots clearly chosen for function rather than fashion, and a simple black-and-white checked flannel shirt, worn to softness but still neat, well-maintained. Black-and-white? *Oh, William, it's you in shirt form.*

"Um, hi." He ran his hand through his hair, a wisp falling over his forehead in a way it didn't usually do, suggesting that he used some kind of product in it when he was at work. "I just parked on the driveway. That okay?" He gestured jerkily over his shoulder, looking to where his tidy navy Honda Accord sat beneath the white oak, tires gleaming black against the white gravel of the driveway. He was shifting nervously and I was charmed by it.

"Hello, William." I waited for him to meet my eyes, then I held out my hand. He grabbed it as if he intended a handshake, pulling a smile from me as I drew him inside. "How was your drive?"

"It was fine."

I closed the door behind him and put a palm on it, arm next to his shoulder, crowding him up against it. His eyes darted from my arm to my face and he swallowed audibly.

"It was, um, pretty. The trees." Now his eyes darted to my mouth. I leaned a little closer to him and his lips parted. Exquisite.

"I'm glad." Just a little closer. "You smell wonderful," I

murmured, and watched a shiver run through him. Watched his eyelashes flutter ever so slightly. Then I stepped away and watched him struggle to get himself under control again.

He cleared his throat. "So, what are we doing?" And did I detect a hint of irritation that I hadn't kissed him? God, I hoped so. "It's kind of early for dinner, isn't it? Unless rich people eat early and I never knew it."

He smiled a bit, like it was a joke and not a dig he'd made to try and assert control in a situation where he clearly felt nervous, so I smiled back. "No. Not unless they're also quite old."

His smile softened.

"I thought we could go on a walk, eat when we're done. The land around my home is beautiful and the weather's fine."

"A walk."

"Yes, William, a walk."

"Sure, okay."

"Unless there's something else you'd prefer we do," I said, dropping my voice low and watching the heat flash in his eyes.

Those narrowed eyes and flared nostrils sent an echoing flash of heat through me.

"Shall we?" And this time when I held out a hand to him, he took it.

It was a glorious autumn day, the sun warm on our faces, then on our backs when we zagged, following the path that picked its way through the hills. The scents of trees and dirt, and just a whiff of William's cologne when the wind blew. The susurrus of leaves, the cheeps and caws of birds, the scrabbling of small things in the underbrush and along branches, and the crunch of footfalls, as we tramped along in harmony.

Will in motion was as glorious as I'd imagined. He had the long, prowling stride of a cat, and the unselfconsciousness of one at ease in his body, accustomed to it being under his command. It was unnervingly hot, knowing what that body looked like, felt like, tasted like when it was under mine.

The crack of a branch I hadn't noticed underfoot made me stumble slightly, and William reached out and caught me by the upper arm, steadying me, though I didn't need it.

He looked open and happy, clearly in his element outside, in nature. It was gratifying to have read him right. I nodded my thanks and he quirked a smirk, as if perhaps he thought I was out of *my* element, before letting go.

"Forgive my clumsiness, William. I hadn't quite accounted for how distracting you would be mounting an incline." I ran my hands over the swell of his round ass and winked. "Really, this should be labeled as a trail hazard."

Will's cheeks flushed red and he inhaled sharply, but instead of pulling away, he dropped his gaze to the ground and a smile played on his lips. "So," he said, continuing up the trail, "I admit I didn't really take you for the outdoorsy type."

"I suppose I'm not, per se. But I've walked these trails all my life. This land is like an extension of me. I've watched certain trees grow, others die. I feel…at home here."

He hummed his understanding and I felt the easy affinity between us. It was what I wanted. The way we were when nothing got in the way.

"That's how I feel when I'm climbing," he said, eyes on

the trees beyond. "At home. Like I'm more myself."

"Rock climbing?" He nodded. It suited him somehow, pitting his will against the very matter of a mountain. "Hmm, I would have cast you in the role of the immovable object, but now I rather like thinking of you as the unstoppable force."

"That's a paradox, isn't it?" he said, single-mindedly striding up the trail. After a few seconds his step faltered. "Oh, sorry, you're joking."

"No." I stepped up to him and squeezed his shoulder. "I'm flirting with you. Attempting to, anyway."

"Ah, right. Sorry."

"Not at all. Come along. We're nearly there."

"Nearly where?"

I ran the hand that was on his shoulder down his spine to the small of his back, and gave him a little push up the trail. "You'll see."

He walked in silence for a minute, then turned around to peer at me suspiciously. "Are you looking at my ass?"

In fact for once, I hadn't been. I'd been watching the way his shoulder blades shifted beneath the soft flannel of his shirt, and thinking about the light smattering of freckles I knew adorned them. Thinking about the kiss I'd placed between them when I'd had him over my desk. Thinking about how I'd tasted his skin there, the slight tang of salt, as he'd come in my hand, clenching around my hard cock. And how I'd wanted to have the right to look at those freckles whenever I liked, to come to know the patterns in their randomness the way I knew the patterns of the trees that surrounded us.

But, "Oh, absolutely," I told him, and smiled.

We reached the clearing just when I'd planned, as the light that filtered through the leaves dappled the ground with shifting shapes and beamed over the drop-off beyond. In this light, it was a magical place, green-drenched and buoyant with life, but quiet enough that we could have been the last two men on earth.

I felt like a boy, suddenly, flush with excitement over a new friend, desperate to share this place with him. Desperate for him to love it as much as I did.

William walked to the edge and gazed out across the gorge, and for just a moment my heart raced to see him that close to the edge.

"It's stunning," he said into the open air.

And I let him take his time with the view as I attended to the preparations. The soft red wool blanket was where I'd left it two hours before, weighted down at the corners with stones so it wouldn't blow away. The picnic hamper sat in the center; a bottle of wine lay beside it. The food was all packed away in airtight containers so no animals would get at it, but I polished the silverware again for good measure as I took it from the basket.

"This is the first time I've actually seen someone use a picnic basket in real life." Will's voice came from over my shoulder before he bent down to sit on the blanket with me, stretching his long legs out in front of him, hiking boots resting considerably off the edge.

"What do people usually use instead?"

"Uh, nothing. Because normal people don't have picnics."

"They don't?"

"No. Well, maybe they do. But not, ah, fancy picnics."

"This is a fancy picnic? You don't even know what I'm serving yet."

Will rolled his eyes, but the gesture seemed indulgent rather than annoyed.

"Whatever. I'm sure it's fancy because you're Amory Vaughn and this is a picnic basket, and these are real, breakable plates, and this is a real, breakable bottle of wine, on a fancy blanket that I'm *sure* is not meant to lie on the ground."

His strong hand ran appreciatively over the soft wool of the blanket and I made a mental note that red looked lovely with his skin tone, though I wouldn't have predicted it, given his coloring.

"I don't know that any blankets are *meant* to lie on the ground."

He snorted. "I bet this blanket cost nearly as much as my rent."

"I'm sure I don't remember the price of this particular blanket, so I'm afraid I couldn't say."

More accurately, I didn't know the precise amount of Will's monthly rent so I couldn't be sure if the blanket cost as much or more… Quality wool did come at a price. I stared at Will's hand on the blanket. Perhaps this hadn't been as good an idea as I'd imagined. Will seemed determined to point out the distance he thought my wealth opened between us.

"Hey."

"Hmm?"

"Amory."

William's hand moved to mine, where I'd paused without taking the food out of the open basket.

I couldn't get over the way it opened something inside me, William saying the first name that only my parents had ever used.

"I'm sorry. I...this is really nice. I didn't mean to make you self-conscious. It's just a blanket. It doesn't matter. Okay?"

He was sincere, absolutely. And I filed away for later the knowledge that, despite being almost cuttingly straightforward, William Fox didn't enjoy hurting people's feelings. Not even mine. Perhaps...specifically not mine?

"Of course. Don't give it another thought," I said. I patted his hand before I continued unbuckling the leather straps that secured the china plates to the lid of the picnic hamper and busied myself with unpacking the food.

Will seemed lost in thought, or perhaps was just enjoying the view, as I pried the lids from creamy baked macaroni and cheese, collard greens with bacon, cornbread and tomato jam, and thinly sliced flank steak. I put a pot of spicy mustard next to the flank steak and set silverware, a plate, and a napkin in front of Will. The clink of silverware got his attention, and the second he saw the food his eyes lit. He looked at me excitedly.

"Is this the mac and cheese you served at the wedding?" he asked, glee evident in his voice.

"Not exactly the same. That caterer only does events, not individual meals. I'm afraid you'll have to make do with the Vaughn version instead."

"You made this?"

I nodded. Then I gave in to the urge to tease him. "Yes, unfortunately my personal chef had the day off." Will put a scant spoonful of food on his plate. "I do hope this is at least edible…"

Then, when I saw the disappointment on Will's face I reminded myself that sarcasm wasn't his forte.

"I enjoy cooking a great deal, William, and I hope I don't flatter myself unduly when I say it is rather a skill of mine. I'm especially fond of classic American cuisine, though my tastes do range widely."

Will snorted as he dug into the macaroni and cheese, but then his eyes went wide.

"Holy shit. That's delicious." He immediately piled more onto his plate, along with some of everything else.

I watched as he tried the greens, the steak, the cornbread. With each new dish, his eyes shot to me, as if surprised anew that I could cook.

"Wow."

"You seem shocked. I'm trying not to take it personally."

"No, sorry, I just thought…" He shook his head. "When you invited me to dinner, I expected you to take me someplace fancy. Stuffy."

"Like me?"

"I don't think you're stuffy, Amory. It just seems like the kind of place you probably go." His confidence trailed off at the end of the statement.

"Because I'm wealthy."

"Well. Yes."

"I do frequent establishments that are both fancy and, as you say, stuffy. But you don't. So I didn't think you'd much appreciate being taken to one."

He hesitated before saying, "Oh."

"Have I miscalculated again?"

He shook his head, looking at his plate. "This is exactly

the kind of food I like. And I love hiking. Being outside. I…"

I took the plate from his hand and laid it on the blanket, then I tipped his chin up with a finger, forcing him to look at me. "It's almost like I pay attention to you, William. Almost like I notice your responses to things and modify my behavior accordingly. Almost like I care about your preferences." I kept my tone mild, but looked right at him.

His smile was just a quirk of the corner of his mouth, but I saw it.

"Thank you," he said quietly. "For all this."

"I assure you, it's my absolute pleasure, William."

I slid my hand along his jaw, then cupped his cheek, drawing him to me. When I kissed him, his mouth opened beneath mine like a flower, and I had the distinct sense that William Fox hadn't had much experience being taken into account. I promised myself I would change that.

I didn't deepen the kiss, but kept it soft, light, appreciative. Then I handed him back his plate, and settled in with my own.

We ate in silence for a few minutes, then Will put aside his plate and lay back on the blanket, dark hair and long limbs elegant against the red wool.

"You know," he said, breaking the silence, "I wish…I wish I had a place like this, close to home, I mean." Only I got the distinct impression he'd started to say something else and changed course.

"Well, I know it isn't exactly close to your apartment, but I'm quite happy to share this one, if you like."

He smiled at me absently. "When Charlie and I were kids, we would climb this tree in the park down the street. It had two spots that were perfect for us, so we could each have our own but sit next to each other. The first time we found it, I was scared to climb it, but she scrambled up like it was nothing. I couldn't let her be braver than me, so I made myself climb up after her, even though my palms were all sweaty."

I smiled at the picture of a young Will, overcoming his fears even as a child.

"But then, when it started to get dark and we knew we had to get home for dinner, I climbed down just fine, but Charlie was scared. She didn't want to admit it, but she was like a cat that'd gotten stuck up there. I had to climb back up and help her get down. It took forever, because each time, I'd climb down and she'd only make it down one branch, so I'd have to climb back up to where she was. I swear, I climbed that damn tree fifteen times before I got her down." He laughed at the memory. "We were late for dinner and Charlie cried so my dad yelled at *me*, said I shouldn't have made her climb the tree." He snorted. "Like anyone ever made Charlie do anything she didn't want to do."

"Did your dad yell a lot?"

"Yeah, I guess. He was a cop. It was kind of second nature. But you know what?"

He turned to lie on his side, facing me. His eyes were bright, his hair tousled. I reached out and traced his lips without thinking. "What?"

"I was never afraid to climb again."

"Now you love it," I murmured.

"Now I love it."

I couldn't have predicted how the word *love* on William's perfect lips would affect me. I felt something kindle in my stomach that wasn't precisely lust, nor was it hunger, exactly.

Longing. My brain finally supplied the word. I felt an unfamiliar longing to know more of these things about William. I wanted to hear all the stories about him and Charlotte as children, to know what their father yelled about. How Will dressed in high school, and who he took to the prom. What books he liked to read, and whether he listened to music in the car. Whether he wore pajamas to bed, or underwear, or nothing. How he took his coffee. Whether he liked Christmas, and what his best birthday was, and what he smelled like first thing in the morning, sleepy and warm and in my bed.

I wanted to know all these things and more, and I was struck with a jolt of panic that maybe he wouldn't let me find out. Maybe, for the first time in rather a long time, all the money and all the charm in the world wouldn't be enough to get me what I wanted.

And the thought of it was unbearable.

I saw the flicker of unease at whatever Will must have seen in my face, and I pushed myself up on one arm and moved right next to him. I pulled his chest against mine and inhaled the intoxicating scent of him, and then I kissed him. It startled a noise out of him, and I did it again.

I kissed William Fox until he groaned and gave way, falling back to the blanket, and letting me press him to it as I eased on top of him. I kissed him deeply and without pause, and I felt his heart pound against my chest and his cock harden against my own. I kissed him breathless, and then I kissed him again, pausing only to drag in a breath of my own.

His cheeks were flushed, his dark hair mussed.

"I was right," I murmured, taking in the sight of him beneath me on the blanket. "You would look wonderful in red."

"What?"

I shook my head. "Nothing, just admiring you." He flushed even pinker.

I fixed the picture of him in my mind—head thrown back, dark hair wild, cheeks pink with arousal, lips puffy with my kisses.

I wanted him so badly. And this time, I wanted to watch his face as I made him fall apart.

I kissed his throat and bit at his jaw, where his pulse was racing, and his breath caught. He grabbed my hips and pulled me into him, grinding our erections together until we both groaned.

"I want you," I breathed into his ear. He nodded quickly.

I reached into the picnic basket for one of the condoms I'd stashed there earlier, and when I turned back to him, he'd loosened his belt and unbuttoned his jeans. I tapped him on the chest with the condom.

"I'll thank you not to make fun of my wide range of picnic accoutrements ever again." I pulled his jeans down over his hips and palmed his cock.

Will gasped. "I won't." He smiled, and then his eyes rolled back as I started to stroke him, slow and firm. "Fuck," he muttered.

I kissed just below his ear, and said, "Your wish is my command."

"God damn it," he said as I rolled the condom on. "The things you say should sound ridiculous. Why don't they? Anyone else would sound like a total—oh, god, fuck." He groaned as I pushed slowly inside him. I wanted him to feel every inch, every second, every thrust.

He blinked wildly, then squeezed his eyes shut, jaw clenching. His breath came shallow, and I kissed him, tasting salt and heat. I reached between us and stroked him as I slid the rest of the way inside, and Will writhed beneath me. His arms came around me and I realized we were close, so much closer than we'd been when I'd fucked him against my desk, or gotten him off against the wall the night we'd met. I rocked into him slowly, letting him get accustomed to my dick inside him, waiting, just kissing him, until I felt his muscles give around me. Until he groaned into my mouth, tongue hot and suddenly desperate, and started pushing even closer to me.

Then I pulled out slowly, watching his face, and thrust all the way back in. And the sight of him, lost in unexpected pleasure, was nearly as potent as an orgasm. He bit his lip, and I forced my mouth there instead. We kissed deeply as we started to fuck in earnest, surging against each other in a rhythm that covered me in goose bumps and had Will shaking within minutes, cock hard and wet between us.

I could have fucked him harder if I'd flipped him over, or faster, but this, right here, this was perfect. The feel of his arms around me, his mouth, infinitely sweet, on mine, his ass clenching around my cock like he wanted to keep me there forever. It was perfect. I tilted his hips up to change the angle slightly, and when he cried out, head thrown back and neck straining, I did it again, and again, and again.

William panted and groaned, and I was on the edge for what felt like forever, shivery bolts of pleasure tickling up and down my spine, each threatening to be the lightning strike that would signal the beginning of the end. I grabbed Will's right hand, kissed his palm, and guided it to his erection, now wetting our stomachs with precome.

"I want to watch you touch yourself as I come inside you," I said against his mouth, and he gasped.

"Yes," he moaned, and, "Keep talking."

And, Christ that was sweet. William begging me to talk to him as I made him come on my cock. It was almost too much.

"I want you to jerk off that gorgeous dick of yours while I fuck you until you come all over yourself. All over me. You're so fucking tight, William," I said in his ear, thrusting deeper. "So fucking tight I could almost think you don't let anyone fuck you but me."

He groaned wildly and then went rigid in orgasm, jetting come between us with his mouth open on a silent scream.

And that was it for me. William's ass clamped down on me and I came like a thunderclap, pouring myself inside him until I saw black.

"Fuuuck," William moaned softly as I came back to myself, my face buried in his neck, my cock still mostly hard inside him.

I blinked to clear the fog of arousal, and kissed his lips gently. "All right?" My voice sounded rough, shredded. Rather like how I felt. As if I'd lost some part of myself inside him.

He nodded, but winced as I withdrew.

I took care of the condom, and turned back to find William still splayed on the blanket, one arm thrown up over his face.

"Darling?" I asked softly, not realizing I'd used the word

until it was out of my mouth. It wasn't something I'd ever called another lover, nor something I'd intended to. I cleared my throat. "Will?"

He nodded.

I pulled his arm away from his face, needing to see him. I didn't think I'd hurt him, but sometimes sex shook things loose that one couldn't anticipate.

The eyes that met mine were wary, confused. And though I didn't mean to, I felt that wariness like a slap.

"I need…"

I kissed him instantly. "What? Tell me what you need. Anything, of course."

But he shook his head and bit his lip. "I need you to not be…who you are," he said, the words opening cuts in their wake.

"Not be who I am," I echoed stupidly.

Being who I was, or at least, versions of who I was, is what I'd spent my whole life insisting I be able to do. Through a childhood where I was known for my family and not myself; through an adolescence when I learned that people wanted my money more than they wanted me; through an early adulthood of losing my parents and having to become the very things I'd tried to distance myself from. Through all that, I'd emerged a man who knew who he was, against all odds. I'd honed myself, always making sure that no matter how much I laid on the charm to elicit donations, or made polite small talk with idiots who had information that would help the foundation, I never lost sight of who I was. Through sheer force of will, I'd never let any of it touch me.

I turned away to pull my underwear and pants back on,

suddenly chilly. I couldn't quite meet Will's eyes.

"I need this to not be a terrible joke where I'm a cop and you're a robber," he went on. "I want to date the guy who throws nice parties and helps the caterer clean up, not the guy who steals art."

And then I could breathe again, the relief so strong I felt my heart rate speed up suddenly and then slow to normal, fight or flight response neutralized, threat gone.

I nodded, and Will peered at me. "I wasn't planning on stealing any more art."

"It's not just the stealing," he said, voice serious. "It's the attitude behind it. The manipulation. I can't...I can't date someone who thinks the rules don't apply to him."

I chose to be happy about the part where he said we were dating.

"Your honor is charmingly naïve, William. Your conviction. Your faith that rules and justice are possible—it's valiant, in a doomed, knightly kind of way."

His eyes went sharp and he started to pull away.

"Yes, all right. I hear you," I said quickly. "I do. No stealing. No acting like the rules don't apply to me. No terrible jokes about cops and robbers. Not that you'd know a joke if it walked into a bar with another joke." I winked at Will, forcing my composure back into place along with my clothes.

"Ha ha," he said, but he did look legitimately amused. A pause, and then his smile slid away and his expression was naked, uncertain. "You promise?"

I went to my knees in front of him and cupped his cheek in my hand. I kissed him, twining my fingers in his hair. "William. I promise that I will make every effort to impress you in areas that do not include breaking and entering. Deal?"

Will nodded.

"Well," I said, considering, and Will immediately narrowed his eyes at me suspiciously. "Maybe *some* entering." I reached around and squeezed his ass as I kissed him again. He laughed into my mouth, and we broke apart, chuckling, lying on our backs in the woods as the sun began to set.

CHAPTER 12

Will

I'D BEEN WORRIED, when Vaughn and I started dating, or whatever you call it, that it meant I'd be attending even more boring parties than I already did for my sister. Luckily, that didn't seem to be the case. He always offered me the opportunity to go if I wanted to, but I very rarely wanted to. Hell, *he* barely wanted to go to a lot of them. But sometimes I'd head over to his D.C. apartment so I'd be there when he got back, and he'd look hot in a suit and amuse me with stories, and then we'd go to bed. That was the best of both worlds in my opinion.

When we actually did go out, we went all kinds of places, from restaurants that were expensive, yes, but worth the price, to local bars, to movie theatres. My only knowledge of people who had as much money as Vaughn did came from television and the movies, so I was a bit abashed to realize I hadn't given him enough credit when it came to dating, and how he'd want to take me places I would like.

One such place was a Japanese restaurant that just opened down the block from his apartment. Sushi was something we both loved, even though I liked the complicated rolls that Vaughn called "Americanized."

We were just settling into our steamed gyoza appetizer when a shadow fell over the table.

"Will?"

I looked up at the familiar voice, and there stood Harris Parks, my ex-boyfriend. Harris was the only serious relationship I'd had, the majority of my romantic encounters since then having been casual dating or the rare one-night stand. Harris and I had broken up more than a decade ago, and we'd only run into each other a few times since then. It hadn't been the worst breakup, but was full of awkwardness and silent resentment nonetheless. "Hey, Harris."

"I thought that was you." Harris looked like he hadn't aged a day since I'd met him in grad school, when he'd been studying non-profit management and I'd been getting my master's in art history.

I stood up and we exchanged the kind of hug you give someone you used to fuck more than a decade ago, but definitely didn't want to fuck again. "This is Amory Vaughn," I said, introducing Vaughn to Harris. "Vaughn, this is Harris Parks." I wondered if he knew this was my ex, if I'd ever mentioned him by name and not just as a prefix.

Polite as ever, Vaughn stood and shook Harris's hand. Though I was over the way things had ended with Harris, I found I felt slightly smug at how tall Vaughn was, comparatively. Harris had always been self-conscious about his height.

"You still at NPR?" I asked. Harris was the annual fund director, soliciting money for public radio by sending an obscene amount of direct mail. He'd always joked that he got his degree in management to fold donation letters.

Harris nodded. "Yeah. For a few more weeks, anyway,"

he said. "Ben got a job, tenure track, at Indiana University."

Harris had always had a thing for academics, and Ben was a history professor. Maybe mentioning the guy he'd cheated on me with—and then married—was his version of me being smug about how tall Vaughn was. Or maybe I was overthinking things, as usual. "That's great," I said. "You have anything lined up?"

"WFIU, yeah. It's the public radio station on campus." said Harris. "I've been promised work-study students to fold all the letters. How about you? Still with the FBI?"

"Yeah." I didn't say anything else, because Harris had never liked hearing anything about my job. "When are you moving?"

"In about three weeks, actually." Harris smiled, and there was nothing unhappy or bitter in the expression. "I'm glad I ran into you."

"Same here. Best of luck. Tell Ben congrats on the job."

We shook hands, Harris gave me one last hug, gave Vaughn a polite "Nice to meet you," and went on his way. I realized that I'd probably never see him again.

It was strange to watch a person who used to mean so much to me walk out of my life and feel nothing. Was I supposed to feel something? Some sense of loss, or what might have been?

Mostly I was just hungry. I dipped another gyoza in the sauce. "That was the only other boyfriend I've ever had," I explained. "Ben, his husband? That's the guy he cheated on me with. And then he invited me to their wedding." I shook my head. "I didn't go. I didn't send a present either." I had, however, sent back the RSVP regret card.

"How vicious of you, darling," Vaughn said. He was

looking at me like he wanted to strip all my bits and pieces apart and spread them on the table. "So I'm your boyfriend, am I?"

Immediately my face went hot and I set my chopsticks down. Oh, god, had I really just—fuck, did I just say that? I cleared my throat, glancing around, anywhere but Vaughn. This was why I hated dating. I liked knowing where I stood with someone. I liked rules. And when it came to dating there weren't any. Especially when you happened to be dating Amory Vaughn. "Um."

He took my hand and I looked up at him. He was smiling widely, and he kissed my hand. "Are you asking me to go steady, William?"

I narrowed my eyes at him and tilted my chin up. It probably looked like I was about to punch him. "Dating, boyfriend, whatever. I just meant—"

"I know what you meant," he interrupted, letting my hand go. "It's fine, of course. I'm teasing you."

Well, great. But now I wanted to know—no, this was stupid. We were dating. In a relationship. Whatever. "You don't have to, you know."

"Tease you?" Vaughn grinned. "I beg to differ."

"Be my boyfriend," I mumbled, because apparently I couldn't let it go.

"I don't do anything I don't want to do," said Vaughn, and his voice was amused. "I'd think you'd know that by now. But I'd like to be. Of course I would," he added.

I gave a theatrical sigh, still embarrassed but also…happy. Very happy. "All right. Great. Glad we got that cleared up."

"I know how you like things to be official," Vaughn

agreed, leaning back in his seat. "Shall I call a notary?"

"*Shall* I suck your cock later, or do you want to keep being funny?"

He winked at me. "So that was your ex-boyfriend, eh?"

Oh, right. The reason for the boyfriend talk in the first place. I nodded, suddenly interested in what Vaughn thought of him. I was fascinated by Vaughn's ability to read people immediately. He liked to figure out what people were hiding. He'd be a good profiler, come to think of it. If we ignored the part where he liked to commit larceny. "What'd you think?"

He thought about it as he sipped his sake. "That it must have ended not with a bang but with a whimper."

That was true, but I wanted to hear his reasoning, so I gave nothing away and just waited.

"Ah, is this your interrogation face, William? All right, let's see. Well, he didn't ask for any details about your job and his nostrils flared at those three letters, so I'm guessing he was never fond of your chosen career."

I snorted. "That's an understatement."

"What was his issue with the FBI?"

I gave him my best Agent Fox expression and said coolly, "Why don't you tell me?"

Vaughn's eyebrows went up; he liked the game.

"Hmm. Perhaps he feared such a traditionally macho job would force him into the closet by proxy...but I know you've never been in the closet at work so I imagine that isn't it."

I gave him a salute with my sake. "You imagined right."

"He was uncomfortable around your coworkers," Vaughn said, and I could almost see him running back over everything he'd noticed about Harris during our brief encounter.

I nodded. "Since I was in the Academy. He came to meet me for lunch exactly once, and then decided not to because he didn't want me to get shit for having a boyfriend."

"Or *he* didn't want to get shit for being your boyfriend," Vaughn said softly.

I smiled wryly. "Right. I'd tell him all the time that I didn't care, that people could think what they wanted, but...I think a lot of the guys I was at the Academy with were the same kind of guys who gave Harris shit for being gay in high school."

Guys like Brett Lawson, who had been in my class at the Academy and now worked in Violent Crimes. Harris had taken one look at Lawson and decided that he didn't want anything to do with the FBI. Never mind that my colleagues in the Art Crimes Unit weren't pricks like Lawson.

"I can't imagine that would be enough for you to stop dating someone," Vaughn mused. "If you truly cared about them?"

"Well, no. It wasn't just showing up at things. Hell, you know how I feel about parties. We had this...insular life in graduate school, right. We weren't the only gay people in our friend group. Everyone there was...pretty liberal, open-minded. We moved in together when we graduated, and Harris got a job at NPR. If I hadn't joined the FBI, I think things would have stayed the way they were."

"But you did join the FBI. And he didn't want you to?"

"He never came out and said it. But I knew anyway. I'd always made it clear I was going to though."

Vaughn gave a low, warm laugh. "And I know how difficult it is to change your mind."

I flushed, but this time it wasn't with embarrassment. "Yeah, well, this wasn't...this wasn't something anyone could have talked me out of. It's what I wanted to do since I first learned of the existence of the Art Crimes team, and I'd planned my graduate career with the goal of joining the FBI after completing my master's. Trying to talk me out of it would have been like telling me to be someone else."

Vaughn's eyes were narrowed thoughtfully.

I sipped my sake again and waved a hand. "Whatever it is, just say it."

"He did want you to be someone else. He was just too afraid to tell you."

"Basically. He never fought with me. He never...he just let me be, and I thought that was the same as letting me be *me*, but it wasn't. We didn't fight, because we didn't talk. I did my thing and he didn't like it, and I didn't like that he was so..."

"What?"

I wasn't quite sure how to say it. "Passive," I said, finally. "Which doesn't make sense, does it? I would have hated him trying to make me someone I wasn't, but I also was mad that he didn't even try."

Vaughn, who had some preternatural ability to know when the server was approaching the table, went quiet as our sushi was delivered. "It makes sense," he said when we were alone again. "We can tell when we're failing to meet someone's expectations, when we're not the person they want us to be. Quiet disappointment is just as hurtful."

"I hate it," I said bluntly. "Yelling, at least I know where I stand, you know? I can deal with conflict, and I'd prefer it to the…whatever he was doing. Suffering? I don't know. But we grew apart, he met Ben, and they were fucking for six months before I found out about it. Which I did, by the way, by walking in on them. I think Harris had been trying to get me to notice and gave up and went for the obvious."

"So you had to break up with him," Vaughn said, selecting a piece of sashimi.

I'd gotten an inside-out fried roll just to watch him squirm, since he'd never be so rude as to insult someone's food. "Yup, because he didn't want to be the one to do it," I said. "I should have done it long before then, anyway. I don't know that it's fair of me to accuse him of being passive when I didn't do anything about the situation either. It's not like I was the one doing the yelling."

"Ah, my William," said Vaughn, affection in every syllable of my name. "Only you would think something like that was supposed to be fair."

"Well, I just meant, you know." I gestured with my chopsticks before picking up a piece of my roll. The hostess sat a loud, obviously inebriated party at the table next to us. Their excitable chatter meant I had to practically shout for Vaughn to hear me. "I should have been clear and said it wasn't working, but I didn't want to hurt him."

Vaughn glanced over at the group seated next to us with an offended frown, clearly annoyed that he had to raise his voice to converse with me when I was right across the table. He had the most impeccable manners of anyone I'd ever met. "Instead, you just assigned him to the roommate category in your mind, and went on with your life?"

I wouldn't have thought of it that way, but…yeah. "That's exactly what I did. I went to work and didn't tell him about it because I knew he didn't want to know. I went climbing—which he hated—and he stopped inviting me to NPR parties. Thank god," I added, which made Vaughn smile.

"For the record, I think it's incredibly sexy that you go mountain climbing," Vaughn said. "And I have absolutely no desire to do it with you."

"Neither did Harris, really," I said. "He just didn't like it that I didn't want him there, I guess. It was a long time ago. We were young. I'm sure I could have done a lot of things better too. I let him have the apartment." I made a face. "And the bed."

"Because that's where you found them fucking?" asked Vaughn. "Subtle."

"Hmm? Oh, no. They were fucking on the couch. The bed just sucked."

Vaughn snagged another piece of sushi. "You delight me, William." He raised his voice to be heard over the raucous table to our right.

Well, that was nice to know. "You delight me, too," I said. "And sometimes you infuriate me."

His slow smile made me want to drop to my knees under the table, slide my hands up his thighs, and suck him off right there. Instead, I shifted in my chair and drank some more sake, getting myself under control so I could excuse myself to the restroom.

When I made my way back to the table, I passed the group of loud diners, now seated on the other side of the restaurant, and a couple of them gave me a glare. Next to our table, I noticed the servers were busy separating the tables and re-setting them for smaller parties. I slid into my seat with a raised eyebrow look at Vaughn. "Did I miss something?"

Vaughn glanced at me. "Yes, I ordered us more sake." He picked up the little carafe and refilled my glass.

I stared at him. "So that group of people just...what? Wanted to move to another table?"

Vaughn's innocent look was laughable. "They moved, yes."

"You know I'm trained to tell when people are lying, right?"

Vaughn's eyes glinted at me. "So I hear."

Before I could say anything, a man stopped by our table. The manager, who apologized to Vaughn for the "inconvenience" and said that he hoped the solution was satisfactory.

I waited until the manager moved away before pointing my chopstick at him accusingly. "You totally made them move that group of people."

"They were rather excruciatingly *loud*, William."

"Right. So...maybe you could have asked for *us* to move? There's just two of us. It'd be way easier than having a group that size be re-seated."

He looked at me, and I saw there was honest puzzlement on his features, as if that had never occurred to him. "I simply expressed my displeasure to the management and asked for them to resolve the issue."

"By moving them," I said flatly.

Vaughn leaned back in his seat and gave me a shrewd glance. "Why do I have the distinct feeling you're about to lecture me?"

"It's not a lecture," I huffed, though fine, maybe it was. "It's just...could you not do that?"

"Did someone say something to you?"

The protectiveness in Vaughn's voice was a little sweet, a lot unnecessary, and just a bit annoying. "No, that's not the point. I just don't like when you do that kind of thing."

"Make an annoying situation go away?"

I couldn't tell if he honestly didn't get it, or was being obtuse on purpose. I sipped my sake. "It bothers me how easily you manipulate people into doing what you want."

"William, I think you're being a bit dramatic," Vaughn said. "They were very rude and it was impossible to hear."

"I know they were. But it still would have been way easier for everyone if *we'd* just moved."

"It wouldn't have been easier for us. And we weren't the ones being intolerable, darling."

"Like I said." I shook my head. "Delightful, and infuriating. Is that how you navigate life when you're rich? You pay to make situations go away?"

"If you must put it so crudely," Vaughn allowed. "From your disapproving tone, I surmise it's not your preferred way to deal with aggravations."

"No. I would have just asked to move."

"Then you're inconvenienced," he argued. "On top of being aggravated."

"Then I've fixed the situation to my liking," I corrected. "In a way that was easier for everyone. Especially the servers. Did you think about how much of a pain that was for them? What if their server lost a table and a large tip because you had them moved into another section?"

Vaughn was giving me an indulgent look. "In future, I will attempt to ameliorate aggravations without inconveniencing others. All right?"

"Or you could stop using your money to manipulate people," I said. It sounded harsh, so I reached across the table and took his hand. "I like being here with you, okay? I'd like being here with you even if you didn't have the money or clout that makes restaurant managers do what you want."

"I want you to enjoy yourself," he said and gave my hand a squeeze. Vaughn never had a problem showing affection in public. "And what is the point of having this 'clout,' as you call it, if I can't make things as pleasurable for you as possible?"

I knew he meant what he said, even if I was still frustrated he wasn't getting the point. "I'm not dating your money or your clout, Amory. I'm dating you. And the world is full of loud drunk people and a thousand other annoyances you can't fix. But you make me happy. Just you."

His eyes softened. "You make me happy, too." He paused, nostrils flaring elegantly. "Even more so when I can actually hear what you're saying."

I rolled my eyes, snorted a laugh I couldn't quite help, and held out my glass for more sake. "Delightful, infuriating, and impossible."

"I'll drink to that," Vaughn said, and refilled my glass.

I was a little drunk as we walked back to Vaughn's. I liked the Falls Church house, but the apartment was more my style. And Vaughn's too, I assumed. Everything was top-of-the-line, simple, clean and modern just like his preferred sushi.

Vaughn took my hand. At my startle, he squeezed it. "Is this not all right? Here I thought boyfriends held hands."

Great, I was never going to live that down. "Of course

it's all right," I assured him. And it was. I just wasn't used to it. Harris hadn't been one for public affection outside of designated areas. "I'm not gonna do that again," I said as we walked, returning to the conversation about Harris. Vaughn's hand was warm around mine. If people gave us weird looks, I didn't notice. "If you want me to be someone I'm not, I need to know about it."

"I don't want you to be anyone else," Vaughn assured me. He tugged me closer. "Well. I do wish you had better taste in sushi. Those razzle-dazzle rolls you like miss the spirit of Japanese food." He had to let go of my hand to pull out the entry card for the building.

"And what's that?"

"Its beauty lies in its simplicity, its perfection, its balance," said Vaughn, holding the door open for me.

"Maybe I just like things that are complicated," I said, eyes glued to Vaughn as he swiped the card that would take the elevator to his penthouse. "After Harris, I dated this guy who was an extreme sports fanatic for about two months. He liked climbing, but then he wanted to jump off the top and go hang-gliding when we got up there."

"And that wasn't complicated enough for you?" Vaughn asked, moving closer, trapping me with my back to the elevator wall as the doors closed.

"That's not complicated," I murmured, shivering pleasantly as he slid a thigh between my legs and moved closer. "That's just having a death wish."

"And do you think I'm complicated?" Vaughn asked, leaning in to kiss me.

"You're an inside-out sushi roll for sure," I agreed, and he laughed against my mouth.

But I wasn't actually kidding. Harris had often bored me, and Rory tired me with his constant inability to be present in the moment unless it involved throwing himself off a summit. I'd always imagined that whoever it was I wanted would be somewhere in between. I'd just given up hope that he existed.

And then I met Amory Vaughn.

CHAPTER 13

Vaughn

THE BOY SCREAMED as the guillotine blade dropped, spattering blood from the severed head onto the plastic-draped floor beneath.

Then he leaned in closer to examine the head. "*Cool*," he said, and moved on to the hallway lined with mummies that popped up from their sarcophagi, trailing their dusty shrouds, to scare people as they walked past and tripped the motion detectors.

I grinned, the mastermind standing in the dark, watching the kids move through my haunted house.

It was two weeks before Halloween, the time of the annual fundraiser for the preservation of historic Virginia homes. And I had to admit, this year it really put the *fun* back in fundraising. Six historic homes in the neighborhood, mine included, had been decorated for Halloween, and were giving out candy and other treats. Those who donated were allowed to bring their family through the tour, and the preservation society must have advertised far and wide because there were more people than I would have expected, including some in their twenties—a demographic notoriously hard to fundraise from. I'd like to meet their new fundraiser and see what her angle had been. It never hurt to swap strategies.

When I'd first received Joanna Madsen's email that this year's fundraiser was to be a Halloween tour, I'd been excited. We'd never celebrated Halloween when I was a child. My parents were always at fundraisers of their own, or attending proper adult parties, and living in a fairly rural area of Virginia, with large houses spread far apart, wasn't conducive to trick or treating, even if my parents hadn't dismissed it as begging for food.

And when I'd learned that Buck and Jennifer Murphy from across the way were also participating, I was doubly excited, because it was a chance to show them up. My decorations simply had to be better. It wasn't a *feud*, per se, because the Murphys didn't realize they were a part of it. But I knew. I knew that they said things like, "We moved here for the schools," to me, and, "We wanted a neighborhood of people like *us*," to Mr. Smithson down the street, who openly flew a Confederate flag. When the Chens moved across the street from the Murphys the next year, they had been chilly at best. I knew they had a *Choose Life* bumper sticker on their Lexus SUV and a nine-year-old daughter who they dressed like a beauty queen even though she really wanted to play soccer.

Which is why, when Buck Murphy first clapped a hand on my shoulder and asked where Mrs. Vaughn was, I lifted an eyebrow and said, "Or the other Mr. Vaughn," and watched him jerk his hand back like my sweater had burned him. And why, when Jennifer Murphy asked me where I got the flowers for last spring's neighborhood association meeting, I slid Eduardo Ortega's card across the table to her and asked, solicitously, if she'd like me to make introductions, watching the slight flare of her nostrils as she left the card where it was.

All battles must be fought on their own terms of engagement. And by the terms of the neighborhood association, having the best Halloween decorations was my opening sally. Oh yes, the Murphys were going down.

Jim and Monica Brubecker had gone with a Victorian Halloween, very prim and proper and full of gourds. Harmon and Janine Tivoli had set up a charming pumpkin patch in their polo field, with scarecrows and bales of hay, and a little cart giving out donuts and apple cider. The Giegers, who had an absurd number of children whose names all began with K, had decorated for a kids' Halloween, with a bunch of cutesy nonsense.

My favorite was Bob and Barbara Chen's Salem theme. They'd set up a kind of history lesson on the Salem Witch Trials, complete with different explanations historians had given for the outbreaks. Something told me the overlap in the audiences for the Chens' and the Giegers' houses would not be large. Something also told me that the Murphys would be offended by anything to do with witches, especially right across the street from them—a fact that I imagined the Chens would be well aware of—and I made a mental note to wink at them the next time I saw them. I made a secondary mental note to arrange a neighborhood holiday gift exchange and manipulate it such that I could give the Murphy kids the entire series of *Harry Potter* books and DVDs.

And me? I had created the haunted house of my dreams. Weeks before, when I'd told William I was going to do a haunted house, he'd smiled and launched into stories about the haunted hayride that he and Charlotte had gone on at the local apple farm as children. They'd sat in hay-cushioned wagons and after being driven through various horrors, left to wend their way through a corn maze that deposited them in the barn, where there was cider, bobbing for apples, and (in the instance of Will and Charlotte's fourth grade visit, and much to Will's mortification) vomiting, after eating an inhuman amount of candy corn, donuts, and caramel apples.

I loved hearing William's stories. I was slowly realizing that though he didn't share much of himself with most people, it wasn't because he was private. It was because he didn't imagine that people much cared. Once I'd made it clear that I *was* interested and I *did* care, he'd begun telling me more and more.

After our picnic, we'd gone on date after date, like we were trying to make up for lost time. Multiple dinners (one at a restaurant fancy enough to make William uncomfortable, a mistake I hadn't repeated); an avant-garde play I'd gotten tickets to as a thank you to the Vaughn Foundation and hadn't wanted to suffer through alone; the movies several times (I let William choose and he picked a moody horror film and an action blockbuster as if he thought I might protest either). We'd even gone to the National Portrait Gallery, and I'd gotten William all hot and bothered by whispering in his ear all the ways a person might perpetrate a theft of one of the portraits. He'd flushed bright red and squirmed away from me, conflicted. He was hard in his pants, confused about how he could be so aroused hearing about something he should condemn.

It was heady, the effect I had on him. Watching him fight his body's reactions, so different from his mind's, I wanted to pin him to the wall, spread him open, and force him to confront the riot of complexity that the world was. That he was. I wanted to overwhelm him, take him out of himself and everything he recognized and give him a mirror that would reflect him back to himself the way I saw him. Beautiful, brave, and scared.

We went on date after date, until we reached the point where it wasn't dates anymore. It was just being together. I couldn't get enough of him, in bed or out. I wanted to learn every inch of his body and know everything about him, hear every story.

Hearing about childhood Will made me want to pull grown Will closer to me and keep him near. Not because his stories revealed anything awful, but because being reminded that he'd been a child, and not always the hyper-competent, gun-toting, stoic FBI agent he was now, made him seem more accessible. More vulnerable.

Then there was the fact that I'd never really had a childhood. Not in the way Will and Charlotte did, with play dates and soccer teams, grocery store birthday cakes and backyard water fights—and, apparently, haunted hayrides, complete with eating until puking. There were just things that Vaughns did, and things that Vaughns did not do. I played golf and polo, socialized with the children of my parents' friends and colleagues, or the other children at boarding school. For my tenth birthday, I'd told my mother I wanted a Pac Man cake, and ended up with a six-tier lemon chiffon affair.

Something about hearing Will's story of the haunted hayride debacle made me more determined than before to have the best Haunted Historical House ever. I'd started weeks ago, ordering the set pieces from various online retailers and renting a few from a special effects company in D.C. When I called Valerie to ask if she wanted to come over and help decorate my house for Halloween, she'd arrived prepared for something very different. What she found was, in her words, "the lunatic trappings of a madman."

"What in holy hell are you doing here?" Valerie had asked.

"I'm making a haunted house. I would have thought that was self-evident."

"I thought you meant 'Come over to decorate' as in, drink whiskey and look at how your staff had decorated for Halloween."

"Ah. Well, I have plenty of whiskey. But we're making a house of horrors."

She'd giggled, but after about two glasses of Lagavulin she'd kicked off her Manolo Blahniks and started squirting fake blood with glee.

It had taken us hours, but I thought the effects looked pretty good. Now, watching children scream and adults clutch each other in fear, it felt completely worth it.

I got a text from Will that he was outside and I went to meet him, sticking close to the walls so I could watch everyone enjoying themselves.

"Well, hello…Count Dracula?" Will was wearing a rayon cape velcroed over his suit. Clearly he'd come straight from work.

He held up a pair of plastic fangs and nodded. Then he gave me a once-over, and his eyes got huge. "Are you…are you Lucius Malfoy?"

I gave him a turn so he could appreciate my costume. "Indeed."

His eyes narrowed and he stepped close. I leaned in for a kiss (since he hadn't inserted the fangs yet) but he spoke softly into my ear.

"How did you…uh, why are you Lucius Malfoy?"

He couldn't *possibly* have thought he could admit to having thought I looked like Lucius Malfoy when we first met and expect me not to tease him about it. I hadn't quite expected the heat in his eyes, however. "Why? Do you like it?"

"Um. I. Maybe."

"Just something I threw together," I said breezily. "Come, let me show you the haunted house." I offered my elbow and he took it, tugging his cape out of the way. As we walked in the front entrance, where there was space to mill about and have a drink for those who didn't wish to enter the house of horrors, Will's gaze darted around.

At first I assumed he was uncomfortable holding my arm in public, but when I moved to ease away, he pulled me closer to his side.

"What is the *deal* with these costumes?" he hissed in my ear.

I followed his eyeline, but all I saw were a few dukes, a Marie Antoinette, the bass player of KISS whose name I couldn't remember, and a smattering of the usual zombie brides, pirates, and animals. "What's wrong with them?"

"They're all…" Will made a gesture with his hand up to the height of his head that I did not understand. "You know, real."

"I hate to break it to you, William, but—"

He elbowed me. "They're *costume* costumes. 'Going to a Halloween party in a movie' costumes. Like...*rented* or something." He spat the words out like they indicated a personal betrayal.

"What's the problem?"

His head drooped a little. "I'm just..." He plucked at his own cape and tossed the plastic fangs next to a jar of candy corn sitting on the buffet table against the wall.

"You're perfect," I said, leaning close. I grabbed him by his cheap cape and pulled him to me, looking in his face for indication that he didn't want to be so close in public. But all I saw was a slight irritation in his eyes, just as I often saw when he realized the gulf between our habits, which quickly gave way to a darted glance at my mouth. I plucked at his cape and smiled. "Just don't get this thing anywhere near an open flame."

I kissed him softly, reminding myself that ravishing one's boyfriend in a haunted house was something better done after the guests had gone home.

When we broke apart, William smiled. "Oh, sorry, probably shouldn't leave those there." He pocketed the fangs he'd dropped.

I bet he put things back in their proper place at the grocery store if he decided he didn't want to buy them, and always returned his shopping cart to the designated area. Hell, he probably returned other people's orphaned carts to the designated area.

"Are these...is that *homemade* candy?" he said accusingly.

"Well, these candy corn and all the jelly beans were commercially obtained." I pointed to the dozen or so jars of candy that glowed like multicolored jewels on the table. "But yes, the candy bars, peanut butter cups, peppermint patties, and truffles are handmade. Not, of course, by me. My culinary aspirations don't stretch quite so far. Would you care to try some?"

William was looking at the candy display like it was either something very distasteful, or something he wanted a great deal. With William it was sometimes hard to tell.

Then he reached out a tentative hand for a Snickers bar, changed his mind and reached toward the truffles. Then his hand just hovered over the table and he turned to me, stricken. I laughed. Something he wanted, then. He looked like a kid faced with the impossible choice between favorites.

"How about you try something now, and I'll have the rest wrapped up for you to take home later?"

Will nodded and leaned into my side.

"May I make a suggestion?" I curled an arm around his waist, holding him close, and handed him a piece of candy from a tray at the back of the table.

He took a tentative bite and then his face lit up, eyes flying to mine. "How did you know?"

"You chose a Milky Way with dark chocolate at the movies," I said. "Twice." I was slightly offended that he would be so surprised I'd noticed. "So I had Priscilla make them."

Will rested his head against my shoulder for just a moment. It was a gesture that I hadn't seen from him before, and it hit me right in the gut.

"Thank you," he said softly, and finished his candy.

"Shall we go through?"

When I took Will's hand, he let me, and I led him through the foyer to where the haunted house began. "Just let me know if you get scared," I teased, squeezing his hand.

Will shot me the unimpressed look I associated with Agent Fox. It said, *Sure, let's see your cute little society version of a haunted house.* I couldn't wait to prove him wrong. Still, he didn't let go of my hand.

We walked down the cobweb-draped corridor and I made a subtle signal behind me for the man in charge of letting people through to hold off for a while, leaving us alone. I'd never been much for horror movies—they bored me. But here, holding Will's hand as we ventured forth into the threatening dark, I could see why people liked to watch them on dates. Will walked half a step closer to me than he usually did, held my hand a little tighter. I felt sensitized to his presence at my side. Attuned to his responses to our environment.

The cobwebs draped down like Spanish moss, and the fog machine made the corridor soupy. We walked slowly forward and came to the room with the guillotine. Cackles and screams poured from the hidden speakers, then the blade dropped and blood spattered the floor.

"Cool," William said, and I bit the inside of my cheek to keep from laughing as he leaned in to look at the severed head just as the kid I'd seen earlier had done. "Where'd you get this?"

"I rented it from a prop house in D.C."

In the hallway of mummies, eerie sounds drowned out all ambient noise. As we walked past the first sarcophagus, the mummy slowly sat up, arms raised, zombie-like, eyes glowing through its wraps. Then the second sat up, and the third, and William grinned, trailing his fingers over the edge of the sarcophagus and peeking inside.

The mad scientist room had lights strung from the ceiling to look like lightning striking and a reanimating the corpse laid out on a medical table. Trays of scalpels, forceps, clamps, retractors, and curved needles, all spotted with blood and gore, lay beside the body.

"You can touch all the organs and blood," I told Will, indicating the bowls on the table that held liver, spaghetti, and more of the blood mixture with red Jello clots in it. He leaned in close, but didn't let go of my hand to touch anything. We left as the lightning struck again.

As we crossed the threshold into the hallway, Will relaxed, seeing nothing coming. Which was precisely the idea.

The man in coveralls and a chainsaw jumped out from behind a curtain, accompanied by chainsaw revving noises. It was the first time I'd experienced it, and it was a *very* good effect.

But rather than grabbing my hand or gasping, when the man jumped out, William pushed me behind him and scrabbled at his side for his gun, tearing his cape off in the process. When he realized that his gun wasn't there, he jumped forward, and the man in the costume dropped the chainsaw, and backed away, hands raised. All told, it only took two seconds, maybe three. Then William backed up, bent down to rest his palms on his thighs, and ran a hand through his hair.

"I'm sorry," he said to the man in costume, voice shaky with adrenaline. "Sorry, man."

I stepped forward slowly, not wanting to get hit by accident, and when I knew I was in Will's line of sight, I put my hand on his shoulder. "Are you all right?"

He nodded, clearly embarrassed. "Yeah, uh, sorry, I just.

You know."

I took William's elbow and led him a few steps down, where I knew there really wasn't anyone else waiting to jump out, and pushed him against the wall.

He wouldn't quite meet my gaze.

"You pushed me behind you."

His eyes flicked up, then he gave a one-shouldered shrug and looked back down.

I leaned forward and tilted his chin up, kissing him deeply. He returned the kiss, grabbing my hands and squeezing them. "It's almost done," I whispered. "Okay?"

"Yeah, yeah, I'm sorry," he muttered sheepishly.

"No need to be sorry. You just almost shot an actor in a Halloween costume, that's all. Good thing you didn't actually have your gun."

"I wouldn't have shot him," William grumbled, but he pulled my arm closer and linked our elbows.

The last room was the haunted library. As we walked in, whispers jumped from the speakers hidden throughout the room. The windows glowed red. Suddenly, there was a creaking sound, and a book flew off the shelf. On the wall next to the grandfather clock, a painting in a large gilt frame tilted on its own, then hung askew.

Will leaned into me. "Even your haunted houses can't resist messing with art," he murmured, and I squeezed his hand.

Then, all at once, a dozen books began to move, their spines sliding slowly out from the ones on either side. Then, one by one, they flew off the shelves onto the floor, and the door slammed shut behind us. William startled slightly. The whispers crescendoed and the lights strobed, making everything appear to be moving toward us. Then a door on the other side of the library opened slowly, showing us the way out.

"That's it," I said softly. And I could have sworn I saw just the hint of relief on Will's face.

"Gentleman," a voice said once we'd exited the library, and an arm pointed us in the direction of the rest of the party.

"Jesus!" William yelled, and jumped backward, almost into me. I grabbed his shoulders to steady him.

I looked where Will was looking, but all I saw was a man in a clown wig and makeup with a stuck-on red clown nose. The man didn't react to Will—or, if he did, his painted on expression hid it.

"What's wrong?" I asked.

William walked in a purposely wide arc around the clown, keeping an eye on him and grabbing my hand. "Yeah, nothing. Just, clowns, man. They're...they smile so big, it's like...I uh. Just. I'm not a super-big fan, that's all."

"Did you read *It* at an impressionable age, William?"

"No, it's not the, um, scary clowns. Just the..." He nodded toward the regular old birthday party clown at the exit.

"I'm trying very hard not to tell you how adorable I find the idea that you rushed in to kill the man wielding a chainsaw, protecting me with your life, but you're scared of children's clowns."

"Shut up," he muttered.

"I did say I was trying very hard, not that I was going to succeed."

William started to give me that look, but I grabbed him and pulled him around the corner, and away from any prying clown eyes. I looked at him for a moment. William Fox, who'd leaned his head on my shoulder, then pushed me behind him to keep me from harm's way. Then...nearly shrieked at seeing a clown, and who was now regarding me suspiciously.

I wrapped my arms around him and squeezed. I held him to me, my nose in his hair, and just stood for a minute, maybe two. He relaxed into it, his body molding against mine, finally hooking his chin over my shoulder. Immediately, all I wanted was for everyone to be out of my house so I could lead Will by the hand to my bed, get him out of his horrible suit, and possibly find some utility for the staff I was carrying as part of this Lucius Malfoy costume. As I began narrowing down its possible uses, Will's stomach growled loudly.

He glared at his stomach as if it had let him down, then looked up, a hopeful little smile playing on his lips. "Hey, can we go back to the candy?"

I kissed him then nodded, leading him back there. He placed one of each of the homemade candies on his plate and grinned at me. I made a mental note that William was very fond of chocolate, and we went to perch at one of the high-top tables in the corner of the room.

"This is wonderful, Vaughn," Charlton Essex said, hand on my elbow as we passed.

"Glad you're enjoying, Charlton," I said. "Have you been through the others yet?"

"Only the Murphys'."

"And how was it?"

"Oh it was lovely. Nothing so dramatic as you have, but quite well done."

Ha. Take that, Murphys.

At the table, Will said, "You look like you just won a prize."

I stood close to him. "I hate the Murphys. Once, Jennifer made a snide comments about how my trees are unkempt. They're weeping willows, for god's sake." Will just raised an eyebrow, like I was ridiculous. "More importantly, they're horrible racists who seem to want their daughter to be the next JonBenét Ramsey. Besides, I don't care for their dog."

Will's eyes got big but he couldn't speak because he was stuffing chocolate into his mouth. Then he groaned around the peppermint patty, a deep, shocked sound of pleasure that shot straight to my dick.

"Oh my *god*, where did these come from?"

"Priscilla," I said, and he rolled his eyes at me. I kissed him lightly just to taste it on his lips.

"So," he said. "That haunted house was amazing. I want to go through again and see how everything works. Like, those mummies were motion-sensor activated, right? And the—"

"You can poke and prod at anything you like."

"But," he went on, "at the risk of sounding…um, just, that all must have cost you a *fortune*. But this was a fundraiser, right? So…"

"I may have gotten slightly more enthusiastic about the project than the budget strictly warranted," I allowed.

He smirked at me. "Don't you do this for a living?"

I raised an eyebrow. "I think people are enjoying themselves, don't you? Appreciating the effort that went into it?"

"Couldn't you just have donated the money you spent

on this haunted house and probably it would've been more than you raised?"

I didn't dignify that with an answer, but I did take half of his homemade Snickers bar.

"Wait, this isn't even about the fundraiser, is it? You just wanted to beat the Murrays or whoever."

"Murphys," I said flatly, and shuddered.

"It is! This is, like, the rich people version of having the nicest lawn," he accused. "Do you have an 'outdo the neighbors' line item on your budget spreadsheet?"

"I filed this under 'unexpected home maintenance,' if you must know." Then I found myself confessing, "I always liked Halloween. I never really got to do it as a kid. Maybe this was my way of making up for that."

Will's expression softened and he smiled at me. He had chocolate in his teeth.

After a minute of concentrated eating, he glanced tentatively up at me. "Wait, do you really have a spreadsheet?"

He was giving me that same suspicious look that I'd seen him direct at the candy display and my Lucius Malfoy costume. I leaned in close, and said in his ear, "If it makes you hot, I do."

He practically choked on a mouthful of candy and I patted him on the back.

After clearing his throat, he said, "You make me feel…complicated things, Amory."

Amory. It sent a shiver through me that pulsed in my stomach and made me feel like I was smiling even though I wasn't.

"Well," I said. "Excel may have powerful tools to deal with complications, but I'm sure we can find more interesting ways to map out your feelings."

Will looked turned on, then self-conscious, then settled at flirtatious. "Tell me about your macros and Visual Basic," he said, and winked luridly, waggling his eyebrows at me.

I laughed. "I'm officially out of my depth with regard to Excel. I pay people to think about those things for me."

"To be honest," William said with a faraway look, "I don't do a lot with spreadsheets, but one time I made one for my climbing expenses and I researched macros because I got bored adding the same columns over and over again." He blinked and refocused on me. "Uh, my stories are...not as charming as yours."

I wrapped a hand around his neck and pulled him in, kissing his mouth that was sweet with chocolate and mint.

"Charm is overrated," I murmured against his lips.

Will looked deep into my eyes and swallowed hard. "Not when it's genuine."

CHAPTER 14

Will

I'D EATEN WAY too much of the most amazing candy in the world by the time the guests finished traipsing through Vaughn's House of Horrors, and I waited patiently while he did the schmoozing that seemed to make up the majority of his duties as a philanthropist.

As I waited, I tried not to think too hard about him dressed like Lucius Malfoy.

Finally, the only people left were those doing post-party cleanup. The lights went on and the fog gradually faded, showing the gruesome props for what they were, the bowls of organs just kitchen scraps and food coloring. Strange how sinister the simplest things could look in the dark.

Vaughn was talking to someone by the door, and I could heard the low timbre of his voice even though I couldn't make out what he was saying. It was unusual to see him with his hair down in public. I'd asked him once why he'd grown it so long if he didn't ever wear it down, and he'd said it was a longstanding rebellion against his father. Vaughn Sr. had very strict ideas about what counted as masculine, and long hair was definitely not one of them.

I loved Vaughn's hair, and I preferred it down. Maybe

because no one else ever really saw it like that. So while I completely approved of his costume, I found myself jealous that other people were seeing him with it down.

To distract myself, I started looking around the house. Not at the temporary macabre additions, but the more permanent décor. It wasn't precisely Vaughn's style, which made sense since, he'd explained, he hadn't changed it after his parents died. It was what you'd expect to find in a historic Virginian home. Like Mount Vernon, but without the velvet security ropes.

I found myself in the study on the ground floor, remembering the day of Valerie's wedding when I'd shown up and threatened him and he'd crowded me against the wall. I'd been so angry at him, for making me want something I knew I shouldn't have. We'd moved on from that, but part of Vaughn's attraction for me was rooted in those first few times we'd met: that strange combination of his charm and that mind like a clock, always ticking. His intelligence was as attractive as his hair, and it was another thing he rarely let anyone see the full extent of.

I rolled my eyes at my mental gushing and helped myself to a glass of excellent bourbon from his stash. I sipped as I ambled around the room, content to let my evil wizard track me down when it was time to show me his magic staff. On a small table was something I'd never noticed before: an ornate pair of crossed pistols.

Eyebrows raised, I picked one up, half expecting to set off an alarm or have someone appear and tell me not to touch them. When that didn't happen, I quickly checked to make sure they weren't loaded before I handled them. They weren't, of course. Yes, Vaughn had his father's firearms stored in a gun safe, but he wasn't a hunter, despite his father's best efforts, and had no real interest in them. Besides, shooting someone was definitely not his style—too much of a mess.

I turned the pistol over in my hand, admiring the craftsmanship, especially of the filigree. My own firearm was a purely functional thing, black and unadorned. A service weapon that I didn't much like having to carry, though it went with the job. I wondered why Vaughn had them in his study, of all places.

A prickle of awareness went up the back of my neck and I half turned toward the door, still holding the gun. There Vaughn stood, hair framing his face, still looking ridiculously hot in that damned Lucius Malfoy costume. My cock stirred, and I had a whole new appreciation for Halloween. "You're not planning to *Avada Kedavra* me, are you?" I asked. I waved the gun. "I'm armed like a proper fifteenth-century duke."

"Like a twentieth-century Italian count, actually," he said, moving toward me.

I looked at the pistol, then back at him. "This is one of those times when you say something and I don't know if you're serious or not."

"I'm deadly serious." He winked at me and laid his staff on the desk. "That's where they came from."

"How did your family end up with dueling pistols from an Italian count?"

"Well." Vaughn seemed to choose his words carefully. "They were a gift."

"For what?"

"My affections." I laughed, but Vaughn didn't.

"Wait, really?" I examined the gun again, more closely this time. "I think all I've given you are a couple of movies and a combo popcorn deal."

At that, Vaughn did laugh, and the sound warmed me. It wasn't the laugh I'd heard all night when we were around other people. It was the one he'd given when I'd been a bit disconcerted by the clown. (Not afraid. *Disconcerted*.) His real laugh, the kind that made him smile and caused faint lines around his eyes. Lucius Malfoy, laughing; who would have imagined it?

"Well, I am quite fond of movie popcorn." He stepped beside me, and I resisted the urge to reach out and run my fingers through his hair. Barely.

With one black-gloved finger, Vaughn traced the filigree on the pistol I was holding. It sent a shiver through me to watch it, a low burn of desire flaring as if it was my cock he was touching.

The sheer power of my attraction to him sometimes shocked me. I'd never felt this strongly about anyone, and occasionally it hit me: that, as well as things were going now, they could go very, very wrong. It spooked me, made me want to pull back, put some distance between us. But now, the bourbon relaxing me (especially on a stomach full of nothing but sugar), I didn't want to be anywhere but here. I wanted him to leave those gloves on and touch me like he was touching this pistol.

"I had a rather…tempestuous affair with an Italian count," he said casually.

"Of course you did." I shook my head.

"I'm serious."

"Oh, I believe you. I mean, I'd never believe anyone else

who said that, but you? Yes." He picked up the other pistol. "Where do you even meet Italian counts?"

"Italy, William." He gave me a look.

Right, of course. "Tempestuous? It didn't end well? I mean, you didn't have to use these, did you?" I joked. I smiled at the vision of Vaughn dueling with a jilted lover at dawn. He didn't even like getting up early for work.

"Well, actually," he started.

I held up a hand. "Don't make me arrest you. There's no statute of limitations on confessions of murder."

"Such little faith you have in me, darling."

I flushed a little, still not used to the endearment. Also, I couldn't help the twinge of discomfort that my initial thought was about Vaughn being a criminal.

"He shot one at me, so I took them with me when I left," said Vaughn simply.

I gaped at him. "He *shot* at you? Someone actually tried to kill you? An Italian count?" Vaughn's history was ridiculous. I wondered what I'd been doing when this had happened. Trying to work up the courage to ask my first guy out on a date? I shook my head. "Why?"

"He didn't want me to leave." Vaughn shrugged. "I wasn't feeling the same, ah, level of attachment. While I had genuinely enjoyed his company, I didn't see myself living the life of a kept man in Italy. Dreadfully boring."

"No aspirations to be a—what would that be, a countess?"

"Not in the slightest. Besides, he already had one of those."

"Are you telling me you got these from a polyamorous Italian count? Because I'm starting to think you got these at a yard sale and you're having me on."

Vaughn gave an elaborate shiver and placed one gloved hand over his heart. "A yard sale," he scoffed. "You know how I feel about getting up early when I don't have to. And on a *weekend*." He sounded horrified.

I smiled at having my logic about his preferences reflected back at me.

He cocked his head, his hair falling around his face. "Polyamorous is rather a formal term for two people accustomed to doing as they pleased. His wife was a lovely woman and a gracious hostess. And preferred women in her bed, or so I was told. It worked out well all around."

"Let me get this straight," I said, ignoring Vaughn's eyebrow-raise at my word choice. "You had…an affair with a gay Italian count who was married to a lesbian countess, and then he was so mad when you decided to leave that he tried to shoot you with an antique dueling pistol, which you then stole?"

Vaughn considered me for a long moment. "Yes, that sounds about right. I can't remember if he was gay or bisexual though. I don't recall the topic ever coming up, and we certainly never invited anyone else to bed with us, given his jealousy issues. But I suppose it could be that he—what?"

I was laughing so hard I had to put the pistol back on the table. "Amory, sometimes I don't think I'm interesting enough to date you. I don't have a single story that is anywhere near that…" I couldn't even think of the word.

"Convoluted? Italian?" He gave me a searching glance and dropped his voice an octave. "Erotic?"

"That is not erotic," I informed him, still laughing. "Well. Maybe you fucking a hot Italian is erotic. But the shooting part, not so much." I sobered at that. "How close was it? Why didn't you have him arrested?"

"That wouldn't have made for a very good story, would it?" Vaughn quipped, moving closer. "And you're very interesting, William. You tried to save me from a chainsaw-wielding maniac, don't forget. Clearly my taste has only improved over the years."

"Well." I took a glance around the room and sipped the last of my bourbon. "I did try and arrest you."

"Oh, we both know you didn't try very hard," Vaughn said.

I didn't want to think about that, so I gave in to my urge to run my fingers through his hair. This really was a perfect costume for him. His hair wasn't quite as long as Jason Isaacs' in the movies, but he still pulled the look off with ease. "I like your costume."

"Your sister suggested you might," said Vaughn, smirking.

I leaned in to kiss him, which meant tugging him down by the hair to account for our height difference. "I had some bourbon."

"I see," Vaughn murmured against my mouth. "And I can taste." He kissed me, and I might have been a little tipsy and a lot stupid with hormones, but I didn't think anyone had ever kissed me like Vaughn. Ever. "Are you ready for bed, or shall I tell you the story behind every antique in my house? I warn you, my parents didn't have the same aversion to early morning estate sales that I do."

Only Vaughn could hear me say "yard sale" and respond as if they were the same as estate sales.

"Do they all have stories involving you fucking counts?"

I murmured, not really paying attention to what I was saying. I slid my hand up into his hair, tugging a little harder. I pushed my hips against his, the pleasant haze of the bourbon making me more aggressive than usual. Or maybe it wasn't the bourbon. Maybe it was the thought of that count, thinking he could keep Vaughn locked away in some castle. Or whatever they called the domiciles of the Italian aristocracy.

"Not quite," Vaughn murmured, biting gently at my lip.

I responded by biting not so gently at his.

"You are in a mood tonight, William. Who knew wizards got you so worked up?"

I smiled and pulled away, breathing a little faster. "It's not Lucius Malfoy that gets me worked up, it's you." I thought about that. "And maybe you...you being a villain is doing it for me." I crossed my arms over my chest, ignoring how impossibly wrong it was for me to say this, given my job. "A little."

Vaughn looked delighted by this admission. "You know I'd never join an organization that required I get a tattoo," he scoffed.

I pitied the organization that tried to require Vaughn do anything. "Not to mention the part where they're racists," I pointed out. "You should take off that costume."

"I intend to," Vaughn murmured. "Upstairs, where we have a bed."

Obviously, I liked the idea of that. Of a bed, and Vaughn in one, his hair sweaty and tangled and in his face. I wanted to fuck him. But I didn't want to wait for a bed. "I don't think so," I said in my agent voice. My agent voice, after a few whiskeys and a dinner comprised entirely of candy. I locked the door to ensure no one still milling about the house stumbled into the study. The drapes were drawn over the windows, which meant we had perfect, glorious privacy.

Vaughn's costume consisted of a suit, a black cloak that swirled in an appropriately stately and sinister manner, black gloves, and a staff. He discarded the cloak, and pulled off the gloves. I shook my head. Here I thought the plastic fangs might have been too much. I should have saved myself the three dollars.

His jacket was fitted, with a wide, tapering collar. It looked vaguely like the tailcoats that would be worn to the symphony. I knew Vaughn had season tickets—was this what he usually wore there? He paused, fingers at his top button, watching as my mind spiraled into nonsense.

"Take that jacket off," I said, and felt a thrill as he obeyed me. It was more intoxicating than the bourbon.

I picked up one of the dueling pistols again, and shook my head as I thought about his story. The thing was, I didn't doubt that every word of it was true. I could see someone getting obsessed with him to the point of doing something dangerous. After all, hadn't I done the same thing in this very room not that long ago?

"You have an interesting effect on people, Mr. Vaughn." I slipped the *mister* in there, wondering if he'd catch it.

Of course he did. He noticed everything. "Are you saying it was my fault someone shot at me, Agent Fox?"

That's when I knew we were playing. He'd barely "Agent Fox"ed me when I'd been about to arrest him for real. "I'm not talking about the attempted murder," I said. Thinking that someone would try and hurt him made me angry on a visceral level. I struggled to keep my voice even. "And anyway, there's no proof of that. All I have is your word that someone tried to kill you with an antique gun."

Vaughn gave me an innocent look. "You could call him, but please not with my number. I went to a great deal of trouble to make sure he can't find me."

Was that true? I wanted to ask, but didn't break character. I put the dueling pistol down and clasped my hands behind my back. "I find it hard to believe that you had the presence of mind to grab a valuable antique on your way out the door when someone was trying to kill you."

"They're not that valuable," said Vaughn.

I almost—almost—smiled.

"Besides," said Vaughn. "It was self-defense."

"You were going to, what, shoot him with both barrels? Like a gunslinger?"

"I took one so that he couldn't use it, and the other to protect myself. Surely you can't blame me for that, Agent Fox." He smiled, that charming smile he gave when he wanted something. Had it ever worked on me? I didn't think so. I liked Amory's smiles, not Vaughn's.

But I was happy enough, caught up in the heady rush of liquor and whatever game we were playing, to pretend. That's all this was, wasn't it? Pretending Vaughn had stolen something, and I was the agent on his case. Was this something I could do? I was still disturbed that I'd let him get away with the Staunton. And—I could admit it to myself if no one else—powerfully curious as to how he'd done it.

He was watching me, gray eyes thoughtful, waiting to see what I'd do. I could carry on with the pretense we were making this about the dueling pistols, and it'd be hot and a little bit wrong. I could drop this altogether and suggest we go upstairs.

Or I could pretend to do what I should have done months ago, in this same room, when I'd confronted him about the painting. Skirting the edge of something that we absolutely shouldn't. Cross a line that I'd insisted be laid between us in steel. Admit that while I knew Amory's moral compass was skewed and possibly cracked, it didn't make me want him any less. I'd never been one to chase the bad boys. I guess I had just been waiting for one to chase *me*.

We were facing each other next to his desk. A few weekends ago, I'd sucked him off while he was on a conference call and bored out of his mind. Then I'd laid on the couch and stroked myself off, giving him something more interesting to concentrate on. And yet when I was alone and I thought about Vaughn, and this room, that wasn't the memory that got me hard and aching.

I rested a hand on the slick wooden surface and leaned in. "Tell me about the night of Keith Oakley's party."

There were so few times I was able to surprise Vaughn. When it happened, I relished it—the way his eyes widened slightly and the skin around his mouth tightened, the briefest falter after which he was forced to rearrange his façade. "That was months ago," he said, and his voice wasn't quite even. He was staring at me, trying to figure out what game we were playing now. I could tell he wasn't quite sure what to make of this.

And I liked it.

"Let's say it wasn't. Let's say it was, oh, three days ago."

"Well, Agent Fox," he said, and I could tell the caution in his voice was honest, and it made my cock hard. "As I recall, I attended that party and met a very charming gentleman who didn't seem to be having a very good time."

"Mmm." I kept my face blank, though my heart was racing. "Tell me about that."

He was watching me like a hawk, and I knew I'd piqued his interest. I'd probably piqued more than that. I didn't know what he liked more—that I was a stickler for following the rules, or that he'd made me break them.

"Well, Agent Fox, I noticed the man watching me as I was enduring the tedium of familiar ass kissing with the hope of receiving funding from my foundation. He was sipping whiskey and standing next to a young woman. He blushed when I caught him staring. I remember that since the woman looked like him, I hoped she was his sister."

I had no idea if that was true or not, but he had no reason to lie. Then again, he didn't always need one. "I see. And then what?"

"He moved around the room but continued to watch me, and I found that…intriguing. Because he wasn't watching me the way so many people do at these events. As if I were a doorway to money or opportunity. He was watching me like I was a man. I decided to see if he'd like to talk, or just keep eye-fucking all night over our cocktails. Not that I'd have been averse."

At any other time, I might have laughed at that. But the memory was there, how I'd felt every time we'd met each other's eyes across the room. I still felt that way. I'd felt that way tonight, when he was off being charming and would look up from whatever group he was with to seek me out. The smile that came after our gazes met was new. Hard-won.

The look in his eyes? That was the same. Possessive,

interested.

"However, as I was on my way to make his acquaintance, he turned and ran away." He smirked at this and I resisted rolling my eyes. "I almost lost sight of him, until I realized he was going downstairs."

"Downstairs," I repeated. "Where Oakley's art collection lived."

"It's hardly a collection," he scoffed. "He paid far too much for that Nedja abstract, and I'm not convinced one or two of the others down there aren't cleverly disguised forgeries."

I blinked. He'd never said that before. Then again, we'd never talked about it. When we spoke of our relationship, when I thought about it in terms of beginning, it was our first date: the picnic after the gala. The day he'd agreed not to take things that weren't his, and I'd let him take *me*. Even my sister didn't know about the Staunton, or Valerie's wedding. No one knew Vaughn was a thief. Just me.

My blood roared for a moment in my ears, my face heating. "And the Staunton?"

"Original," said Vaughn, "but hung too low. And the lighting, as you know, was abysmal."

I stepped closer and ran my finger down his lapel, like he'd done to me that night. "And what else do you remember?"

"Seducing the man I'd come down there to find." Vaughn stared at me, shrewd, the telltale flush on his face signaling he was turned on. "Getting on my knees for him. The rug Oakley referenced as the impetus for purchasing a painting he thought would match. I imagine he overpaid for that too." Vaughn's tone dripped with derision.

"You were focused on the rug? Must not have been that memorable of an encounter."

"Oh, believe me, agent. It was."

We were getting to the part that might be dangerous. Oakley's Staunton was back where it should be—though Vaughn was right about the placement, and it had nearly killed me not to raise it up a few inches. I supposed, technically, I could haul Vaughn in if I wanted, and use his confession as probable cause. But that wasn't the point, and it wasn't why I wanted to do this.

I wanted to let myself have him. Not just the Amory Vaughn who had elaborate theme parties ostensibly to raise money but really so he could outdo the neighbors. Tonight, just for tonight, I wanted him to be the liar I'd once accused him of being. I wanted the thief. The villain.

And I wanted to be the one who brought him down.

I edged closer, sliding a hand to my hip. I didn't have my gun, and my badge was in the car, but it was a typical agent stance, the same one I'd use if I had both on my person. "And then he left without giving you his number."

"Mmm." Vaughn's eyes were as sharp as cut glass. "Imagine if he'd only given it to me. We might not be here today."

We probably wouldn't be, and we both knew it.

"So, what did you do, Amory? Instead of asking his sister, who you knew was the party planner, what did you do instead?"

Vaughn went still, likely at the use of his first name. I wondered if it bothered him that I'd used it. If it was throwing some hint of uncertainty into this whole thing. Good. I hoped it was. "William," he said, softly.

I pressed my fingers to his lips and moved in, kissing them and by extension, his mouth. "You knock me off balance all the time, do you know that? I'm beginning to see why you like it."

I pulled back and we stared at each other, the tension ratcheting up a few uncomfortable degrees. The safety net of our relationship was new enough that I didn't trust it not to tear if we fell.

"What did you do, Amory? Tell me."

He stared down at me for so long I thought he wasn't going to, and then he said, "I left a wedding invitation outside his door."

Casually, I grabbed a fistful of his hair. I loved doing that, especially when he was above me, fucking me. I loved how it felt on my thighs when he was sucking me off, silky and slightly ticklish. And I loved remembering how I'd pulled it in anger and frustrated wanting the night I should have arrested him. "Why?"

Amory Vaughn was not the kind of man who backed down from a dare. "Well, Agent Fox, I suppose I wanted to make an impression. From one art lover to another."

He still wasn't saying it. I moved in closer, catching a moan at the last minute as I felt how hard he was. I pulled on his hair again, brought my mouth to his ear and murmured, "Tell me what you did, Amory."

"I stole Keith Oakley's Staunton, and left it for him."

The air between us vibrated and I leaned in closer. "How?"

"Well," Vaughn said, and one hand slid down and around my waist to pull me closer. "I think I'd prefer to have this conversation with a lawyer present."

I paused, ensnared by my own game and unwilling to back down. "I don't think that's necessary, Mr. Vaughn. Surely we can come to some kind of understanding."

Vaughn gave a quiet laugh. "I've seen enough television to know that's absolutely not possible, Agent Fox."

He was right, and part of me was glad to hear that. "Well then. If that's what you want."

I kissed his neck, then moved quickly, pushing him face-first over the desk, holding his hands behind his back. He looked at me over his shoulder, hair half in his eyes, and a smirk playing on his mouth.

"Amory Vaughn," I said. "You're under arrest for grand theft larceny. You have the right to remain silent. Anything you say can and will be used against you in a court of law. You have the right to an attorney. If you cannot afford an attorney, one will be provided for you. Do you understand the rights I have read to you?"

"Mm," said Vaughn, eyes flashing up at me.

"With these rights in mind, do you wish to speak?"

"Oh, probably," he said as I moved to stand behind him.

I pressed my erection against his ass. "Tell me how you did it."

"I don't see my attorney present, Agent Fox. I'd call, but you've got my hands restrained." He tugged against my grip. Not hard, but enough that I had to tighten my grip to keep him where I wanted him.

"Tell me how you did it," I repeated, eyes closing briefly as I rubbed myself harder against the firm muscles of his ass. "I want to know how you walked out of there with a painting and no one noticed."

"People are surprisingly nearsighted," Vaughn said, pushing back against me. His own voice was breathless. If he hadn't figured out that what was getting me hot was hearing the details of how he'd done it, then he wasn't half as smart as I thought.

I let go of his hands and reached around him to fumble at his pants. It took me a few tries to get them undone, then I shoved them down along with his underwear. I didn't have any restraints, so I said, "Put your hands behind your head, and keep them there."

I looked around, wildly, after he'd complied. There was something I was forgetting, something I needed…

"Top drawer. I've plans to fuck you over every desk I own, William."

I smiled because he couldn't see, then retrieved the lube from the desk drawer. He had fucked me over a desk, and if I wanted to even that score like I had with that blowjob, I could do the same to him. But that wasn't what I wanted. Amory wasn't in charge of the game. Not this time. "Stand up."

He did, and I put my hand in the small of his back and scanned the room, finding a spot on the wall that wasn't blocked by a table full of knickknacks or boring, stuffy portraits. "Over there." I gave him a bit of a shove, and he shuffled toward the wall, shackled by the pants around his ankle.

His hands were still behind his head like I'd told him, and I knew he hated this—stumbling around, being mussed, out of control. Hated it, and I'd bet anything if I reached around and grabbed his cock it'd be slick.

I pushed him against the wall. "Keep your hands there." I closed my eyes and let myself rub my cloth-covered erection against his naked ass. "Now tell me how you did it." With one hand, I undid my own pants and pushed them down, the lube clutched in the other.

"I told you," Vaughn murmured, voice muffled. "People see what they want. The caterers were packing up, so it was easy to move around the house. I went up to Oakley's bedroom, found his closet—atrociously disorganized. I wouldn't want him anywhere near *my* bank account—and found a garment bag. Then I went downstairs, put the painting in the bag, and left through the back door."

I was lubing my cock with one hand and keeping Vaughn pressed against the wall with the other. I blinked. That was it? "You just walked out of his house, with a painting in a garment bag?"

"Yes." His voice was choked. I kicked his legs apart and fitted myself against him, holding his hips tight as I slid my slicked cock up and down his crease.

"And, what, walked home?"

"I don't live that far from Oakley, as you know, Agent Fox. I simply went home, found your address and a crate big enough for the painting, ordered some sushi, and waited for a time I thought any sensible person would be asleep."

I pressed the tip of my cock to his hole. "And then you drove to Arlington."

"And then I—drove to—Arlington," Vaughn agreed, breathless, the muscles in his back shifting as I pushed inside. He tried to angle his hips but I put my palms on either side of his head, stilling him. He could bend slightly to adjust for our height difference, and steady himself when I pushed in, but I was in control of our movements.

"And no one ever noticed you were carrying a painting in

a bag," I said, sweat stinging my eyes as I started to thrust. God, he felt so good—and something about hearing this, hearing the *sheer audacity* of it, was getting me as hot as the sight of him, naked from the waist down, hair everywhere, pushing back to try and get more of my cock as I fucked him.

"Of course they noticed the bag. That's the thing, Agent Fox. It doesn't matter if they see you. What matters is that they think you belong wherever you are."

That was so perfectly *Vaughn* that if I'd been able to think past the haze of lust and the feeling of him so tight around my cock, I might have laughed. Instead I groaned, pulled his hips back, and tried to fuck him through the wall. I was already dangerously close to coming. "Why?"

"Why, what?" He was panting now, using his leverage on the wall to fuck himself on my cock. I spit in my palm, reached around, and took his dick in my hand. Vaughn's cock was wet with precome, and the spit and remnants of the lube on my hand gave him a nice, slick fist to thrust into. I heard something fall off the wall next to us as I fucked him hard, but I didn't stop to look.

"Why did you *do it*," I hissed, moving my hand faster, feeling his legs shake and those frantic pushes of his hips stall as he neared orgasm.

"I didn't know—what you did—for a living," he managed. He looked at me, face red and sweaty, hair a tangled mess, eyes wild. I wasn't sure I'd ever found him more attractive, falling apart and telling me things he probably would've preferred I never know.

He came in my hand, gasping, before I could say anything, and it made him tighten around my cock so that I nearly saw stars. I was incapable of speech, and I struggled to support him as he moaned through his orgasm.

I grabbed his hands and shoved them behind his back, fucking him flat against the wall, graceless as I neared the edge. When I came, the roar in my ears was deafening, my shout harsh and honest. My knees buckled, and my vision went white, and I bit Vaughn's shoulder through the sweat-dampened fabric of his shirt.

I moved away from him, sweaty and overheated, and pulled at my clothes until I was in my undershirt and suit pants. I sat down heavily on the couch and caught my breath, looking up only when I'd stopped gulping at air.

Vaughn was leaning against the wall, strands of his fair hair sticking to his face. He'd pulled his underwear and pants up, but hadn't bothered with anything else. He was also out of breath, staring at me with a look that bordered on unfriendly. It was, I thought, one of the most honest expressions I'd seen since I'd met him.

"I did it because you made an impression," he said, finally. "No one ever does. Not on me. So I wanted to do the same."

I'd fucked a confession out of him. It wasn't admissible in court, but that was fine. That wasn't why I'd needed it. I nodded, elbows on my knees. I wondered if we'd gone too far. If I'd crossed a line I shouldn't have. If I'd fucked this up.

"I'm going to have a shower," he told me, and he was all Amory now, no pretense and no charm and no arrogance. In that moment I realized I loved him, and wondered if I'd just lost him.

"That wasn't—" I winced at the sound of my own voice,

rough with emotion and sudden self-doubt. "I wouldn't ever—"

Turn you in. I couldn't finish that sentence, choked suddenly by the knowledge that I meant that, absolutely.

Some of Vaughn's tension eased, though I was now paralyzed by how willing I was to compromise my ethics when it came to this man. He gave a brief nod, then pushed away from the wall and headed toward the door. He was going to leave me there, I realized. He wanted space, because whatever that was we'd just done, whatever game we'd played…it had affected him too.

I waited a few moments before climbing the stairs. I saw someone scurrying by with the last of the Haunted House cleaning-up. He glanced at me and I nodded, too exhausted and too raw to care.

In the bathroom, I stripped the rest of my clothes and climbed in the shower with Vaughn, who stood with his hands against the slick tile, head bowed, letting the water run over him.

"Let me wash your hair," I said, overtaken by the unfamiliar urge to take care of him. I'd gotten him to confess to the crime we both knew he'd committed, and now I wanted to touch him, soothe him, bring him back from wherever he'd gone in his head. Uneasiness thrummed through me as I reached out for his shampoo.

I squirted some into my hand and frowned. It was as blue as the bottle. "Is this from the drugstore?" I'd only ever seen shampoo that color if it was Pert Plus, and something told me Vaughn did not shop for hair care products at Rite Aid.

"William," he said, a hint of his usual self in the recrimination. "Honestly." I smiled with a rush of sudden affection for him and began working the shampoo through his hair. "The blue takes the brassy tones out of my hair," Vaughn said, leaning into my touch. He was quiet and let me wash his hair, and we found ourselves kissing after the suds had washed away.

"Are you—"

Vaughn kissed me, his equilibrium clearly returning. "I'm fine. That was very...unexpected." He smiled. With his hair wet and his lean body covered in suds and glistening with water, he looked younger than I was accustomed to seeing. Maybe just a little bit more vulnerable than he ever had.

Telling me that he'd stolen the painting, telling me how... Even if he'd been factual—maybe part of that was a game. But telling me *why* he'd done it? That meant something. "I know." Now that it was over, I wasn't sure if I wanted to talk about it. I felt tired, drained, but somehow at peace. "I can't even explain...what you do to me," I said, fingers tracing patterns on the smooth skin of his chest. He had very little body hair, and what he did have was so pale it was nearly invisible. "You make me...want things. That I shouldn't."

"Oh, William," he said, and caught my hand. He carried it to his mouth and kissed it, an odd, courtly gesture considering we were both in the shower and his stupid blue shampoo had stained my hand. "Believe me. The feeling is mutual."

It wasn't until we were in bed, both dry and tangled together in easy familiarity, that he spoke again.

"Are you disappointed?"

I frowned, turning to look at him behind me. "About what?"

"My confession. I realize it wasn't all that exciting. No *Thomas Crown Affair* master plan."

I rolled my eyes in the dark. "If you think that wasn't exciting… You know what? I'm not finishing that sentence." I stared out of the window, trying to think what to say. "You want to know what I think? I think it was reckless. Reckless, and arrogant, and unnecessary."

"Unnecessary?" Vaughn mouthed at my neck. "How do you mean?"

"You could have just asked for my number," I huffed, tilting my head to give him more access to my neck.

"William, I've just confessed to a crime," Vaughn murmured against my skin. "So do me the favor, please, of conceding it was necessary."

That wasn't true…was it? "I would have been happy to hear from you, if you'd gotten my number and called me," I said. That was true. Wasn't it?

"Would you have called me back?"

I didn't answer right away. Would I have? Or with the rush of our initial encounter over, would I have slid right back into my daily life, everything predictable and ordered, and told myself it'd never work out? That I was bad at flirting, and relationships were a romance, and… "I don't know," I murmured. It felt like a lie.

Vaughn bit gently at my ear. "You wouldn't have. You climb mountains for fun, William. A simple invitation wouldn't have been enough to get you to take a chance on me. You like a challenge just as much as I do."

"Larceny is not—ow!"

"Let's not pretend you didn't find that confession of mine hot, darling." He nuzzled the spot where he'd bitten me.

"Fine." I was huffy for a moment, but I reached around and found his hand, holding it tight to my chest. After a few long moments, I said, "I wasn't disappointed."

I could feel Vaughn's smile against my neck as his arms tightened around me.

CHAPTER 15

Will

I T WAS A Saturday afternoon, and the clouds outside Vaughn's apartment hung heavy and gray, a light drizzle pattering the windows. Vaughn was muttering at his paperwork—he did a lot of paperwork. His hair was pulled back in a ponytail and he was scowling at the pages spread out on the low coffee table. I thought it was cute that he talked to himself while working.

He must have felt me watching him, because he looked up from his papers. He was wearing his reading glasses, which I secretly wished he'd wear all the time. They were frameless with a silver nosepiece—simple and elegant, like everything of Vaughn's. "I'm talking to myself again, aren't I?"

I smiled and nodded. "Yeah, you are." I didn't say it was cute, but surely he heard it in my voice that I thought it was. After all, he'd gotten to know me pretty well. We'd begun spending most weekends together. In fact, lately I'd been spending more time at his homes than at my own.

He yawned, and made a sound of pure frustration. "I'm sorry I have to spend time doing this when you're here."

I shrugged. When he put it like that, it made me feel like

a guest, which wasn't how I wanted to feel. I wanted him to just…be himself when I was here. Do whatever he usually did on Saturdays. Think of me as belonging here.

He was wearing jeans and a sweater even though I was still in pajama bottoms and an old FBI t-shirt. I knew Vaughn owned pajamas, but I'd never seen him wear them out of the bedroom. I had a feeling if I wasn't there, though, he'd be lounging around in his PJs and a bathrobe. I wanted him to do that too. I didn't want him to dress up for me, or think he needed to impress me.

"It's probably better than this book," I said, holding up my paperback. "I should know better than to read anything featuring FBI agents. They either get everything wrong, or make us out to be unlikeable dicks who just want to ruin the lives of the local sheriff or whatever." I glanced at the table, where I'd set my messenger bag. There were files pertaining to my latest case in there, and I supposed I could be looking over them. Instead, I'd opted to read something mindless, unsure if it was because it was the weekend or if I felt conflicted doing my job around Vaughn. Especially since it was a reminder that I *hadn't* done my job when it came to him.

Vaughn gave that elegant shrug of his. "You've mentioned a few unlikeable dicks to me."

"Yeah, but we're not all like Brett Lawson," I groused, referring to my least-favorite colleague.

"Maybe you should stick to something that doesn't aim for realism," Vaughn suggested. "Paranormal romance. Space opera." He gave me a sly smile. "Pornography."

"Do you have pornography around here somewhere?"

"William, I have Google Fi and you have a laptop."

I snorted and shook my head, standing up. "I meant in book form."

"I repeat. Google Fi and laptop."

I rolled my eyes at him and pointed him back to his papers spread out on the coffee table. The coffee table that he would never, in a million years, allow anyone to drink coffee on. Even me. Because the coffee table was on the rug.

I didn't know what the rug was made out of, but I knew that the first time I'd stayed the night here, I'd wandered over to look out the window the next morning while holding a cup of coffee and seen a look of apprehension on Vaughn's face ten times that which I'd seen when I'd accused him of grand larceny. Vaughn, who had made a point of fucking me on furniture from every century since the founding of America, had been watching me with my cup of coffee like I was a child with a bowl of chocolate sauce.

"I didn't realize the rug was an antique," I'd said, teasing him.

"It's not," he'd said. "It's an Alanna Vale Allen."

After explaining (needlessly, I was sure) that I wasn't up on the latest names in rug design, Vaughn had told me more than I'd ever needed, or wanted, to know about the rug. Which was white—because of course; why have a ridiculously expensive rug in any other color? Admittedly, it was very soft, but my joking suggestion of having sex on it had been vetoed severely and without Vaughn's usual humor. I was amused to have found a weakness. Something Vaughn actually worried about ruining.

"I can stop working, if you'd like to do something else," Vaughn said. I glanced meaningfully at the rug and raised an eyebrow just to watch the panic flicker over his face.

"William, we've been over that. But I'm not adverse to going back to bed."

"Do your paperwork, and I'll blow you. On the couch. Unless…" I teased, running a fingertip up his thigh. "Unless that's too close to the rug?" He gave me a severely put-upon look and went back to his papers. I went into the kitchen and started rummaging through the cabinets. I was thinking about how good a few of those handmade chocolates from the Halloween fundraiser would be right now, and that's when I got the idea to make cookies.

Which was odd, because I couldn't remember the last time I'd baked anything.

Ever since Charlie discovered that you could make up your own recipes at the age of twelve, she'd been the one to do all the cooking and baking. From that moment onward, she was constantly tinkering in the kitchen, doing whatever our mom would allow, from birthday cakes to cookies to elaborate dishes with names I was pretty sure she made up. Once she began Fox Fêtes, and got to dream up the ideas and have other people do the dirty work, she liked it even better.

I usually got home from work starving, so the last thing I wanted to do was cook anything elaborate. Somewhat to my surprise, Vaughn actually enjoyed cooking. He had someone who kept his house stocked with food and prepared meals when he entertained at home, but when it was just him—or us—he usually cooked. I poured the wine. It worked out well for us.

But suddenly, I remembered a time when I'd been sick and stressed out over a case at work, and Charlotte had baked me cookies. Just the smell of them baking in my subpar oven had made me feel comforted, cared for.

"Hey, what's your favorite kind of cookie?" I asked Vaughn, thinking I could make him feel as cared for as I had. Make him feel like I really did belong here.

"Hmm? Oh. Well, I'm not sure." Vaughn chewed on the end of a pen distractedly, a gesture so unlike him that I found it charming.

God, if I stopped to think about how much time I spent smiling around Amory Vaughn, I'd probably freak out. It was just that I'd never liked anyone quite so much. Which scared the hell out of me.

"I had some brandied fruit tartlets at a tea in London," Vaughn said vaguely. "Do tartlets count as cookies?"

I had no idea. "Nope."

Vaughn wrinkled his nose and stared up at the lofted ceiling. "Those pine nut cookies with rosemary your sister served at the gala were very good. People still ask me for the recipe."

I crossed my arms over my chest. "They were good, yeah, but seriously, they can't be your favorite. That wasn't that long ago."

"Well, I'm very sorry, Agent Fox, I didn't realize your question came with so many codicils."

I rolled my eyes, but hearing him call me *Agent Fox* after what happened in his study back in Falls Church made my cock stir. "Your favorite cookie, Amory. This shouldn't be that hard."

"Green tea shortbread?" I could practically see him running through a list of Vaughn Foundation function desserts.

"When was the last time you had those?" I demanded.

"I can't recall. Why? Are you asking me for a cookie

alibi?"

I laughed. "No, I just meant…your favorite cookie can't be something like green tea shortbread."

"Why not?"

"It's like…" I waved my hand. "The cookie you ate when you were a kid. The ones you always hoped would be waiting for you when you got home from school. You know." Then it struck me that he probably didn't. From what I'd heard about Amory's childhood, he probably *had* mostly eaten cookies at Vaughn Foundation functions. His parents seemed to have treated him like a business partner since the time he could walk.

"My mother always served Venetian butter cookies at parties. Everyone loved those," he said vaguely. He was staring out of the window at the rain and didn't meet my eyes.

I didn't think that was the answer. In times like these, I wondered how lonely he must have been as a child. Who took this long to answer a question about cookies?

Someone who never got to have anything just for himself.

Every single answer he'd given me was something other people chose, something other people found delicious.

"Yeah, but Amory." I made my voice soft. "What was *your* favorite?"

He bit at his lip, and darted a glance up at me, then looked away. This time when he answered his voice sounded different. "Chocolate chip." He still wouldn't look at me, like he was afraid what my argument with that answer might be.

"All right, then," I said softly, feeling a surge of emotion. "Chocolate chip it is."

I changed into jeans and grabbed my jacket, and when I kissed him goodbye he still wouldn't quite look at me. At the corner market a few blocks down I grabbed the ingredients I needed, got half soaked on the walk home, and changed right back into my pajamas before going to the kitchen.

I caught Vaughn looking at me a few times, but he never said a word. I fixed him some coffee, and when he came to drink it *far* away from the rug, his eyes strayed toward the mess I was making. "You have flour in your hair."

"Don't worry. If I get it on the rug, it'll blend in." I winked at him. I'd said the same thing about having sex on the rug too.

He just shot me a look over the top of his glasses and went back to the paperwork. I put a dozen cookies in the oven, wrapped the rest of the dough in Saran Wrap, and put it in the freezer. When he was there during the week, he could bake some more.

"I'm not bringing these near your precious Allen rug," I said, placing two freshly-baked cookies on a plate on the counter.

"Vale Allen," Vaughn said without thinking. He stretched and his sweater rode up so I could see the muscles of his beautiful torso shifting as he reached toward the ceiling. He padded over, slid onto the barstool and looked at the plate. I couldn't read his expression as he bent slowly over the counter and inhaled the smell of fresh-baked cookies. But his eyes flew to mine and there was something open there. Something raw and unmanaged and just for me. He picked up a cookie and slowly took a bite, like he was afraid of what it might taste like. Then he closed his eyes with a smile that passed through appreciative and landed on happy as he ate the rest.

That was the face of a man enjoying his favorite cookie. *Green tea shortbread.* Honestly. "They're good, then?"

"They're delicious," he said, opening his eyes. He snagged the second cookie—which I'd put there for myself—and dug in. "Is this a Fox family recipe?"

I blinked. He had to be kidding. The empty bag of chocolate chips with the recipe printed on it was right there on the counter. Then I realized that Amory Vaughn had probably never eaten a chocolate chip cookie made from the recipe on the back of store-bought chocolate chips in his life.

I turned to get myself a cookie, suddenly at a loss for words. I had a million memories of helping my mom, my dad, my grandparents and my sister make these. Being ten and making them with friends at a sleepover, just to eat the cookie dough. "It's…your standard recipe," I said, clearing my throat and nonchalantly whisking the empty chocolate chip bag into the trash.

"Well, now you know what my favorite cookies are," Vaughn said, and smiled at me so sweetly it made my heart pound. He grabbed another cookie off the baking sheet and ate it too.

"I left you the rest of the dough in the freezer," I told him. When he kissed me, he tasted like chocolate. "You done with that paperwork yet?"

"Almost." He snagged another cookie and went back to the sofa to finish up. I set about doing the dishes, and my phone vibrated on the counter, distracting me from the cookie-dough-laden spoon I was cleaning. With my tongue.

It was an email from Patty, our constantly overworked secretary. This one was a reminder about the upcoming seminar in Durham, on diversity and sensitivity in the workplace. She wanted to know whether we'd be arriving Friday night or Saturday morning, and if we were bringing a significant other.

I stared at the message, and then looked at Vaughn. I thought about how I'd been reticent about anything pertaining to my job around him, and yet, how badly I wanted to be part of his life. Maybe I should stop trying to keep my job so separate, especially if this was going to work long-term. If I wanted him to just be himself around me…then that meant I had to do the same.

Not that I was going to go over my latest case with him—a stolen painting that had turned out to be a forgery. There were laws governing how much I could share, after all. But that didn't mean I had to keep him away from the FBI completely. Maybe, if he wanted, he could come with me to this diversity seminar. Work trips were terrible. This one even more so because diversity wasn't something many agents were that open to discussing. But it did mean a weekend away and paid-for accommodations.

Nothing fancy. Nothing that would meet Vaughn's standards, to be sure—he was a complicated man in a lot of ways, but the fact that he was a snob was pretty damned straightforward. This was the final reminder about the seminar and accommodations, and I'd been putting off answering because…well, should I ask Vaughn to go with me to an FBI retreat? Would he think spending a weekend with me was worth having to do so in below-his-standard accommodations? Probably not.

There was also the small fact that next weekend was my thirty-fifth birthday. I didn't necessarily want him to know that. I hated people making a big deal out of it. Imagine growing up with a budding party planner, extroverted twin with a thousand friends. But I wanted to be with him for it regardless.

"You busy next weekend?" I asked before I could stop myself.

"Let me see." Vaughn had a lot of engagements and obligations, so I knew it was likely he wouldn't even be able to go with me. "No, it appears I'm free. Why?"

"I, uh." I couldn't believe this was making me so nervous. "I have a thing. A work thing, in Durham. I was thinking maybe…if you wanted…you could come with me." The instant I said it, I felt incredibly stupid.

But Vaughn looked intrigued. "Is it about catching art thieves?" He winked, and his eyes flicked to the wall, just momentarily, where *Oliver*, the James Novack painting from the student art show, was now installed.

I flushed and gave him a severe look. "No. It's about diversity and sensitivity in the workplace. You know. How to do my job with respect for all races, religions, genders and sexualities."

Vaughn cocked his head at me. "Do you require that lesson?"

"Just because I'm gay doesn't mean I couldn't be racist, or prejudiced against Muslims or women."

"William, you're not any of those things." Vaughn's voice took on that low, warm quality that made me shiver with pleasure. "Shall I produce letters of reference to free you from this tedium?"

"Sometimes you talk like a character in a novel," I told him.

"Well, there is a character in an F. Scott Fitzgerald novel

with my name. Not the one everyone knows." He took off his glasses and folded them. "It's a lovely area. Have you been?"

"No, two years ago it was in Asheville. They try to make it…not tedious, I guess. By having it somewhere nice, and telling us we can bring someone. If we want." I was beginning to feel stupid that I'd brought it up, but I kept talking. "I have the training during the day on Saturday and Sunday, and a dinner thing on Sunday night, but Saturday evening free." Which was my birthday.

"I won't be expected to attend the seminar, will I?" Vaughn asked. "I have participated in many a diversity training already."

"I think we've got rich white male covered, but you might step in for bisexual."

I shook my head and Vaughn walked over to join me in the kitchen. At first I thought maybe it was to make good on the blowjob I'd promised him for finishing his paperwork, but he went right for the plate of cookies I'd set on the stove. "I'd be delighted to accompany you to Durham. I have some work I can get done while you're learning how to be sensitive."

"Yeah? All right, if you're sure. I can pick you up here Friday after work, if that's all right? I'll have to drive, of course, and we have to stay in the hotel where the conference is, but they're usually pretty nice."

"I'm looking forward to it," said Vaughn. "As I am to this blowjob I believe I've now earned."

But as I reached for his pants, Vaughn took a step in and wrapped his arms around my shoulders. He held me close for a long time, the smell of fresh-baked cookies mingling with the scent of his hair.

CHAPTER 16

Vaughn

I HAD AGREED that we'd play this William's way. It was his business trip; he had to drive the company car, stay at the company hotel. I knew the drill.

I hadn't complained about the lack of leg room in William's Taurus. I had graciously accepted the brackish gas station coffee he had procured for us, though it made my teeth feel gritty and burned behind my sternum in a disturbing reminder that I wasn't twenty-five anymore. I had managed to hold my tongue when we turned into the parking lot of a hotel I'd only ever seen advertised via signage at highway exits. Hell, I'd even used the towels they provided without asking Will if they were intended as some kind of punitive measure.

However. A man could only bear so much. And this? This was where I drew the line.

"William."

"Hmm." His attention was on the television over my shoulder.

"These are not eggs, William. These are a nightmare that chickens have."

"Mhmm."

I winced at my plate. "Complimentary Continental Breakfast!" the sign in the lobby had insisted. But the weak coffee was an insult, not a compliment, and the mealy corn muffins and hardboiled abominations were about as continental as eating dinner at five p.m. Clearly, Will's mind was on other things. I tipped my untouched food into the trash, briefly eyed the waffle maker with its dirty plastic tub of batter, and shuddered.

I poured myself a glass of orange juice and reluctantly filled a paper bowl with Raisin Bran from a bulk cereal dispenser where it was the only sane option among three neon-colored cereals. God knew how long it had been sitting in the dispenser, absorbing the taste of plastic and the germs of the room. But at least you couldn't overcook Raisin Bran.

Back at the table, Will was fiddling with his phone with one hand and mindlessly eating a muffin with the other. I hated the cheap-looking suits he wore; his watch was a sports timepiece, completely unsuited for business attire; and he was wearing navy blue socks with his black suit. It was almost as atrocious as the La Quinta's garish green-and-purple modernism. But it didn't matter in the slightest, because when he glanced up at my return, and smiled at me, he was the loveliest thing I'd ever seen.

William Fox might not have been objectively the handsomest man I'd ever been with, but there was nothing objective about what I felt for him. His appeal was in the whole package. How his seriousness made his full lower lip look like it was getting away with something sensual. The moment when the calculation in his eyes gave way to acceptance. The way he trained his body as a weapon of enforcement, protection, and let me turn it to an instrument of pleasure.

The way his voice changed from barking, "This is Agent Fox," to curling around "Amory" when he realized it was me on the phone, caressing the word like licking a sweet. I called his work phone instead of his cell so I could listen to him change from Agent Fox into William, just for me.

Not that I'd ever admit it. I was almost certain he had no idea he did it, and would make every effort to stop if he did. But it made my heart beat fast every time.

I took a bite of Raisin Bran while I watched him, his beautiful eyes narrowing and the smooth golden skin of his forehead creasing at whatever he saw on his phone.

"Ugh," I said, mid-chew. "What on earth?"

"Hmm?"

"This…this…William, I cannot."

"What?"

"This…raisin bran is not even Raisin Bran! These raisins are…what on earth *is* this?!"

"What? It's probably just an imitation brand, Vaughn. Snobby much?"

I started to open my mouth on the running list of offenses against decency and taste that this trip had committed thus far, when Will checked his watch again and lifted his phone to his ear. He had eaten his muffin with seemingly little difficulty and I felt slightly petulant.

I plucked one of the desiccated thorns masquerading as raisins from my bowl and dropped it onto the table in demonstration and disgust.

"Hey!" Will's face lost its FBI seriousness as he grinned at whoever was on the phone. "Happy birthday!…I know, right?…Yeah, in Durham…Yes, I realize it's problematic terminology, believe me."

Will gave me a quick look and smiled as whoever was on the other end spoke. His eyes lingered on my mouth, then slid down my body to where my hand lay on the table next to the offending raisin. I could tell that he wished he could slide his hand over mine and squeeze. For a moment, I nearly did it for him, to spare him having to struggle with the choice. Will wasn't in the closet, in life or at work, but I knew he weighed the costs and benefits of his actions in ways that wore on him at times. As this was his milieu, I would follow his lead.

"Okay, cool, see ya then," he said, and ended the call. He got to his feet and shook out his suit jacket before sliding it back on. Not that it helped. "Ready?"

I stood and buttoned my own coat, snatching the bowl of cereal from the table at the last minute. Our aerobic sex the night before had left me hungry. In the parking lot, I picked out another raisin and threw it on the ground, eating a few of the flakes. Will shook his head at me.

"Who was on the phone?" I asked, giving in to the desire to slide a hand up his spine.

"Oh, Charlie."

"Charlie…as in, your sister Charlotte."

Will shot me a look like I was an idiot. "Yeah, as in my sister, Charlotte."

"Today is her birthday."

"Yup."

"Your twin sister, Charlotte."

I pulled Will around by the arm so he was facing me, and he squinted into the sun, then rolled his eyes.

"So then—and please correct me, unless I've been laboring under a misapprehension about twins—that would mean that today is also your birthday."

"Uh…" Will fidgeted. "Uh huh."

"God damn it, William, how could you not have said?"

"Oh. It's no big deal, really."

And the way he was looking at me, I could almost believe him. Had he ever celebrated just for himself, or had he always thought of it as primarily Charlotte's birthday? I had a vision of them as children and teenagers, planning every birthday together, Will letting Charlotte—nascent party planner—make the decisions for them both. I wondered how many people ever wished William a happy birthday and thought of it as only his.

Then again, some people simply didn't care about their birthdays.

I pulled him to me by the arm I still held, and bent to kiss his lips. "Happy birthday, William." I kissed him again, and smoothed his hair where it had dried a little mussed.

"Thanks," he murmured, looking down at the pavement.

"Well. I hope you will enjoy spending your birthday learning how to be a minimally decent human being and seeing that your coworkers are—no doubt—not nearly as up to the task. My condolences in advance."

"Yeah, these things are always…not the best." He glanced over his shoulder at the entrance to the La Quinta's conference room, then down at his watch. "But I should." He indicated the doorway.

"Of course. I'll see you back in the room when you're done?"

He squeezed my hand, then turned and strode purposefully across the parking lot, immediately in work mode. As I made my way back to the room, I shook my head. If only we'd been at home, I could have celebrated him in style! Better yet, had we gone away to somewhere of my choosing for the weekend, even if I hadn't known it was his birthday, I would've had wonderful things planned.

But I was almost immediately distracted from my annoyance at not having the upper hand in Will's celebrations. Because it was so dedicated, so loyal, so utterly *William* to agree to go on a work retreat over the weekend of his birthday and not even think to complain about it.

I allowed myself a brief moment of fantasizing that perhaps he'd been especially pleased when I'd jumped at the chance to come along, because at least he'd get to enjoy being with me for his birthday, even if it was spent in a horrible motel that served inedible breakfasts. Perhaps he'd thought of me, just for a moment, as a birthday gift.

And then I brushed my teeth to get rid of the taste of the worst continental breakfast on the continent, canceled my next phone meeting, shot the purple and green room a glare for good measure, and went to procure a cab. Because I had some planning to do if I was going to have things ready by the time the birthday boy got back.

✧　✧　✧

EVERYTHING WAS READY when William let himself into the room. The food was keeping warm in its insulated bag. The champagne was chilling in the cheap plastic La Quinta ice bucket. Bath products, candles, and soft towels awaited in the bathroom. And the bed was remade with new pillows and sheets that didn't feel as though they were cleaned via carwash and left to dry in a pile on the floor. Will's gift hung in the closet, still zipped in plastic in case he should open the door unexpectedly.

My first instinct had been to take him out for dinner, or to a club or a show, but I'd forced myself to think of what had gone so well about our first date. It had been my guiding principle since this whole business with William had begun, and I was trying hard to stick to it. It even had a simple acronym: WWWW. What Would William Want. Not what would I want, or Valerie, or any of the number of other dates whose birthdays I had celebrated. But William, and only William. And in the case of today, I imagined that after a long day of unpleasant work-related socializing, Will would likely want to relax. So I'd brought the relaxation to him.

As the door closed behind him, I was met with a decidedly not-relaxed sound. He yanked his tie off, nearly strangling himself in the process, dropped his suit jacket in a heap on the ground, and kicked off his shoes, before falling face-first onto the bed with another irritated groan and mumbling something unintelligible into the new Italian sheets.

I eased onto the bed next to him and rubbed a hand up and down his spine. His shirt was tacky with sweat and his muscles were tight.

"What's that, darling?"

My hand stilled on Will's back as he flipped over. "I hate Brett Lawson."

"The gentleman who needed reminding that sexual orientation was not an accurate predictor of personality traits?" On the drive to Durham, I'd heard all about Brett Lawson and his lack of enthusiasm at having to participate in a sensitivity training. And I'd heard a lot of things that

William *hadn't* exactly said, about how Lawson had treated him over the years. I gritted my teeth as he nodded, but couldn't help notice that Will sounded less vitriolic than...whiny. And it was just the slightest bit adorable to see him reduced to pouting into the bed. "And what transgression of sensitivity did he perpetrate this time?"

"Oh, uh, nothing...he's just a dick."

But this time when Will rolled onto his face, I was nearly certain it was so I couldn't see the truth in his eyes. William was a wretched liar.

"William." I kept my voice low in his ear as I stretched out beside him on the bed. He shivered. "Darling, tell me."

"'S stupid," he muttered. But he turned into me, throwing an arm over my waist and tucking his nose to my neck.

I could probably lull him to sleep like this, with my fingers in his hair and his lips against my skin. But it was late enough in the day that if he napped he wouldn't be able to sleep, and he'd be annoyed that I'd let him. "What happened?" I asked softly.

A sigh.

"I didn't exactly think about how having you here would be...uh, a topic of conversation."

Before I could wrangle the specifics from Will, he forcibly changed the subject.

"Hang on...are these...did you get housekeeping to change the sheets?" Will pulled the top sheet down and ran his hand between them. "Oh, god, Vaughn, did you ask them to put a different kind of sheets on the bed?"

I scoffed. "You can't possibly imagine that the La Quinta Inn, however convenient its proximity to the highway, keeps Pratesi sheets in its housekeeping carts."

Will's eyes narrowed. "I don't know what that means, but I think it implies that you went out and bought new sheets to put on a bed in a hotel that we're staying at for one more night."

"It's your birthday, William. I couldn't possibly let you spend your birthday between sheets that—ah, in anything less than whatever comfort I could provide. Are you hungry?" I asked before he could comment further.

"Yeah, I'm starved, actually. I got caught up talking to the trainer at lunch and lost track of time."

"Excellent. Would you like to take a quick shower while I set out the food?" Will always liked to shower the day off.

"Okay." He kissed me gently, then went into the bathroom. I wondered if he'd notice the new towels and robe I'd swapped for the wretched ones the hotel had issued.

I also wondered if he'd notice the other swap I'd made. I'd promised Will no more art theft, and of course I had every intention of keeping my promise—even if the oversized photographs of water droplets and bamboo stalks were such an offense to the eye that if I *had* stolen them it would only have been to the aesthetic advantage of the next poor souls to check into room thirty-three. But, no. Swapping wasn't stealing. All I had done was put the one in the place of the other. Sure, it had required unmounting what was never meant to be unmounted, but it was the work of only fifteen minutes or so. And now, though I was stuck in this horrid room with this horrid art, at least I had the satisfaction of knowing I'd left my mark.

And I had. On the backs of the pictures, I'd added my own signature: a discreet *W&V* to commemorate our stay. Like signing a guest ledger, really, had this been the sort of place that would have one. They looked good together, *W&V*. And as I'd rehung the paintings, I'd imagined our monogram on other things we might share. Hand towels, bathrobes, Christmas cards. Wedding invitations?

I tapped the cumbersome frame of the photograph of water droplets that was now above the desk, then I moved the desk out from the wall so I could put a chair on either side, set it, and laid out the food and champagne. Will came out of the bathroom in a gust of sweet-smelling steam just as I put the finishing touches on the table. He was wrapped in the thick robe, drops of water visible on his muscular chest where the fabric gaped, and his skin was flushed from the heat. He looked even more edible than the meal I'd procured.

"Great water pressure," he said.

"Yes, my chest thought so too. If only I could say the same for my hair." I kissed him, feeling the heat from his skin.

"What? Oh. Ha, you're too tall."

"I would prefer to say that the shower is too short."

"Wow, where did all this come from?"

"A restaurant called Luna. I got the recommendation from a friend of mine in D.C. It's South America meets the American South."

Will put his nose to a container of carnitas and inhaled blissfully.

"Here, sit."

I put my hands on his shoulders and pressed him into the seat, gesturing that he should serve himself first. I popped the champagne and poured it, handing a flute to him.

"Cheers, William. To, I hope, a very happy birthday, and

many more to follow. I can't tell you how pleased I am to be sharing it with you." *Even though you weren't going to tell me it was your birthday.* I touched my glass to his and sipped, the champagne wonderfully dry and bright, with just a hint of fruit on the swallow.

"Amory, I—" Will shook his head and sipped his own champagne. "I can't believe you did all this. Thank you."

"This is a far cry from what I could've done with some notice." I shot him a look. "But I'm glad you're pleased."

We ate and talked and it wasn't too terribly hard to imagine that we were in a beautiful hotel room, in a resort somewhere, or at one of my properties out of the city. The food was good, the champagne was good, and whatever was lacking in ambiance, the beauty of the man in front of me more than made up for it.

After, I sat Will on the bed and told him to close his eyes.

"You didn't have to get me anything," he said, and I kissed him until he shut up.

I got his gift from the closet, where I'd clipped its tags and removed its pins earlier, and stood in front of Will.

"Okay," I said, feeling suddenly self-conscious.

He opened his eyes, then they opened even wider when they saw what I held. The Zegna suit was a navy blue slim-cut, two-button in a wool-mohair blend. I knew the color would look gorgeous with his warm brown hair and eyes, and the narrow cut and side vents would show off his broad shoulders and lean hips to perfection.

"Because it's you, I *know* that's a nice suit," he said, smiling. "And where the hell did you get it on such short notice?"

"Thank goodness for Nordstrom," I said. In truth, I'd had to go to two different Nordstroms and follow their sales associates into the storeroom to find anything passable. It was just the best I could do in one day.

"Try it on?" I asked. "There's a shirt there too."

Will looked at me with an expression I couldn't quite read, then nodded, and took the clothes into the bathroom. I wasn't sure why, since I'd seen him naked from every possible angle—and a few I'd thought impossible before I met William. But I supposed seeing the whole package at once would be nice.

He was right: it *was* a nice suit. But it was *nothing* compared to what I wanted to give him. As I'd walked through the unimpressive shopping malls today, I had been regretful that I couldn't have a bespoke suit made for Will, the way I would've preferred. Not because I cared overmuch for how he dressed—hell, if I had, it would've been a problem the first time we met. And not because I thought his life would be better lived in a more breathable fabric and flattering cut.

But because of what it represented. That I could intercede between William and the very material of the world he came in contact with. The world that I couldn't control. That I could look at my lover and see evidence of my care upon his body. It was a possessive thought. Perhaps even a jealous one. But it had been all I could think of. The Zegna suit, nice as it was, was merely a stand-in for a better one. And that one, in turn, merely a stand-in for the frustrating reality that I couldn't keep Will in my arms every hour of every day.

"Did you get my measurements out of my other suit?" Will asked, stepping out of the bathroom slowly. The suit fit him beautifully. Not bespoke, but nearly perfect.

I scoffed and crossed to him, running a finger down the soft lapel.

"I didn't need measurements," I told him. "I know you by heart."

I'd expected him to laugh at that, or to mock me for flirting with him. For saying something cheesy. But he didn't. He stepped into my arms and cupped my cheek, kissed my mouth.

"Thank you," he said softly. "It's a beautiful suit. Nicest I've ever had. I—thank you."

"My pleasure," I murmured. And it was. It really was. "Can I talk you out of it as easily as I talked you into it?"

At that, he snorted. But he spread his arms wide and smiled at me. "I know you think you can talk your way out of anything. But you might have to actually use your hands for this one." I loved his clumsy attempts at banter.

"You don't say."

I undressed him slowly, hung the suit back up in the closet, and encouraged him down onto the bed. Then I crawled between his legs and kissed him deeply, canting his head back and running my fingers down his bare throat. We kissed until we were panting and Will was tugging at my clothes. Splayed naked beneath me on the soft Pratesi sheets while I was fully clothed, Will looked decadent and de-bauched. Hair mussed, mouth puffy, eyes heavy, he was a vision.

I stripped my own clothes off and reached for the cham-pagne bottle. I took a sip and then kissed Will so he could share it from my mouth. Then I slid back between his legs and kissed the insides of his thighs until he was moaning and trying to press his hips up to get my mouth where he needed it. I kissed his low belly, and the creases of his thighs, not touching his swollen erection.

"I want you, please," he said, tugging at my shoulder to try and pull me up.

"No, this is just for you."

I tilted his hips up and finally sank down, taking his erection into my mouth. He groaned and clutched the sheets as I worked him. I luxuriated in the taste of him, salty-sweet and clean, and the feel of that velvet skin stretched taut around his thick need. There was something so vulnerable about a man with his cock in my mouth. Having control over his pleasure with the single flick of my tongue or touch of my lips.

William went wild beneath me when I scraped my teeth lightly along his length. I pressed my fingers to his lips and he sucked on them as I was sucking him, getting them slick. I slid two fingers inside him, stroking his ass in time with the rise and fall of my mouth on his cock. When his broken whimpers and pants signaled that I'd brought him to the edge, I backed up, playing with his balls, stilling my fingers inside him until he made a sound of frustration and wriggled beneath me.

"Impatient, William?" I asked.

His response was inarticulate.

When he'd backed away from the edge, I started up again, sucking him to the hilt and spreading my fingers inside him until he was a shuddering mess, sweating and moaning. I backed off again and he let out a needy cry, a hand reaching out for me. I pressed a kiss to his palm and his palm to the bed, licking the insides of his thighs softly to feel them tremble.

When I put my mouth back on him, I slid a third finger inside and nailed his prostate directly. He clenched around me and cried out so I did it again and again until he was panting my name and leaking a steady stream of precome. Then I took him deep and moved on him, hollowing my cheeks on the downstroke and swirling my tongue around his sensitive head as I came up. I kept up pressure on his prostate and after a minute or so, he was crying out over and over, straining his hips to meet my mouth, clenching around my fingers, and, finally, exploding into my mouth as he groaned his release.

"Oh, fuck," he whimpered. I gently cleaned him with my tongue as he came down, tiny shivers of pleasure still running through him. "Oh, god."

"Mmm." I slid a hand up his thigh, over his hip, up his belly, and rested it on his chest where I could feel his heart still pounding. "Happy birthday, love," I said softly, and pressed one last kiss to his belly. He whimpered in response.

"Here, let me," he said, reaching for me. My erection was a hot brand against my belly, almost painfully hard from watching him fall apart. I went to push him away, but he got a hand around me and jerked before I could. I groaned and lost it in two more strokes, shooting all over his stomach and chest, my own thighs now trembling with release, my ass clenching as I shuddered through my own aftershocks.

I leaned down and kissed him, brushing his hair back.

"We made a mess," I murmured.

"Mmm. You made a mess," he said, and I smiled into his neck.

"Yes, true. But I made it on you, so now we are both

rather in need of a shower."

Will made an unimpressed sound and I moved off him and started the shower, so it would be warm by the time I got him into it.

I kissed his neck and up his jaw, then kissed his mouth.

"Come," I said, and pulled him up. He was boneless in my arms, languid, and I got him under the hot spray before he even opened his eyes. He sagged against me and it was a rare moment of vulnerability outside of bed. He wrapped his arms around my neck and let me hold him under the water.

"Can't believe you did all this for me," he said sleepily into my neck.

"Of course I did." I didn't tell him that it had been nothing, because I knew that to him it hadn't. "Maybe next year, with a little more notice, we can go on a trip that doesn't include sensitivity training for your birthday."

He laughed softly. "Kay."

And that was all. A low, sleepy indication that Will *didn't* think it was ridiculous to imagine that we would still be together a year from now. It warmed me to the gut. I lifted his face to mine to kiss him, imagining he could taste my smile even with his eyes closed.

"I love you, William," I murmured against his mouth.

His blinked his eyes open, brows drawing together. "You do?"

It was such a very William response.

"I do."

I worked shampoo into his hair, then tilted his chin up so I could rinse it out without getting shampoo in his eyes. He blinked dazedly at me, arms still around my neck, water sluicing down his neck and chest. I could see the gears turning as he considered his options, and I had the urge to tell him more. To make the case for *why* I loved him so I was positive he believed me. But this was William, so I stayed quiet, and I spoke with my body.

I conditioned his hair, though I knew he never used conditioner. I washed him, sliding the cloth over every inch of his beautiful body and kissing my way back up. I worshipped him.

When I got back to his mouth, he looked confused. Overwhelmed.

"You must be so tired," I said. "It's been a long day."

Will nodded, and let me lead him out of the shower, dry him off.

"Do you want to watch a movie? Or some mindless show?" I held the covers aside so he could slide into bed, but he stopped in front of me, scowling in concentration.

I touched a finger to the lines in his forehead and he refocused on my face.

"I love you too," he said, like he was proposing the answer to a puzzle he'd just worked out.

The moment the words were out of his mouth, his brow smoothed out and the shadow in his expression passed.

"You do, huh?" I slid an arm around him as he nodded, and we climbed under the covers.

"Yeah, I... Yes."

The sheets were soft, the mattress was lumpy, and I had never been happier to be exactly where I was. I kissed Will softly. A kiss about love and appreciation. We sank down to the pillows together, his head on my shoulder. Then he let out a small laugh, like a kid at a sleepover, and buried his face in my neck.

"What?"

"Nothing." He kissed my neck. "Oh, can we watch *Forensics Files*?"

"I hate that show," I muttered. "But yes."

Will grinned at me wryly. "I'm pushing the whole birthday thing with that one, huh?"

"No," I said. "There's not a thing you could ask me for right now that I wouldn't willingly give you." And I meant it. "Not because it's your birthday though."

"I love you," he murmured, softly, like he was trying it on for size after the initial purchase.

"I love you, William."

CHAPTER 17

Will

THE REST OF the seminar took up all of Sunday, and I was more than ready for it to be over. I would much rather have been back in the room with Vaughn, rolling around on our six-million thread count sheets and drinking champagne. The thought made me smile down at my notes and smooth the front of my new suit. At least I knew I looked like a million bucks in it, even if I was doing so in a sea of green and purple that was starting to turn my stomach. Every time I thought about how it was a gift from Vaughn…and that he loved me, it went a long way in making the end of this seminar bearable.

But even thinking about those three words that Vaughn had murmured again as he fell asleep with his arms around me didn't have the power to make Lawson disappear.

"So, did you bring your boyfriend as some kind of example?"

Jesus Christ. Though we had one every other year, Lawson had decided that my being gay was the reason we were having *this* diversity training, and he clearly had no problem punishing me with passive-aggressive commentary for his trouble. I just wished he'd go away, and spent a moment fantasizing about him being transferred somewhere else. Somewhere very cold and without viable public transportation. Or any of the sports teams he was so invested in.

"I'm not sure why you're asking me this," I said to Lawson, doctoring my terrible coffee at the refreshment station. The problem with my amazing birthday dinner was coming back down to earth and eating normal-person food.

"Just curious, is all." Lawson's eyes glittered at me and his smile was snide. "If the taxpayers were paying for it, or what."

Was he kidding? The idea of Vaughn depending on the taxpayers subsidizing his bill for the La Quinta Inn made me snort. "Or what," I answered flatly. "Excuse me." I was trying to move past him, but he stopped me.

"Look, I don't have a problem with what you do on your own time, Fox. But when you go and do this, shove it in my face?" He was still talking quietly, and I was starting to get pissed off.

It's what he wants, I told myself. "I didn't realize my boyfriend staying in the same hotel as you counted as shoving it your face, Lawson. Believe me. I don't want to shove anything of mine anywhere near you."

Maybe I shouldn't have added that last part. But I was pissed, and Lawson's continual attempts to rib me about my sexuality *at a diversity seminar* were getting old. I sipped my coffee, found a seat, and vowed to ignore him.

Of course, he was perfectly appropriate during the actual training. That was the problem with people like Lawson. It wasn't like he wasn't aware that it was frowned upon to be a homophobic dick. So he just toed the lines, aced the tests, took his certification hours, and never applied a single thing to his actual life. Lawson would not become a less homo-phobic, less racist, or less misogynistic person because of this stupid waste of time seminar, no matter how sound the intentions behind it. I wished I'd gone on vacation with Vaughn instead.

The futility of sitting here, knowing that for so many of my coworkers it wouldn't change anything, was making me crankier than usual. Or maybe it was because it was Sunday and my boyfriend had told me he loved me and I had to sit here breathing the same air as Fuckhead Lawson. I resisted the urge to send Vaughn dirty text messages and calmed myself until we were finished with the seminar by daydream-ing about him fucking me in those sheets.

The last thing we had to do was a team-building dinner, and then I was free. At least I had Monday off for travel.

"All done being diverse for the day?" Vaughn asked when I returned to our room.

"I know we technically have this room until the morn-ing, but we can just leave after dinner?" I sat heavily on the bed.

"That good, was it?" Vaughn was reclining on the bed, reading a book. I wondered what he'd done all day. I didn't think I'd ever seen him watch television. And while he liked movies, I didn't think I'd ever heard him reference watching a particular show. The TV was off, and his phone was on the bedside table, and I guess he really did love me to put up with this voluntarily.

I leaned over and kissed him. "If you want to skip out on dinner, I won't blame you."

"But you won't, will you?" he said against my mouth, hand settling at my neck.

"Blame you? I already said I wouldn't. Oh, skip out?" I smiled and nipped at his bottom lip, sucking it lightly into my mouth. "You know I won't. Besides, Lawson was being an ass and I don't want him to think I'm afraid of him."

"My William," Vaughn murmured, resting his forehead on mine. "Of course I'm going with you. Unless you'd prefer I didn't."

"I'd prefer neither of us going, but." I shrugged, some of my tension easing. I was still a bit giddy remembering last night. The knowledge that I loved him, and that he loved me, filled me with a happiness as bubbly as the champagne we'd shared last night. "Some of the other people brought their significant others. No one else is queer but me though."

"No one else is anything like you," Vaughn said, and I felt my face heat. He was charming, and for a long time, when he said things like that I'd thought he was being glib. Now I knew he wasn't.

"Well, you either." I pulled back and grinned at him. "My coworker Lawson thinks the taxpayers are footing the bill for your half of this splendor." I gestured around us.

"Then they're all fired," Vaughn said, looking around the room.

I laughed. He was such a snob, but I'd slept pretty well on those sheets. It might have been the sex and the champagne though.

"Where are we going to dinner, dare I ask?"

"Ryan's Steakhouse," I answered.

"Is the steak decent?"

I laughed, then realized my joke had gone right over his head because—well, because when would Vaughn ever have been to a Ryan's Steakhouse? "I was joking. Look it up on your phone," I teased. "I'm gonna change."

"You didn't tell me where we're going," Vaughn said, picking up his phone.

"Conference Room B," I answered. "It's catered. Sorry, I thought I told you that yesterday."

"Ah, Conference Room B. Right." He waved a hand at me. "Get out of that suit before I take you out of it."

"You like this one," I reminded him. "I thought you only wanted to get me out of the bad ones."

"I want to get you out of your clothes ninety-nine percent of the time I'm around you," Vaughn informed me, not looking up from his phone.

"And the other one percent of the time?"

The look he gave me and my new suit was covetous, filthy, destructive. Then he winked.

I was finishing up in the bathroom when I heard him say, "A buffet steakhouse? William. You're an FBI agent. That should be illegal and you know it."

I smiled at my reflection in the mirror. "They have good yeast rolls."

"I don't know you," Vaughn said huffily, and I laughed.

WE MADE OUR way down to the conference room. It was nearly identical to the one that had housed the seminar, only with linen-covered round tables instead of the long, rectangular ones we'd been forced to sit at for the last two days.

"My sister would be horrified at the pleating on these table linens," I murmured to Vaughn as we found our table.

"As well she should be," Vaughn murmured, and pulled

my chair out for me in a ridiculous, gallant gesture that should probably have made me mad. It didn't, especially as I realized we were sitting at the table with—who else?—Brett Lawson. There were almost a hundred and fifty agents here, from both HQ and field offices close to the area, and I had to get stuck with Lawson. Of course.

Also at the table were a guy whose name I didn't catch from Organized Crime, my colleague from Art Crimes, Cindy Maloney, and her husband, Trevor Sandy from White Collar Crimes, and his wife, Amy. I might not have been the only one who'd brought a significant other, but I'd bet mine was the only one who'd brought his own sheets.

I introduced Vaughn to the table. When I got to Cindy, Vaughn shook her hand and said, "I believe William's mentioned you."

I hadn't, ever. I was sure of it. But she smiled at Vaughn and then at me, clearly pleased.

"This is Brett Lawson," I said. "Lawson, this is my boyfriend, Amory Vaughn." I couldn't help the thrill of pleasure I felt at using the word "boyfriend" to his face.

Vaughn shook his hand with a polite smile and a "Lovely to meet you," as if I hadn't spent the last two days bitching about what an asshole he was.

Of course Vaughn would never be so crass as to express how much he loathed someone directly to their face. But I was sure the handshake he gave Lawson was a shade too firm, and his gaze was direct, his smile and eyes equally chilly. Vaughn was taller than everyone at the table, including Lawson. To macho types like Lawson, I was sure that mattered.

I knew there were plenty of people Vaughn didn't like,

but I'd never watched him systematically cut someone to ribbons with the sheer force of his disregard. By the time the catering staff was filling our water and iced tea glasses, Vaughn had charmed the entire table, and my fellow agents and their significant others were putty in his hands.

Except for Lawson. Vaughn managed to *just* keep him out of conversation, managed to give a *slightly* dimmer smile, an obviously polite laugh, any time Lawson thought to contribute. I was watching Vaughn destroy a man through microaggressions, and I was so turned on I was hard under the table and wanted to get on my knees and blow Vaughn right then and there.

Lawson was an irritating human being but he wasn't oblivious. There were tells we were all taught to look for, but while I believed Vaughn to be capable of completely fooling Lawson, I didn't think he wanted to. He wanted Lawson to know exactly what he was doing.

"...from, Mr. Vaughn?"

I blinked, realizing Cindy was speaking, and turned my attention back to the table. Cindy was smiling at Vaughn in a way that made me think she might have had a little crush on him. She wouldn't be the only one.

"Just Vaughn, please," he corrected with a smile. "Falls Church, Virginia."

"Huh," said Lawson, who'd had a few drinks by now and was staring at Vaughn with enough ill-concealed dislike that I hid a grin in my glass of iced tea. "That accent, I would have thought Alabama."

"Would you?" Vaughn asked. "It's common to be unfamiliar with the intricacies of Southern accents. From your accent, I'm guessing you're a midwesterner? Missouri, maybe?"

I snorted before I could stop myself. Lawson was from L.A., and he definitely wanted everyone to know it. He didn't sound at all like he was from Missouri.

"Hell, no," Lawson answered. "The armpit of America? I'm from L.A."

"Ah," said Vaughn. That was it, nothing else, and yet there was a wealth of feeling layered in the simple syllable.

"I'm from St. Louis," Trevor's wife, Amy, said. She gave Lawson a bit of a frosty smile. "It's a very nice city."

"Flyover country." Lawson laughed, but no one else did.

I reached down and surreptitiously rubbed my hand over Vaughn's knee as he referenced Tony's, an Italian restaurant on the Hill in St. Louis with which Amy was familiar. It once again cut Lawson out of the conversation and I noticed him shooting a glare at Vaughn, which I knew Vaughn couldn't care less about. He was probably enjoying every minute.

I slid my hand up a little higher in his lap. Oh, yeah. Definitely enjoying himself.

He turned his head slightly, winked at me, and went back to his conversation.

Dinner was delivered a few minutes later, and I noticed that Vaughn and I were not served the chicken I'd signed us up for. Instead, the server came over with two plates and presented them to us with a flourish. The man glanced at Vaughn, who gave a polite nod and discreetly tipped him. I had a moment to wonder why Vaughn had gone behind my back to choose the vegetarian meal, and then the smell hit me. Vaughn had ordered food in from Luna, the restaurant we'd eaten from last night. He must have had it delivered to the kitchen and served on the same plates as everyone else. For a moment I was shocked by his audacity, not to mention his effort—the restaurant must have been who he'd texted in the room. But shock quickly gave way to head-shaking because, of course he had. Of course.

Suddenly, even with Lawson glaring daggers at me across the table, dinner was looking up, just a bit. Vaughn being a snob definitely had its benefits. Every bite I took would remind me that we were a team.

"What on earth did you get?" Amy asked, leaning over. "It smells way better than this chicken."

"They were kind enough to accommodate my dietary restrictions," said Vaughn. "I'm abstaining from meat at the moment."

I raised my eyebrows, since "dietary restrictions" meant "desire not to eat the tasteless slop you caterers call dinner."

"Doesn't seem like a compliment to poor Fox," Lawson said. It was a cringeworthy attempt at a joke, like most of Lawson's barbs.

Vaughn gave Lawson a sharp, cold stare and said nothing. Lawson had the grace to flush, and I forked up some of my...whatever it was.

"It's barbeque jackfruit," Vaughn murmured as I took a bite.

"It's delicious." I recognized the side of hominy mac-n-cheese. "This is from the same place as last night, right?" I kept my voice low.

"You liked it," Vaughn said simply. "And I have wasted too many taste buds on bland banquet roast beef."

"I signed you up for the chicken," I told him, closing my eyes in bliss at the jackfruit. It was the consistency of pulled pork, with an earthy bite, and the tangy barbeque sauce was heaven. The hominy was salty, cheesy perfection, and the kale with smoked salt and slivered almonds a thousand times better than the boring green beans and new potatoes everyone else was eating.

"It would have been indistinguishable from the roast beef," Vaughn said. "Trust me." And I'd been to enough FBI events to know he was right.

I made it a point never to drink too much at these things because I didn't want to let my guard down, and it always surprised me that a bunch of FBI agents—who should be paranoid, given the crimes we investigated on a daily basis—would feel comfortable getting soused around each other. Or maybe they figured since we were the good guys, it was all right.

They weren't sitting with a drunk Lawson though.

"Have you two been together long?" my colleague Cindy asked, as we had post-dinner coffees and Lawson had yet another beer. I was vaguely offended that he was getting bombed off domestic beer, but hey, I wasn't dating him. Vaughn and I each had each stuck to a glass of what Vaughn muttered was "dregs of bottles mixed and called table wine."

"A few months," I answered.

"You were dating someone else when we were at the Academy, weren't you?" Lawson interjected.

He must have been drunk if he wanted to talk about my love life. "Yeah," I said.

"Didn't work out?" Lawson prodded.

"We broke up ten years ago, Lawson," I answered, sipping my coffee.

"He wasn't into dating an FBI guy?" Lawson continued,

sounding snide.

Actually, no. But I wasn't going to get into that with Lawson, for fuck's sake. "He was a great guy, but things ran their course," I said, shrugging it off. Let Lawson make an ass of himself.

"I heard somewhere gay guys date a lot," Lawson said, emphasizing the word *date* in a manner that suggested he meant something else entirely. "That true?"

The rest of the table looked just as uncomfortable as I felt with this line of talk, and I thought for a moment about how to deal with it. He was clearly going for attention, either by getting a rise out of me or having me ignore him and look like I was bothered by the conversation.

"Are you the victim of a recent breakup, perhaps?" Vaughn asked without missing a beat. "I notice most men who are overly concerned with other people's romantic situations and drunk off cheap beer at dinner are usually nursing a broken heart. Or simply being rude."

That made everyone quiet, but I could see Amy smile as she ducked her head. Trevor met my eyes and glanced upward. It was gratifying to know I wasn't the only one who didn't like the guy.

"Hey, man," Lawson said with a fake laugh. "No need to be a dick. Even if you're into that."

"I'm mostly into manners," Vaughn said smoothly. "You might find them a bit of an acquired taste, but I'd suggest looking into them instead of another glass of beer."

Lawson muttered something and pushed away from the table without a word, stomping off to the bar.

"Ugh," Trevor said. He gave me an apologetic smile. "Sorry about that."

"You don't need to apologize for him," I said. "He hasn't liked me since the day we started at the Academy. I'm used to it."

Vaughn gave me a sharp look, but didn't say anything.

"Still. We're at a diversity seminar," Cindy huffed. "What the hell is his problem?"

"I'm gay." I shrugged. "I guess it offends him that I get a gun? I have no idea. I've never asked. Whatever it is, it's *his* problem."

We didn't stay long after that, and Lawson didn't come back to the table. I excused myself to go to the bathroom and on the way back to the table, saw that Vaughn wasn't there. I scanned the room and found him on the other side, talking to Deputy Director Rice and laughing his fundraiser-laugh. I wondered how he knew Elizabeth—but then, he knew everyone.

Cindy leaned in to me, her eyes wide. "You didn't mention he was one of *those* Vaughns."

My guard was immediately up on Vaughn's behalf and I resisted the urge to ask Cindy if she'd thought to tell me what her husband did. As Vaughn finished talking to the deputy director and made his way back over to me I realized how exhausted I was.

"Are you ready?" he asked politely, hand on my lower back. I felt his touch all the way to my bones, and I wanted to be out of that room, naked, and on my back in as little time as possible.

"Yeah," I said, leaning against him for a moment. "More than."

I couldn't wait to get back between those ridiculously expensive sheets.

The expensive sheets that, after Vaughn's not-so-subtle comment that they were much nicer than the ones I had at home, I later stripped off the bed, folded neatly, and put in my suitcase.

CHAPTER 18

Will

THE FIRST I noticed of Brett Lawson's absence was my suspiciously peaceful morning getting coffee in the café at work. I was used to him being there and smirking at me.

I was ostensibly researching an urn that'd been stolen from a Venetian glass exhibit in Chicago and asking myself why, of all the exhibits to rob, a thief would pick one where everything was made of glass. My instinct told me it was fraud, but since it was four thirty on a Friday, I was thinking more about the weekend than my case. Hey, even FBI agents needed some time off to visit their boyfriends' historical ancestral homes and drink bourbon on their decks under heat lamps. I headed to the break room for a late-afternoon cup of coffee. I had a feeling I'd be up late.

Jodie Sayers was also fixing herself a cup, and she smiled at me. "So much more pleasant in here without Lawson, isn't it?" Lawson had been hitting on her since we were all in training together and she disliked him as much as I did.

"Yeah," I said. "Is he on assignment or something?" I hadn't noticed him all week, now that I thought about it.

"You didn't hear?" Jodie was in the Cyber Division, which I always thought sounded sexy and exciting. Jodie said it was the reason she needed bifocals at thirty-six. She had been gung ho to do Organized Crime when she showed up, but when the higher-ups found out she was some kind of computer super genius, her fate was sealed. She seemed happy though.

"Didn't hear about what?" I felt a vague flash of worry that he'd been killed in the line of duty. I didn't like him, but I didn't want to be happy he was gone if he was...*gone*.

"He got transferred to Illinois. The field office in Spring-field."

I blinked. "Stop teasing."

"I swear!" Jodie put her hands up. "He really did. I'm friends with a couple of people in his department. He and his swagger are headed to the Land of Lincoln." She laughed and I couldn't help my answering grin. "You look so delighted. I don't think I've ever even see you smile that big, Fox."

I gave her a slight salute, but I *was* smiling and I couldn't help it. "I'm not going to pretend I'm broken up about it."

"He was an ass to you from training on," she said. "I'm surprised you never reported him."

I shrugged. "Didn't want him to know he was getting to me."

She rolled her eyes. "Macho bullshit. I should be used to it by now, and yet."

I held my hands up. "Hey, it wasn't that bad. Just him saying stupid shit. If I reported everyone who did that, we'd be working with a skeleton crew."

"Half my department would be gone," Jodie agreed, but winked.

"I wish him well, far away from us," I said, raising my

coffee mug.

Jodie snorted. "You do not. Neither do I. And I send my condolences to the entire state of Illinois, in advance of his arrival."

Lawson was the kind of guy who thought working in HQ made him a tough guy, big-shot agent. I'd once heard him talking about making deputy director before he was forty-six, so it was *possible* his career aspirations had taken him to Springfield, but I doubted it. Especially given the opinions about "flyover country" he expressed at dinner in Durham. Nope, it looked like Lawson had finally pissed off the wrong higher-ups in the Bureau and paid the price. It was only a matter of time, really, given his toxic combination of ego and mediocrity. I smiled at the thought that finally justice had been done.

"What are you up to this weekend?" Jodie asked. "I always mean to see if you want to grab a drink with me and Hank. I think you guys would get along."

"Going to visit my boyfriend," I said.

"Aw, how long have you guys been together? Where does he live? How did you meet? Wait—did you meet him online?" Her questions had come rapid-fire, but at that, she frowned, looking concerned. "Wait, seriously, did you? Because I can tell you some stories, Fox."

"I didn't know Cyber Division got involved in online dating gone wrong. I thought you guys were more about espionage and online terrorism."

"Yeah, uh, I meant, like, personal stories. Never mind." She flushed but recovered quickly. "Anyway, did you?"

I laughed. "Nah. We met at a party. One of my sister's things. He splits his time between here and Falls Church, so

I'm going out there for the weekend."

"Yeah?" Her eyebrows went up. "Nice. I think I heard about him—tall blond guy?"

Of course she'd heard about Vaughn. The tendency toward office gossip combined with the tools of career investigators? Good luck having a secret around here "That's him."

"Good for you," she said, with a smile. "And thanks for the coffee break. I think it's probably time for us to head out. Have a good weekend. Drink a toast to Lawson—our loss and Illinois'…well, loss."

CHAPTER 19

Vaughn

WE WERE SNORKELING, William and I. In my dream, the sun-shot blue water was so clean that I could see straight to the bottom, where improbably bright fish swam peacefully and the sand glinted gold. Will was as lithe and smooth as a dolphin, and he put his face right up to mine, so close our goggles clicked. He kissed me, and I felt it, even through our snorkels. Then he pulled away and tried to tell me something. He was yelling it, gesticulating wildly, flippers churning the water white, but I couldn't hear him.

"Get to a safe place, and call the cops!" Will yelled as I slammed awake.

"What?" The sun was freshly risen, and I could smell sex and warm bedding and Will's hair.

Will was on top of me, which was nice. But he was yelling again, which was not.

"I'm going for my gun. Vaughn, you have to get up and call 9-1-1."

"What's wrong?" I said, coming up on my elbow, instantly alert. William's eyes were wide as he stared up toward the window he couldn't see while lying on top of me.

That's when I heard it—*pop, pop, pop.*

Gunshots. Followed by yelling.

I flopped back onto the bed with a chuckle. "It's fine," I said, and tried to pull William down on top of me in a position that was more early-morning-cuddle and less shielding-me-from-an-attack.

"You don't understand." He pulled at my shoulders, trying to get me to—what? Roll onto the floor and under the bed? No, not happening.

I pushed his hands away and groaned when he shook me.

"There's an active shooter on the lawn. Possibly more than one."

"Uh huh, I know. It's the British army."

"What. The. Hell. Are you talking about?"

"Don't worry, darling, they lose this one. C'mere." I wrapped my arms around him, already well on my way back to our underwater paradise.

William levered himself off me and peeked out the window, keeping his head low as if he might be shot at any moment. "Amory."

"Mmm?" I slid my palm up his back. His tensed muscles relaxed, though his voice was still tight.

"Why are there people dressed up in costumes and shooting each other on your lawn?"

"This is the Battle of Spencer's Ordinary. Fascinating battle. Are you familiar? Lieutenant Colonel John Graves Simcoe was on the road for Williamsburg, when—"

"Amory!" I heard the residual irritation in his voice. "I don't need to hear about that battle right now."

I sighed, and opened my eyes. Clearly William was not going to be mollified by anything less than an actual explanation, even though it was too early for anything but sleeping, cuddling, or being half woken briefly for a dreamy blowjob. None of which were the direction this line of questioning seemed to be going. I pulled myself up on my knees next to him and looked out the window, where we watched as fifty or so reenactors ran out of the woods in period garb, yelling. Will flinched when a volley of shots rang out.

He turned on me, eyes narrowed, nostrils flared, mouth grim. Not amused, then.

"They film things here sometimes," I said, and put a hand on his shoulder. "These are scenes for a historical reenactment. For a PBS show."

He turned back toward the window and peered out. A horse trotted out from the tree line and Will shook his head. "Your life is ridiculous."

"Barry will be thrilled to hear how accurate it was, I'm sure." I tried to compose my face but William was too adorable, too grumpy.

"This isn't funny."

"You'll think it's funny after breakfast," I told him.

"We are going to have a long talk about home security," Will hissed. But he let me coax him back into bed, muttering until I drifted off to sleep.

AFTER THE RATHER explosive start to the day, William soothed himself by lecturing me on emergency evacuation routes and musket safety protocol and I soothed myself by shutting him up with my tongue in his ass.

Clearly, he still needed to burn off some energy, so I lured him out for a walk with the promise that he could pick up any spent shells the reenactors had left behind, which could possibly pose a danger to the neighborhood children. Who would never dare set foot on my property without invitation.

It was a gorgeous November day, cold and sunny, with a snap in the air that made the promise of a post-perambulation hot toddy in front of a fire—and hopefully wrapped in a shared blanket, beneath which I could grope my grumpy boyfriend—feel like heaven. After pocketing two cartridges and a granola bar wrapper with obligatory muttering, even William wasn't immune to the bright sun, chilly air, and earth-scented breeze that ruffled our hair.

I followed Will through the trees and allowed my thoughts to settle into the fantasy that I'd been spinning more and more often recently. In it, the Falls Church house was *our* home and we walked these paths nightly, arm in arm, swapping tidbits about our days and making plans for the future. The walks terminated in dinner, and then in the kind of sex that you can have if you know you are both staying. The kind of sex that says, *You don't need to leave in the morning so it's okay if you can hardly walk*, and *There will always be more time.*

Of course, that fantasy didn't take into account the fact that William wouldn't want to live here during the week any more than I did, given that work was in D.C. The commute was hairy enough even without winter weather and traffic. But someday, perhaps. After all, it was just a fantasy. In the meantime, there was always the chance that the D.C. apartment could be our home base. That wasn't unrealistic. William's apartment was horrible—cramped, and dark, with furniture more befitting a college student than the beautiful, strong man I knew. But William didn't care about things like that, not really.

For someone who appreciated art as much as he did, he didn't consider his own environment an aesthetic opportunity. Maybe he'd been trained not to, through years of scrimping and brutal practicality. But I thought it was more likely that he simply never thought he was worth it. Never found his desire for beauty weighted more heavily than the impulse that the aesthetic was unnecessary.

I wanted to live with William because I found myself rather helplessly in love with him, of course. But I also wanted to live with him so that I could give him an excuse to have all the comforts and delights that he'd never let himself acknowledge he desired. He'd grumble and mock me for how much my armchair must have cost. But then he'd sit in it while he read the paper and sipped his morning coffee, and he'd be comfortable. All day, he'd carry the comfort of those few minutes with him.

I wanted to make comfort and beauty and joy the baseline of William's life, not the exceptions to it. I wanted my life and William's life to be *our* life. But he wasn't ready. He felt things were unbalanced between us, and not just in terms of money. He was so used to being the capable one, the unflappable one, the dependable one, that he didn't yet know how to share burdens without feeling that he was obviating responsibility.

But the moments when he did...the moments when he allowed himself to loose his hold on the person he thought he had to be, and give himself over to what he *wanted*, what he needed...they leveled me. In those moments, his desire was pure and needy and he was desperate to fall apart, secure that he wouldn't be punished for it.

And I had made it my mission in life to create a whole world where he could feel that way.

To our left, just off the path, came the rustle of underbrush and a tiny mewl of urgency. Will dropped into a crouch and peered intently.

"Oh, aw." He rocked back on his heels and looked up at me. "Kitten," he said, as if making an identification at work. "Seen any female cats around the property lately?"

I smiled. William was the only person who could say "female cats" and actually mean female cats.

"I'm afraid I haven't noticed any cats. Nor would I be likely to check their sex if I did."

I crouched next to him as he made a kissing sound, and quelled any disappointment that it wasn't directed at me.

From the underbrush slunk a kitten. I had always operated under the assumption that "kitten" described an unerringly cute category of creatures, if one were into that sort of thing. This kitten forced me to revise that assumption. It was painfully skinny, with a torn ear crusted in dried blood, wild orange eyes, and matted brown-black fur. As it moved toward Will, the knobs of its hips stuck up through the fur, and its mouth hung open. Then it mewled again, and my heart gave an involuntary twinge for the pathetic thing.

"C'mere," William said, his voice low and soothing. Clearly the kitten found him as irresistible as I did, because after a minute's wariness, it bumped its head against his outstretched hand and allowed itself to be pet. I made a mental note to disinfect every part of William that had touched it when we got home.

Will looked up at me, one hand scratching under the kitten's chin, the other cupping its skinny ribs, and the twinge in my heart became a flutter.

"It got in a fight, or got attacked," he said, fingers curling protectively around it. "But mostly it's just hungry." He trailed off, eyes on mine.

"Okay," I said, resigned. "Bring it along. I'm sure there's some tuna in the pantry."

William's smile turned the flutter to a palpitation.

He scooped the kitten up and cradled it. It fit in his open palm and he held it gently, until it started to squirm. Then he pinched its nape and it went docile in his hand.

Back inside, I rummaged around the pantry until I found a can of tuna, and tipped it into a shallow soup bowl so the kitten wouldn't cut its tongue on the rough edge of the can.

"Did you just serve a stray cat tuna on fine china?" William asked, gaping at me as I set the bowl on the floor.

I shook my head at the notion that he could consider this old set of Wedgwood "fine china."

He set the kitten down next to the bowl and it immediately shoved its tiny face into the food.

"It's like a damn Fancy Feast commercial," he muttered, and I snorted. The matted, starving kitten with its face covered in tuna was far from the delicate-nosed white fluffballs those commercials featured, china plate or no.

After the kitten finished its food, it practically sagged in exhausted relief, and William was able to scoop it up and give it a bath in the kitchen sink, massaging suds into its matted fur, and gently cleaning its torn ear. He wrapped it up in a dish towel and it closed its eyes immediately. At Will's raised eyebrow, I sighed long-sufferingly and waved him into the living room.

"Just until it wakes up. Then it can go back outside. Cats are a menace," I said sternly, picturing its needle claws snagging my upholstery and its fur all over my cashmere.

William nodded stoically.

An hour later, he obligingly set the kitten down outside the kitchen door, where it shivered in the cold, then straightened its spine. He didn't even pout about it.

"Bye," he told it, and "Be careful." Then he flushed as if he hoped I hadn't heard.

Two hours after that, we were ensconced in amicably rooting for opponents in the finale of a cooking competition, William trotting out culinary trash talk that proved he did listen to Charlotte when she told him about her catering decisions. When I muted the show at the commercial break, there was a scratch at the kitchen door.

William was immediately at attention, but with a glance at me, he said, "I'm sure it's fine." But he kept one ear on the kitchen door for the remainder of the program. When we went into the kitchen to heat up leftovers for dinner, a meow came from just outside the door. Instead of the pathetic, plaintive mewl of earlier, this sounded questioning. Will bit his lip and concentrated *very* hard on the chicken warming in the oven.

When the meow came again, along with a scratch at the door, William clenched his jaw and didn't look at me. The meow grew in volume and then turned plaintive. Will's mouth turned down at the corners. I slid my arms around his waist from behind and kissed his ear. He turned in my arms and kissed me, but I could feel his concern, his distraction.

The meow came again, and it sounded sad. Lonely. William tensed.

I brushed his hair back and looked into his eyes. "Fine," I said. "Let it in."

His face immediately brightened.

"Really?"

"Just in the kitchen."

He kissed me sweetly, grinning, and I wondered when I had turned into a complete pushover when I had never been in danger of it before.

When he opened the door, the kitten bounded in, sliding across the tile in its excitement and butting its head up against William's ankle. When it made contact, it started purring so loudly I couldn't help but smile. Its fur looked softer and its torn ear wasn't so grisly without the crust of dried blood. Even the one meal had seemed to fill it out a little—or perhaps that was just the fluff of its fur.

It was clear that further dinner preparation would be mine, as Will and the kitten had eyes only for each other.

When the food was ready, I moved to carry our plates to the small table in the living room that looked out over the back garden and Will's face fell. He recovered quickly, but once I'd seen it, I put the plates on the kitchen table instead, and pulled out a chair for Will. As we talked, the kitten inched closer and closer to his leg. Then suddenly it pounced onto his lap and then onto the table, sniffing at the chicken.

"Um."

Wide eyes met mine. William's. The cat didn't even know I was in the room.

And that's how it went for the rest of the weekend. The kitten scratched at the kitchen door when it got hungry, and we spent hours in the kitchen. By the time I kissed William goodbye on Sunday evening, the creature seemed to have doubled in size. Which seemed especially unfair, since my sex life seemed to have been inversely affected.

I went up to read in bed soon after, and had forgotten about the kitten by the time I wandered blearily into the kitchen the next morning, ready to make coffee and head into D.C. myself. But as I flipped the percolator on, a small meow came from outside. I ignored it, gathering my things for the week while the coffee brewed. I didn't need much— for convenience's sake, I had most everything I needed in the D.C. apartment as well. But there was always errant paperwork that I shuttled back and forth.

But when I went back into the kitchen to collect my travel mug, the meow came again.

I opened the kitchen door and the kitten pranced in as if it had lived here its whole life. It sniffed around for a moment before it realized William wasn't there, and then it drooped slightly.

I knew exactly how it felt.

I knelt and extended a hand to it. When it approached and rubbed its face against my fingertips, I realized I'd somehow avoided touching it before. Its fur was downy and I could feel the heat from its little body close to the surface, despite the cold outside. I couldn't remember the last time I'd pet a cat.

I opened another can of tuna into the cat's bowl, and set it just outside the door, and closed the door behind it. Then I added tuna to the grocery list and shook my head at myself all the way to the car.

✦　✦　✦

ON TUESDAY, MY meeting finished early and Will had to work late, so I decided to go to Falls Church for the night. The fact that I had seen a stray black cat outside the restaurant where I'd had a lunch meeting had absolutely nothing to do with my decision. The kitten wasn't mine. It had lived this long outside on its own, and it had to keep its survival skills intact so it could continue to live outside.

And if I found myself in the kitchen as soon as I got home, that was just because I was hungry.

As I seared a filet of salmon and steamed green beans, my mind wandered to the look on William's face as he'd fed the kitten a morsel of chicken from his hand. He'd cut his gaze to me as if doing something he knew he shouldn't and wondering if he'd get called on it. I'd raised an eyebrow at him. Watching him care for the kitten had inflated something just behind my sternum. A warm balloon of...something, that had prevented me from saying a word.

I added a buttered hunk of bread to my plate, and poured myself a glass of Châteauneuf-du-Pape Blanc. Before I could grab my plate, a familiar meow came from outside the door.

"Don't let it in," I muttered. "It'll never leave." But even as I spoke, I was opening the door. The kitten was sitting on its haunches just outside the door, like a dinner guest who'd rung the bell.

"Come in," I found myself saying.

And it did.

I ate in the kitchen, feeding the kitten bits of salmon with my fingers and resolutely not texting William to inform him that his cat was ruining my life.

After dinner, I picked it up and set it down gently outside. It was cold. The kitten nuzzled my hand as I let it go.

The next morning when I opened the door for it, the kitten barreled inside mewling. It had a scratch on its cheek and it whimpered when I tried to touch it. I googled "How to clean a scratched cat," and reasoned that I could do all the work I needed to do from the Falls Church house. All my meetings for the day were phone meetings anyway.

✧　✧　✧

FRIDAY EVENING, WHEN the crunch of tires on gravel meant William had arrived, I poured him a glass of wine and met him at the door.

His arms came around me and he tucked his chin into the crook of my neck. The warmth of satisfaction—of *rightness*—settled over me like a blanket.

"Welcome home," I murmured, wishing it truly were his home, and he squeezed me. After a kiss, and a grateful smile in exchange for the wine, we settled on the couch in the living room and Will finally satisfied my curiosity about the case he'd closed that week. When he'd finished and his stomach started growling, we made our way into the kitchen.

"Um, have you happened to—" Will began, but he was interrupted by the now-predictable meow and scratching at the door.

I cleared my throat and opened the door. The kitten bounded inside and rubbed itself against my ankles.

"Aww, has it been coming back?" he asked. Then he seemed to catch himself, and amended, "It really should learn to hunt for itself. If you're not going to keep it, that is."

I said nothing, and he bent down and offered his knuckles to the kitten. It seemed overjoyed to have another playmate, and bounced between Will's knuckles and my ankles for the next few minutes. I served it tuna and William and I ate in the kitchen without discussing it. I loaded the dishwasher as Will went upstairs to change out of his work clothes, and brought the bottle of wine into the living room, where he met me.

He threw his legs up over my thighs and sighed happily, clicking on a show he knew I didn't mind as background noise, and I grabbed my book from the table, resting a hand on his leg.

I was just losing myself in the book when a small weight plopped up on the couch next to us.

The kitten.

William looked at me, horrified.

"Shit, sorry," he said. "I forgot." He grabbed the kitten and petted it, walking back to the kitchen. I bit my lip so I couldn't tell him to let it stay.

"Sorry," he said again as he settled back beside me.

"No harm done," I said, running a hand up his thigh.

Suddenly, with the feel of hard muscle beneath soft flannel, reading didn't seem all that appealing. I stood and held out a hand to William, eyes on him in a way that had him scrambling up off the couch and into my arms.

✧ ✧ ✧

I WOKE WITH my arms full of solid, sexy man. For a moment, I wasn't sure what had woken me, since William was still asleep, his leg flung over mine, his head heavy on my shoulder, the smell of sex all over us.

Then lightning ripped through the sky and a crack of thunder followed. I tightened my arms around Will a moment before he woke harshly, and held him to me. We both peered out the window as the storm blew in.

I loved to watch the lightning illumine the sky, trees flashing in relief, skeletal black branches reaching toward the clouds. Wind whipped the branches, and blew gusts of leaves in whorls on the ground. Rain lashed the windows.

"Probably the last storm before the first snow," William said, voice sleep-creaky in the darkness. He spoke about the weather this way sometimes, as if it were something knowable.

An errant branch scraped the window with a screech.

"Do you think…" I began, then muffled my mouth with Will's shoulder.

"What?"

"Oh. Well. What do you think the kitten does in the event of a storm?" I pulled away slightly, so Will wouldn't feel my heart pounding.

"Amory."

"Hmm."

Will grasped my chin and pulled me so he could look at me in the moonlight. "Have you been letting the cat in?"

"Hmm?"

"Have you been letting the cat come in farther than the kitchen? Is that why it jumped up on the couch? Have you been letting it sleep inside at night?"

Busted.

I cleared my throat. I supposed I should've expected such dot-connecting from a federal agent. I cleared my throat again, then felt the press of Will's lips to my jaw.

"Softy," he murmured.

I sighed.

Will's lips met mine and he pulled me back down beside him on the bed. I felt his breathing start to slow again, but I was suddenly wide awake. "William?"

"Mmm."

"She's so little."

Will pushed himself up on an elbow and looked at me for a minute. Then he slid out of bed and pulled on jeans and a sweatshirt. I scrambled to follow suit, then followed him downstairs.

We pulled on coats and shoved our feet into boots, then Will wrestled the kitchen door open. Rain blew inside, along with a damp spattering of leaves, but there was no sign of the kitten.

"C'mere," Will called into the shrieking rain, but the sound was swallowed up and nothing came. A lightning strike split the sky, and I couldn't see anything kitten-shaped. "Okay, let's go," he said, pointing and yelling over the storm. "Check under things. It's probably hiding." I nodded.

We were soaked and freezing within seconds of being outside, and the wind whipped my hair around my face and shoulders.

"Cat!" Will called, and grabbed at my elbow as I slid on wet leaves. He shook his head. "I feel like an idiot calling it *cat*."

"It's very Audrey Hepburn of you, William."

He cocked his head and went back to searching. I tried to look under bushes and behind terra cotta pots, but my hair kept getting in my eyes and I couldn't see a thing.

When I caught up with Will, he was shivering in the cold.

"It's okay," I said. "Thank you for trying."

But he had that look on his face. That stubborn look that usually thwarted my attempts to buy him things, or telemarketers' attempts to get him to upgrade his cable service. He walked to the tree line and called out again, louder this time. The wind tossed his voice into the trees. He stood for a while, a black shape silhouetted against taller, slimmer black shapes. Then he crouched.

When he rose and made his way back to me, he was cradling something against his chest. I opened the kitchen door and it wasn't until I shut the storm out that I could hear it. The whimpering mewl from inside Will's coat.

I grabbed at his hand, peeling the coat away.

And there was the kitten, a bedraggled, shivering mess, its fur plastered to its body and its little face just huge eyes. William didn't look much better. I helped him strip off his coat, did the same with my own, and left them with our boots on the floor, tugging Will upstairs. I turned on the shower and closed the bathroom door, then dried the cat with a towel, until its fur spiked damply and it was purring in my hands. Then I pushed Will under the hot water, and made a nest of the towel for the kitten on the floor.

I stepped under the spray with William, sighing in relief as the icy fall of my hair was warmed. When I opened my eyes, Will's were on mine. He looked amused, and he put his hands on either side of my neck tenderly.

"We should take it to the vet and get it checked out," he murmured in my ear.

"Her," I said, shutting off the water and drying William off. He didn't take to it as easily as the kitten.

I scooped her up and took them both into the bedroom.

My hair would be a mess come morning, but something told me Will wouldn't care, so I slid beneath the covers without braiding it.

"She needs a name too," Will said. "If you're going to keep her." He shot me a wry look. "Which you obviously are."

"*We* are," I corrected. He opened his mouth like he might quarrel, then dropped his eyes to the kitten, who had snuck out of her towel and curled between us on top of the coverlet.

He settled himself into my arms as he usually did, leg thrown over mine, head on my shoulder, but this time he moved slowly, so as not to dislodge the kitten, now curled on his hip.

"Thank you, love," I said, running a hand up and down his back.

"Softy," he teased, but he cuddled closer and kissed my neck.

"My hero," I said.

CHAPTER 20

Vaughn

"I CAN'T BELIEVE I let you talk me into this," Will muttered, indicated our first class seats.

"William, you know I appreciate the extra leg room. Besides, you accepted the complimentary whiskey quickly enough."

"Well. I might feel like a tool sitting in first class on an hour-long flight, but I'm not an idiot," he grumbled.

I smiled and patted his hand.

In truth, I was surprised and relieved that Will hadn't put up more of a fight. When he'd asked me if I would accompany him to his parents' home in Ohio for Thanksgiving, I'd been delighted, but surprised. I knew Will cared for me a great deal, but I also knew that his family represented a different life than the one he was living. I hadn't had any confidence that he would want to share that side of himself with me, or me with it. He'd fumbled through the question, studding it with *If you're not doing anything* and *You probably won't want to.*

I'd had to kiss him to shut him up long enough to tell him that I would love to spend Thanksgiving with him, and that I'd be honored to meet his family. He'd gotten very quiet then. A pleased kind of quiet that looked good on him. It spoke of confidence and satisfaction. And a confident, satisfied William was an irresistible William. Of course, I rarely bothered trying to resist.

The next day, I'd called him into my study to consult about airline tickets, expecting his usual noble insistence that he would pay for his own ticket. But he'd just gaped at me and said, "Oh. I always drive." Then we'd spoken at the same time. He'd said, "It's only about six hours" at the same time I'd protested, "It's over six hours!"

Will had laughed nervously and I'd grimaced in anticipation of a car ride that Will said was six hours but that would, certainly, with the bad luck that attended holiday car rides, find us with a flat tire in the middle of nowhere, or stuck in an early blizzard, or in gridlock traffic because somewhere someone had misplaced a traffic cone.

But after a few minutes, Will had shrugged and agreed that we could fly. It was less of a fight than he usually put up, but I'd been too relieved to question it. Later he'd admitted that he'd realized if we drove that Charlotte would certainly want to come with us and that the last thing he needed was to *begin* the holiday pre-stressed out. Since he and Charlotte were forever in each other's pockets, I could only assume that it was my added presence that would turn the twins' ride oppressive. But I took the win, booked our flights, and emailed William the information.

And if I'd happened not to include our seat numbers with the reservation, well…really what difference did it make if he had that information in advance or not? Besides, it charmed me that he felt guilty flying first class. It charmed me that he apologized to the flight attendant when I handed her my coat to hang in the closet at the front of the aircraft so it wouldn't get wrinkled, and refused to let her hang his, though I could see he was overly warm with it on his lap.

As he finished his whiskey, I discreetly signaled the flight attendant, and when she collected his empty glass, I handed her his coat with a small smile, and she went to hang it up before he could protest. I captured his hand in mine and rested them both on my thigh.

Will squeezed my hand as the plane took off, and looked straight ahead.

"Are you afraid of flying?" I asked, never having considered that might be the reason he chose to drive.

"No, I'm fine. Just, it takes a minute to get used to it, is all."

I squeezed his hand in return and decided on distraction being the better part of valor. "So, what do your parents think of you bringing me home?" William's father had been a police officer and his mother an elementary school art teacher. Both had retired several years before.

"They're fine with it," he said, still staring straight ahead.

I grabbed his chin and gently turned him to face me, running my knuckles over his cheekbone. His warm brown eyes went soft at the touch. "You all right?"

He nodded, but there were subtle lines of stress around his eyes and a tightness to his forehead that I wanted to smooth away.

"You brought your ex-partner home for holidays, yes?" I asked.

"Harris? Yeah." He shook his head. "Poor Harris. He liked my mom okay but he was scared to death of my dad."

I slid my hand to his shoulder and massaged gently,

willing him to keep talking as I reached behind him and slid the window shade closed.

"Fear, to my dad, is like blood in the water. He can smell it and it just makes him double down. Like, once he realized Harris didn't know anything about football but was too scared to admit it, he'd talk to him during the game. Make comments that Harris would try to respond to but couldn't. Don't get me wrong, my dad's not mean. He just…has certain ideas of how men should be, I guess."

I nodded.

"Harris loved my mom. She was sweet to him, and his own parents weren't the greatest. And I think she felt sorry for him, a bit. But after we broke up she told me she was relieved because she'd always known he wasn't right for me. Not that she'd ever said."

"Why not?"

"It's just not the kind of thing my mom would ever say."

Which was such a William thing to say. Such a William thing to accept that some people simply *were* a certain way and that was that.

"And what did your father say when you broke up?"

"Nothing. My father never said anything about Harris. No, wait. That's not true." Will got a faraway look. "The first time Harris came home with me, it was for Easter. I was helping my dad clean the gutters while my mom made dinner, and I tore my hand open on a nail. Here." He traced a scar beneath his thumb with an absent fingertip. "I needed stitches, a tetanus shot, there was blood everywhere. And they couldn't numb me up because I'm allergic to lidocaine."

"I didn't know that," I murmured.

"No reason you would."

But I wanted to know everything.

"Anyway, it hurt like a motherfucker to get the stitches, and I…" His brow furrowed and he looked down. "I guess I reached for his hand. I don't know. I don't even remember it, honestly. I just remember the part where he pulled away. He didn't want my father to see us touching. And that night, when I ran into my father in the hallway going to bed, he said, 'Don't depend on a man who fears judgment more than shame.' I've never forgotten that. And Harris came back maybe five more times, but he would never touch me in front of my family. Not even a hug, or a kiss at New Year's."

Will shrugged uncomfortably, and my heart ached for this years-gone-by version of him, left aching for a touch that never came. And I vowed to myself that he'd never suffer its absence again.

✧　✧　✧

WILLIAM'S MOTHER ANSWERED the door looking so exactly as I'd pictured her that I almost laughed. She was of average height and weight, wearing light pink lipstick, mascara, and no other makeup, her thick, blunt-cut, wavy brown hair shot through with gray.

"Hello, darling," she said, hugging Will. "Where's your sister?" she asked immediately, peering around him and finding only me. I had a sudden vision of all the hundreds of times he must have heard this same question.

"She's coming," he said. "Mom, this is Amory Vaughn."

"It's so nice to meet you, Amory," she said, and my stomach lurched as I realized that *of course* Will's parents would call me Amory. But aside from Will, no one but my own parents had called me that in a very, very long time.

"It's my pleasure, madam," I said, kissing Mrs. Fox's cheek. "Thank you for inviting me into your beautiful home."

"Well," Mrs. Fox said, smiling. And she stepped aside so we could enter, telling me to call her Karen.

The Foxes had a split-level house, the living room to the right of the entrance, and the kitchen to the left. Will's father materialized from the living room as we removed our shoes by the door.

"Will," he said, and gave William a hearty handshake that he used to pull his son into a quick hug with a firm pat on the back. He was a couple of inches shorter than Will's six feet, with a thicker build and meaty hands. His mostly gray hair was receding, but still full, and his eyebrows were brown. I could see the resemblance between them, but where William's eyes were watchful but warm, his father's were suspicious. The eyes of a cop who'd long ago learned that trust was dangerous.

"Dad, this is Amory Vaughn."

"Pleasure to meet you, sir," I said, shaking his hand firmly. "Thank you for making me welcome."

"Call me Henry."

His eyes tracked me up and down and I could practically read his thoughts on his face. I supposed I had found where to lay the blame for Will's inability to hide anything he thought. From me, anyway.

Henry took in my height, and my clothing, and my gray hair—he couldn't have known it had silvered at age twenty—and his eyes cut sideways to his son, then narrowed slightly as he looked back at me. If Harris Parks had been scorned, he had also shored up Henry's vision of his son:

masculine, normal, able to pass as straight. Now, when he looked at me, his own prejudices were forcing him to question what he'd thought he knew. I was older, larger, clearly made more money. And what, then, might that say about his son?

Of course, it said nothing at all about Will in reality. But in Henry Fox's mind, it was forcing him to entertain notions about William that were making him distinctly uncomfortable.

"Of course, Henry," I said, infusing my voice with warmth. I turned away from him and slid a hand up Will's back, squeezing his shoulder. "Babe, can you point me toward the bathroom?" I asked.

"Yeah, it's just past the living room, on the right," Will said. I could feel him ease, muscles relaxing under my hand. And his eyes spoke of a gratitude I wasn't sure he was even aware of.

✧   ✧   ✧

KAREN WOULDN'T LET me help with dinner, though she gave Charlotte a pointed look when she settled in to watch football with her father and brother.

"I'd love to help, Karen," I tried again. "I've never been much of a fan of games." I winked at Will, and Charlotte grinned; Henry pretended not to notice.

"I suppose, if my daughter can't be bothered," Karen said, resigned.

Charlotte was sprawled on the beige corduroy couch, feet up on the blocky coffee table, a beer in her hand. She didn't even take her eyes off the game as she said, "Busman's holiday, Mom, come on. I coordinate with caterers every day for work. Besides, you know I can't stand making things the same over and over. Remember last year? The mashed potato experiment? You said I was barred from the kitchen."

"Whatever did she do to the mashed potatoes?" I asked solicitously, linking my elbow with Karen's as we walked into the kitchen.

We worked in companionable silence for a few minutes, Karen peeling potatoes and basting the turkey while I put together an unpleasant-looking green bean casserole from the ingredients she indicated.

After a while though, I got the feeling that she was psyching herself up to talk to me. I didn't endeavor to make people uncomfortable, but in my experience it was often necessary to discourage conversation in the pursuit of peace. However, this was Will's mother, and though I didn't get the sense they were particularly close, I certainly wanted to make Will's life easier by encouraging her to like me. And a surefire way to make someone like you was to make things easier for them without them realizing you were doing so.

"It's a treat for me to have a real Thanksgiving dinner," I said casually. "The last few years I've had to attend such stuffy, catered dinners, for work. It's wonderful to be able to relax." I smiled warmly at her and watched her glow.

"That's terrible. Everyone should have a home-cooked meal on Thanksgiving. I swear, I don't know where my children get it—the fast-paced life, never stopping to eat properly, always in the middle of five different things. Charlie hasn't been home in a year! And Will—well, you know Will." She shook her head.

"I love Will," I said softly. Her head jerked up, and the shock was clear on her face. "Your son is a wonderful man.

Thank you, for the hand you had in making him who he is."

I was aware that I was laying it on thick. But that didn't mean I wasn't sincere. I'd never met a lover's parents outside the circles I usually ran in. Of those, I'd run into a few at galas, or work events. Another few at golf tournaments or parties. I'd even invited a few to my home in Falls Church. But I'd never been invited home with anyone except Valerie, and we'd been friends since we were children.

Seeing where William came from—the habitat that had produced the man I'd lost my heart to…it mattered to me.

"Thank you for saying that," Karen said, disconcerted but clearly pleased. "I suppose…" And here it was—whatever comment or question I'd eased the way for. "I suppose all this must seem quite simple to you? Will told me you're quite cosmopolitan."

I would bet my considerable net worth that Will had never used the word "cosmopolitan" in his life, unless it was in reference to statistics about urban crime, but the fact that he'd told his parents enough about me that Karen would get that impression surprised me. I hadn't gotten the sense that Will was particularly confessional with them. Wasn't he just full of surprises this weekend.

"Simple? Well, in the best way, perhaps. In that it's a family who love each other, in a house full of memories, sharing a meal together."

Karen smiled and I knew I'd said the right thing.

"Do you usually spend holidays with your own family? When you're not at…stuffy events, was it?"

How long had it been since I'd spent time with people who didn't even know enough about me to know about my parents? Long enough that I'd forgotten how much it always hurt to disclose. How, even though I hadn't had anything like a simple relationship with my parents, on days like this, I still thought of them. Still mourned them.

"I'm afraid I really haven't any. Not anymore."

Karen's face fell and I started talking about other things until the tension dissipated.

Dinner was a cheerful affair, with a Thanksgiving meal that could have been snatched straight from a child's drawing. Turkey, stuffing, gravy, mashed potatoes, cranberry sauce, green bean casserole, and a salad of iceberg lettuce and ranch dressing. I wasn't sure I'd ever eaten ranch dressing before. Along with the meal, the Foxes all drank Budweiser, even Karen, though she commented that it was naughty of her. Will smiled, and Charlotte rolled her eyes, and they all toasted me, their aluminum cans thumping together in welcome.

Will squeezed my thigh under the table. He was happy and relaxed, possibly a little tipsy from the pre-dinner beers he'd had while watching football. I couldn't wait to taste his mouth, search out the lingering taste. As if he could read my mind, his eyes darkened, gaze flicking to my mouth.

Charlotte was chatting about the new location she'd found for an event she was planning, and Will was shooting not-so-subtle looks at me when Henry pushed back from the table and announced he was ready for pie and he'd have it in the living room. I jumped up to help clear the table, but Karen waved us all out of the kitchen and told us we'd simply be in her way.

"Do you want to take a walk?" Will asked, and I could see Charlotte wink at him as she made her way to the living room.

We got our coats and headed out into the Foxes' suburban neighborhood, the air cool, and fresh, and blank-smelling. I took William's arm in mine as we walked in silence for a few minutes until we passed a school.

"That's my elementary school," he said. I was overcome with a rush of tenderness for the pavement William had run across, the woodchips he'd surely scuffed, and I tugged his arm toward the playground.

He laughed and grabbed ahold of the monkey bars, swinging up to perch on top.

"I busted my chin open on these monkey bars in third grade. Charlie saw from all the way over there." He pointed to the swings on the hill opposite. "Came running over like I was dying."

I ducked beneath the structure, and was tall enough to rest my chin on his knees as he sat atop the bars. Looking up, I could see the small scar on the underside of his chin gleaming in the moonlight. I touched it, and he pulled me closer, leaning down and running his hands over my hair.

"You don't have any scars," he murmured, looking down at me. It was rare we were in this position because of our heights. "It's like even your skin is impervious."

I shook my head. "There are lots of kinds of scars."

"I know," he whispered. Then he kissed me, and slid down from the monkey bars into my arms.

"Did you and Charlotte stick together at school?" I asked as we walked back to the road.

"Yeah, mostly. My dad kind of had a fit if Charlie wanted to hang out with me all the time. Just like he hated when I started taking art electives in high school. He just...you know, gender roles and all that. Sometimes I think having boy-girl twins makes it even starker. Like, one of us had to do some chores and one of us had to do others, so it was easier to make Charlie do the dishes and me take out the trash. It really sucked for her. She hated it."

"It doesn't sound very nice for you either, love."

"I guess." He shrugged. "Mom was better about it when we were little. My dad was so intense about work that when he got home he was wound pretty tight. Mom would let us play, or do art projects. On the weekends, my dad just wanted to watch sports. Sometimes throw the ball around with me. I wasn't really into it. He never asked if Charlie wanted to."

"You're not much for team sports."

"Nah, I'd rather compete against myself, I guess."

That certainly rang true. I'd always thought Will was one of the least competitive people I knew, but that hadn't quite comported with his intense drive, both in work and play. It made sense that he *was* competitive, but that it was an internal competition that disregarded the standards set by others in favor of those he set for himself. And god knew his standards for himself were more exacting than anyone else's...except perhaps his father's. I identified with that too. Rarely did I use societal standards or the expectations of others to measure my success. In fact, I took perverse pleasure in disregarding them altogether.

Back at the house, we ate a Mrs. Smith's frozen pumpkin pie with Reddi-wip, and watched the news. It was a kind of normal I'd never known. And William and Charlotte had fled from it as soon as they'd had the chance.

When the news was exchanged for a professional football game, I zoned out, idly stroking my fingers through Will's short hair, drowsy with travel and bland food. I began woolgathering about William's time here, wondering if high school William had ever made out with a boy in his bedroom, heart racing with lust and the fear of his parents coming home and interrupting.

I was spinning a fantasy that I doubted I'd ever get to act out when Will's voice startled me.

"I think I'll turn in," he said casually, but he'd pressed his knee into mine on the couch, a subtle request. I stood when he stood, smiling.

"Thank you again for a wonderful meal, Karen. Henry, Charlotte," I said, nodding to each of them.

Charlotte waved sleepily, her eyes on the game, but Henry and Karen exchanged a vaguely uncomfortable look.

"Will you both be in your room, then?" Karen asked.

"Uh, yup. Where else would we be?" His voice was calm, but I could hear the edge of irritation creeping in.

My fierce William. Always defending me. I squeezed his shoulder and he sniffed.

"Night," he said, and turned away.

I followed him up the stairs and down a hallway carpeted in thick brown shag, then through the last door on the right. Once inside, he dropped our overnight bags on the floor and began fussing with the bedcovers, the line of his shoulders tense.

I slid a hand up his back and leaned over him.

"I've been cooking up a fantasy while sitting with your family and watching football, William."

"Oh?"

"Oh, yes." I crowded him, bending him forward over the bed, spread with a navy blue comforter trimmed in red.

"We're in your childhood bedroom," I murmured into his ear, kissing the skin behind it until he shivered in my arms.

"Mmhmm?"

I slid a hand under his sweater and splayed my palm against his warm stomach. His back was pressed to my chest and I could feel his heart beating. "We're in high school. You're a junior and I'm a senior. You invited me over to do homework, so we brought our books upstairs."

I licked a line up the side of his throat and pulled him more firmly against me so he could feel the evidence of what this fantasy was doing to me.

"What subject?" he asked, pressing his hips backward.

"History. The Revolutionary War." I gave his earlobe a nip and saw the corners of his mouth draw up. "You're very studious. Serious. You're concentrating."

"Mmm, and what are you doing?"

"I…am being very distracting."

I slipped a hand inside his dark jeans and ghosted my fingers over the ridge of his hard cock.

"I keep bumping your knees with mine. Touching you. I can't help myself. You're so damned hot."

He moaned softly, shuddering as I took a firmer grip on him. He made no attempt to turn around, just ground his taut ass back against my hips, teasing my swollen flesh. I pulled my hand from his pants and he gave a plaintive whimper. I kissed the back of his neck, feasting on soft skin until his hands clutched at me.

"What," he gasped. "What do you do next?"

"Well, that all depends." I dropped my voice low, knowing how much it turned him on. "You're a junior, William. Are you a virgin?"

He gasped and craned to look at me. He nodded, sunk fully into this game. Lust shot through me at the idea of being Will's first; of sliding inside his body where no other man had been, opening him, owning him.

"Well then," I murmured. "I'll have to be very." I kissed his neck. "Very." The skin under his jaw. "Gentle," I whispered against his mouth, and felt his moan.

I pushed him forward enough to pull off his sweater, then pressed against him again.

"The first time I touch you," I told him, "you aren't sure what to make of it. Am I teasing? Should you react? Or am I just being friendly?" I ran my hands up his sides, tracing his ribs. "But then I touch you here." I circled his nipples with my fingers, plucking them until he arched against me. "And you know I'm not just being friendly anymore. You know that I'm going to do things to you no one has ever done before."

Will shuddered and I drank his reactions like the finest whiskey.

"Have you thought about them, William? Alone in your room, in your bed. Have you thought about what it would feel like to have another boy's body against yours? A man's hand around your dick instead of your own? The sensation of a man kissing your mouth, kissing you everywhere?"

Will shook his head, mouth open.

"No? You haven't thought about it? Or you haven't wanted to?"

He froze in my arms.

"It's okay, love. I've got you."

I pressed him down, chest to the mattress, and kissed up his spine.

"When I can't take it anymore, I push my hand into your pants and I touch you." I pulled him up against me, back still to my chest. I wanted him to feel. Just feel. I slid my hand back into his jeans and squeezed him. He jumped, then groaned. "I've only done this with a few other boys," I said, trying to stay in character by making my grip a little too firm, my movements unpracticed.

William ground back against me, lost in his pleasure. He needed this. I pulled his hip back with my other hand, and ran a finger over the tip of his erection, smearing the liquid I found there. Then I brought my hand to his mouth, feeding him his own taste. He licked and sucked at my fingers, sloppy with arousal. I knew what he wanted, and I was desperate to give it to him.

"William," I murmured in his ear, voice dark and teasing. "Do you want me inside you? Do you want me to take your virginity?"

"Unnghh," he groaned, and it was a measure of his arousal that he was beyond speech.

"You want me to touch you where no other man has ever touched you?" I pressed my hips forward, rubbing my erection along the crease of his gorgeous ass.

"Yessss," he hissed.

"Tell me," I said. "Tell me I'm the first. That no on else has ever been here."

He shook his head, panting now. "Just you. Nobody. I never even kissed anyone before."

I stilled myself, his words pulsing sweetly in my stomach. "Well. We must remedy that."

I turned his chin gently and kissed his mouth, trailing my fingertips down his throat and over his jaw. He opened to me, touching my tongue with his own, the sweet taste of him and the pie he'd eaten making me lick into him, deep, kiss him until we were both breathless.

"I take your pants off," I said, "because I can't wait to see this ass I've watched for months at school. When you walked down the hallway, talking to your friends. When you changed for gym. When you bent over to pick up the notebook you dropped in our history class."

I squeezed the globes of his ass in my hands and knelt behind him.

"What are you—"

"Shhh," I cut him off. "You've never done this before, but I have. You just relax."

I licked at Will's hole and his hands fisted the covers as he bucked forward. "No, no," he groaned. "I can't. I'll—"

I pressed his face into the mattress to muffle the sounds he was afraid would escape, and he sagged against me. I licked at him until he was wet and shaking and pressing back against my face. Then I backed off.

"I touch deep inside you next, William. So deep, and you never thought it would feel this good, but it does."

I slid two fingers inside and groaned softly at the heat clenching around me. I went right for his prostate, stroking it as I cupped his balls and felt him shudder, hands groping, mouth open and panting against the bed.

"I slide in and out of you with my fingers, and all you can think about is how much better it will feel when it's something else inside you. When it's my cock deep inside your body, owning you. Isn't that right, William?"

"Yesss," he moaned, legs as shaky as his voice. "Yes, please, that's what I want. Just you."

"Just me," I murmured. I rubbed more spit inside Will, not willing to stop touching him for even as long as it would take to find the lube in my dopp kit. "This will hurt a bit, since it's your first time. But I've got you."

He nodded frantically and pressed back against me. I pushed my pants over my hips, and slicked my erection with the copious precome I'd leaked, watching Will, touching him. Fuck, he was the most gorgeous thing I'd ever seen.

"I'm going to put myself inside you now, William. My body inside yours. My cock in your ass. We'll be as close as you've ever been to anyone. Connected."

He whimpered. I pulled apart his cheeks, lining myself up with his slick, clenching hole. When I surged into him, I thought for a moment that he'd come, but it was a stream of precome sliding down his dick as he writhed beneath me, so turned on he forgot to be quiet.

I covered his mouth with one hand and grabbed his hip with the other. This wasn't going to take long at all. I bent my knees to ensure a good angle, then I rocketed into his willing body, the slide of slick flesh milking my swollen dick until I had a hard time staying quiet myself.

"Oh, fuck me, you feel amazing," I whispered. William's broken sound was muffled by my hand, and he kissed my palm. I could feel the orgasm threatening like a thundercloud gathering in my belly and groin. "I'm going to touch your cock," I growled. "And when I do, you're going to come all over yourself. All over this bed. With me buried so deep inside you that you'll never, ever forget your first time."

Will's moan was not quiet and I was past caring. I took my hand away from his mouth and reached between his legs, feeling the slick, iron heat of him pulse in my hand. I jerked him hard and slammed into him, every muscle clenched. He buried his face in the blanket and shouted out his release, his cock erupting all over the side of the bed, and his inner walls milking me so hard it was like the grip of a fist. I came inside him like a freight train, my vision going black and my head full of cotton, heartbeat pounding in my ears. I shuddered against Will's back as I poured myself inside him then collapsed, pressing him to the bed.

I kissed every part of him I could reach, lying on top of him until I could find the strength to move. When I pulled out he stayed boneless, relaxed on the bed like I'd fucked him to sleep. Maybe I had. I grabbed tissues from the box on the desk and cleaned us up. Just as I was wondering if he'd actually passed out, he murmured something into the covers.

"What's that, love?"

He turned his face to the side. "Are you gonna ignore me at school tomorrow?" he said.

I lifted him up and rolled him under the comforter, hitting the light and following him.

"No," I said, wrapping my arms around him. "No, never." And I drifted to sleep with my face in Will's hair, the slightly musty comforter wrapped tightly around us.

CHAPTER 21

Vaughn

AFTER A CASUAL breakfast of cereal and Entenmann's coffee cake, I found my attention split between wondering what we'd do for two entire days at the Foxes' house, and trying to figure out if the dismal state of my hair was due to the way William had slept with his fingers tangled in it or the Foxes' unfortunate hard water.

We watched the news for an hour or so, William and Charlotte cursing the state of the world, their parents largely silent, and then Charlotte went to her room to return some phone calls. Karen started to clean, and Will and Henry began restlessly attempting to fix a sticky drawer on the television console. It seemed no one was quite sure how to spend the time together.

I watched as William and Henry performed a tango of competency. Each new project—rehanging a crooked picture, sanding out a burn in the kitchen table, recaulking around the downstairs toilet—was a microcosm of father-son competition. Henry had clearly taught Will to do these things and, over time, Will had developed his own methods. Each time William did something as Henry had taught him, Henry was quiet, proud, relieved. Each time he questioned, or proposed an alternative, Henry was defensive, judgmental, and—when Will's suggestions turned out to work—embarrassed.

William had been right when he'd said his father wasn't mean. Henry wasn't in any way nasty or conniving; to the contrary, he struck me as a thoroughly straightforward and staunchly ethical man. Much like Will.

But unlike Will, Henry seemed to lack creativity and empathy. His beliefs, his ethics, his standards, and his expectations were all deeply rooted in his own limited experience. His world was blinkered, and thus so was his capacity to understand anything that fell outside his scope. Including his son.

William was clearly used to their dynamic—aware, but resigned. Seeing them together gave me a whole new admiration for my lover, who had taken the oppositional values his parents had instilled, and used them as the foundation for his understanding of the world, rather than as limits.

I hadn't even done any of the work, but I was mentally exhausted by early afternoon, when Karen interrupted the Home and Garden Channel weekend fix-it-up show starring William and Henry.

"Will, dear, could you and Amory go pick up the trays from the grocery store? Your aunt and uncle will be here in a few hours and the basement is still a mess. Your sister is apparently incapable of taking a single day off. She's been on the phone for hours."

William's mouth quirked, and I wondered if he was generally amused by his mother or if he had some inside information that Charlotte might be on the phone with someone not strictly work-related.

"I didn't know your aunt and uncle were coming," I told Will as he backed his mother's Toyota Camry out of the driveway.

"Oh, I guess I forgot to tell you. They always come. It's my mom's sister, Lisa, and her husband, Gary. Their kids—my cousins—used to come. There are three of them. But I think only Megan is coming. Rick lives in Arizona and Jana just moved to…maybe Florida? So I think it was too far. Megan's the youngest. She's always been all right to me, but she irritates the hell out of Charlie."

"Oh? How come?"

"She's a bit…" I could see him searching for a descriptor that wasn't too mean. "Superficial," he settled on finally.

We pulled into the parking lot of a Kroger, and I realized it was the first time William and I had ever been grocery shopping together. I appreciated the cheerful domesticity of it, though supermarkets were something I usually avoided at all cost. Seeing a throng of harried shoppers stuffing their carts with flats of juice boxes, bags of Doritos, and family-sized boxes of sugary cereal made subsequently enjoying a meal difficult. Give me the dignity of a specialty market any day.

Will was clearly familiar with the layout of the store and went right to the deli section, peering down at trays of cold cuts encased in plastic domes. Rolls and lines of sliced meats, chunks of artificially orange cheeses, and dry-looking baby carrots made my nose twitch in distaste. Will piled three of them into a shopping cart the size of his mother's car and walked to the bread.

I breathed in deeply through my nose and out through

my mouth to distance myself from this awful place, but quickly regretted it when breathing in through my nose resulted in smelling the chemical tang of plastic mixed with meat. So I breathed shallowly through my mouth, and pictured myself in a better place. On the beach, with William sprawled in the chaise longue beside me, his sleek chest gleaming with oil in the tropical sun.

"Oh Vaughn, with all this travel stuff, I completely forgot to tell you that Brett Lawson got transferred," Will said, and I opened my eyes. We were still in the fluorescent-lit hellscape of the supermarket. "Jodie told me he got transferred to Springfield. Bet he wasn't pleased about that." Will smirked.

"Good, good," I said. "I didn't like how he spoke to you at all."

William was off, and I trailed after him, attempting not to look at anything, or breathe. He piled the groceries on the checkout counter, still talking about Lawson as a tired-looking woman rang us up.

"I swear, he got exactly what he deserved too. Remember that crack he made about the Midwest when we were in Durham? And they say people don't get what they deserve." He grinned as we walked to the car, handing me a bag.

"Yes, I'm so glad you agree it was the right thing," I said absently, forcing my shoulders to relax as I could finally draw a breath that didn't smell like processed food and desperation.

"Well, it was certainly good for—wait, what do you mean the right thing?"

"What? Nothing. What were you saying?" *Oh dear.*

William stopped outside the car and whipped around to

look at me, eyes narrowed. "Did you have something to do with Lawson's transfer?"

"Why on earth would the FBI take anything I had to say into consideration?" I said, damning all supermarkets to the darkest corners of hell for getting me so out of sorts that I'd walked right into that one. This was not a thing that I did.

"Amory." Will's voice was low and threatening. "Did you have something to do with it?"

I evaluated my options under Will's glare. I didn't like to lie to him. But I could already tell his feelings on the matter were not favorable. I decided to try one last attempt to simply shut this down, in the hopes that he would see it would be better for everyone if we simply drove back to his parents' house so that everyone (who wasn't me) could eat meat and cheese from these horrifying plastic sarcophagi and enjoy family togetherness at the holiday.

"Brett Lawson was a bigoted menace and I'm very glad that neither you nor anyone else will have to put up with his bullying and his prejudice. Surely we should get home before your mother worries."

William's face went cold, but he unlocked the car and we loaded the groceries in the back seat. This was not going to go well. Will had no sense of self-preservation in such things. His principles, much though I admired them in the abstract, prevented him from ever letting things go when it was easier to do so. *Damn, damn, damn.*

His jaw set and his nostrils flared, William drove out of the parking lot.

"Let me get this straight," he bit off. "You yet again decided that you could determine the fate of things that have nothing to do with you, because you think you can just do whatever you want. No consequences, even when it's playing with people's lives."

"You have something to do with me. I was protecting you."

His laugh was a bark. "Yeah, I feel very protected, Vaughn. I definitely don't feel humiliated because my boyfriend thinks I'm so incapable of dealing with a coworker that he has to go behind my back, to my boss's boss, and no doubt wield some unholy combination of money and influence to get that coworker transferred out of the state. Who's the bully now?"

"Hold on. I didn't do it because I think you are incapable. You're the most capable man I've ever met."

"But you did do it."

"Look, love," I sighed. "The FBI reeks of systemic homophobia. Brett Lawson was never going to be appropriately dealt with when the organization itself doesn't value the safety—"

"No. No, do not make this about the FBI. *You* did this. *You* chose this. You went behind my back and I don't care why you did it. You lied to me. You managed me. You did what you always do, which is decide that you know what's best and damn anyone who doesn't agree. After you promised me you wouldn't. This isn't having the manager move a group of drunk diners, Vaughn. This is someone's life."

The words tore through me like bullets. Everything he'd said was true. And none of it was. How could I explain to him that the world wasn't fair? That it was all rigged anyway, and I was only doing what I could to tip it in the favor of someone I loved. That there was no honor in playing by the rules of a rigged game.

"William, pull over," I said softly.

I was sure he'd tell me to fuck myself since I'd just told him what to do, but apparently anger outweighed spite, because he pulled the car to the side of the road, and rocketed from his seat, slamming the door behind him, and I followed.

"I can't believe you," he ranted. "I honestly can't. I thought...I thought we were past this! I thought we agreed."

He was genuinely upset, and everything in me yearned to make it go away, if I only knew how. "I didn't...I didn't steal anything. I just—"

Will wheeled around and glared at me. "It's the same thing, Vaughn. You *did* steal something. You stole Lawson's right to his job, for one thing. My chance to handle my own problem, for another. People are not just chess pieces you get to manipulate! Or paintings you can shuffle around when the mood strikes you to redecorate. You—god, how dare you?"

I shut my mouth and I did what I rarely ever had to do. I forced myself to acknowledge that, from William's perspective, I had behaved badly. If he cared more about the unfairness perpetrated upon Lawson than on the fact that Lawson deserved it, there was nothing I could say to change his mind. William wasn't like me; he needed to trust the system. He needed to believe the rules and laws he worked to uphold every day meant something. Because if he stopped believing that, what would he have left? If I accepted Will as he was, I had to accept this about him too, no matter how much it hurt to see myself the way he saw me.

"I admit, I didn't consider it from your perspective," I

said slowly. "I hear where you're coming from. I apologize."

I put my hand on his shoulder, wishing desperately that we could start the whole day over again. Return to the morning sun peeking through the window of William's childhood bedroom and alighting on our intertwined bodies. To the minutes I'd spent watching him wake slowly, his face young in sleep, then irritated at the sun, then deeply, purely, almost heartbreakingly joyful when he opened his eyes and remembered that I was there. There was a softness to him at such moments that I stored deep inside, in a part of me no one had ever touched before. I wanted so desperately to take care of him. To make him happy. To give him everything.

If it were possible to create for him a world where things were fair and the rules did apply equally to people, I would have given up every scrap of wealth and comfort to do so. Tinkering behind the scenes to approximate one was all I could do. But I would give that up too, if it was what he wanted. If it would mean I could wake up with him like that every morning in the future.

"I need you to leave." William's tone was flat, his voice strangled.

"What?"

My heart began to pound and a vast emptiness opened where my stomach should be.

"I can't have you here," he said. "I can't...it's Thanksgiving, and my family, and—I need you to go because I can't deal with this here."

"William, I—"

He shook his head sharply and looked away, getting back in the car.

I stood for a moment, looking at the brown paper bags

in the back seat. Suddenly, I was overcome with the desire to be forced into eating those cold cuts. I would have given anything for the chance to make a face at their slimy texture and processed taste, and hear William call me a snob, smiling at me.

I slid into the car and he began to drive before I even had my seat belt on.

He pulled into the driveway and turned to me. His expression was tortured, his eyes tired. "Now, please," he said softly.

I reached out to cup his cheek and he didn't pull away. He just closed his eyes as if it were too much.

"If that's what you need," I murmured, and he nodded once. Then he set his mouth, grabbed the bags from the back seat, and blundered into the house without looking back, leaving me in the passenger seat.

CHAPTER 22

Will

THANKSGIVING WITH MY relatives was a nightmare, and all I wanted to do was wake up.

First, I'd had to tell my parents that Vaughn was gone, and why he'd had to leave so suddenly that he couldn't say goodbye or get the rest of his stuff. I didn't want to get into specifics, and "work emergency" was clearly not the real reason. My mother, bless her, took one look at my face and didn't ask. My father, well…he hadn't known what to make of anything about Vaughn from the minute we'd walked in, and Vaughn's exit was no exception.

Charlie, though. There was no getting around *her*.

She'd hauled me into her bedroom, still full of posters from her teenage obsession with Hole, and crossed her arms over her chest while she demanded to know "everything."

That was the problem. I couldn't tell Charlotte "everything." Because telling her everything meant starting with Vaughn's penchant for art theft, and his promise that he wouldn't ever steal again. With how I'd once called him a liar, and he'd just proven, once again, that he was.

"We had a fight," was all I'd allowed, followed by, "I don't want to talk about it right now."

If we'd been back in D.C., no doubt she would have ignored my protestations entirely and badgered me until I confessed. But we were at home, and at home we were a team. She had my back, and the second I gave her a plaintive look and said softly, "Please, Charlie," I knew she'd back off in favor of protecting me from our inquisitive family.

I didn't know how I'd managed to get through the family get-together without losing my mind. I stood there with a beer and nodded along with my uncle's hockey talk.

Every now and then, my eyes would search the room for Vaughn's tall form, his silver hair. Then I'd remember why and get another drink. I was torn between fury and loneliness, two terrible emotions that went terribly together. Everything made me think about Vaughn: the food, which he'd have hated and eaten without a complaint; my cousin Megan's long diatribe about the resurgence of nineties fashion, which would surely have inspired some hidden barb from Vaughn about my own lack of fashion sense; the game of euchre I lost because I could barely concentrate on my hand, at which Vaughn would have trounced everyone effortlessly. My father prided himself on his euchre skills, so I wished I could've seen that. Then I'd think about Lawson and get mad again, because how dare he do this? How dare he assume I couldn't take care of myself? How dare he play god?

Luckily, my family was used to me being the quiet one, and with Charlie there to distract them with stories, it wasn't so different than any other holiday.

And that was the problem. This one was supposed to be different. This was supposed to be the one where I introduced my boyfriend to my parents—the boyfriend I'd been thinking more and more about asking to live with me. And not because rent in D.C. was outrageous, which had been my reason for moving in with Harris. No, this time I wanted to live with someone because I loved him and wanted to share a life with him.

I was in my room, packing my things and Vaughn's in a larger suitcase, and Charlie couldn't have picked a worse moment to barge in, because she found me standing with Vaughn's shirt in my hand, my eyes burning.

"Jesus, can you knock, Charlotte!"

"Oh my god," she said, when she got a look at me. "What *happened*?"

"I told you I didn't want to talk about it. Still don't."

"But you look miserable." Her eyes searched mine. "Is it—it's not over, right?"

The thought of that nearly brought me to my knees, but what the fuck choice did I have? How could I stay with someone I couldn't trust?

"I don't know," I said honestly. "I really don't. And please, I can't—" My voice got choked. "I can't."

"Okay." My sister knew the last thing I'd want was a hug, so she backed off and left me alone, closing the door softly behind her.

I pressed Vaughn's shirt to my nose, inhaled his scent, and cried. I'd hoped it would make me feel better, but it didn't. Not at all.

✧   ✧   ✧

MY SISTER'S UNDERSTANDING of my need to be left alone with my emotional turmoil lasted exactly one week before she started badgering me to talk. I put her off without much creativity, citing a huge case at work and a dead phone battery. I knew I didn't have long before she'd find a way to corner me.

Honestly, it was only the holiday season that was keeping her from showing up at my door. Her days and nights were full, so I was safe—for the moment.

I'd thrown myself into work manically, but my last two cases had been clear-cut instances of insurance fraud. I knew I should've been glad that I'd prevented people from getting away with fraud, but instead I wished I would get assigned something on par with the Gardner Heist, to really take my mind off things.

Vaughn had texted me apologies, and left voice mails on my cell, which I hadn't listened to because I didn't think I could handle his drawl in my ear without breaking. He hadn't tried calling me on my office phone; still, every time it rang my heart pounded and my mouth went dry as I thought about what I'd do if it was him. Every time it wasn't, I was breathless with relief—but I couldn't deny that I was disappointed too.

Finally, afraid I was going to lose my mind, I sent him a text asking him to give me some time to think without contacting me; that I'd be in touch when I was ready to talk. I half expected him to ignore my request—maybe I half hoped too—but he didn't. My phone was bereft of messages, and though I'd gotten just what I'd asked for, it made me feel worse.

When Charlie showed up at my apartment the day before Christmas, armed with Thai food and determination, I was such a wreck that I was a little bit glad to see her. Because if she was here, that meant she was going to make me talk. And if I talked, maybe…I didn't know.

"No more hiding, and you're talking," she bossed, waving a carton of khao phat at me. "Or you don't get this."

I'd barely tasted anything I'd eaten for weeks, so it wouldn't matter. But that sounded too pathetic to admit, so I just leaned against my door and stared at her, making a last-ditch effort to look mad. "If I wanted you to come over and talk to me, I would have asked you."

She rolled her eyes. "In what reality would you ever do that? Come on, Will. I know you're miserable. Look at you." She chewed on her lip. "He's miserable too."

My sister had been doing a lot of work for Vaughn, including some winter fundraiser thing, so I guessed she must have seen him and that was how she'd know.

"Well, it's his fault." Great. I sounded like I was twelve. This was exactly why I hadn't wanted to talk to her.

"What happened? I've never seen you with someone who just…you guys just *worked*," she said, and I felt my stupid stomach drop, felt a burn in my eyes, and wished she would stop talking.

Just like the millions of times I'd wished for that growing up, it didn't work.

She went to the kitchen, telling me all sorts of things about relationships needing challenges to function, that whatever happened we could work through. I wondered how the hell she knew about any of these things, since, of the two of us, I was the only one who'd ever had a relationship last longer than a few months. We weren't easy to be with, us Foxes.

"I just don't get it," she said, dumping the khao phat into a bowl and pushing it at me. "Did he cheat on you?"

Her eyes narrowed. "Because if he did, fuck that guy and don't take him back."

"He didn't cheat on me," I assured her. Oddly, that had never been something I'd worried about with Vaughn. "He—it's not really something I feel comfortable explaining."

"Tough. You're so miserable I can barely stand to look at you. Tell me why."

I caved. Of course I did. Oh, I put up a good front at first and tried to get her to leave me alone, but it didn't work. It never did. Finally, I gave up and came clean about our fight at Thanksgiving.

She listened to me tell her how he'd gotten Lawson transferred with a surprised expression. "Wait, what? How did he even do that?"

"He's rich," I said, shrugging. "That's how."

"It's not enough to be rich. You need like...an in or something. With the FBI."

I recalled the diversity training in Durham, and how I'd seen Vaughn speaking to the deputy director.

"I think he does have a contact. But it doesn't matter—even if he didn't, he'd get one. You don't know Vaughn. When he's determined, he makes it happen. He doesn't give up."

"Wasn't that guy a dick though?" My sister frowned. "Lawson. He hit on me that one time and you went ballistic."

"I did not go ballistic. I just told you why you should throw a drink in his face and tell him to fuck off."

"That's the Will Fox version of ballistic," she pointed out. "But, like...why are you so mad about this? It seems like a bit of an overreaction."

This was the part that was hard to explain, without getting into Vaughn's less-than-legal activities with art. "Because, Charlie, it's patronizing and manipulative, and it shows lack of moral character—"

"To not want your boyfriend harassed by a homophobic jerk every day?" Charlie interrupted, scoffing. "That shows a lack of moral character, really?"

"No. Treating people like he can manipulate them as he sees fit," I bit out, shoving my bowl aside. It tasted like dust, anyway. Spicy dust. "Like my life is something he can step in and rearrange to his pleasure. *That* shows a lack of moral character."

"I mean, I get that," she said slowly, but she still sounded unsure of what my problem was, looking at me with raised eyebrows while eating my abandoned khao phat.

"Amory's used to getting what he wants, Charlie. And he thinks the rules don't apply to him. That's the opposite of what I believe. Maybe we're just too different to work."

"Maybe you are," she said, and it knocked the air out of me to think it. "I saw that. But I saw your face just now. You aren't done with him, Will. No way. So, listen, bro. You think in absolutes. See the world in black and white. Stuff is right or wrong, people are criminals or victims, et cetera. Vaughn strikes me as a gray area kind of guy. Of course that's gonna mean disagreements about stuff. But, honestly? You could use a little damn gray in your life because otherwise…"

"What?"

She shook her head, shoving food in her mouth instead.

"Charlotte, what?"

"Fine, Jesus." Her eyes flashed. "Otherwise you're gonna end up like Dad!"

That had *not* been what I expected to hear.

"What the hell, Charlie? I'm nothing like Dad and you know it!"

"Yes, you are, babe. You have these...rigid ideas about people. How they should act, how they're allowed to fit into your world. Sure, maybe your ideas aren't the same ideas as Dad's, but it's still this way of meeting people with ultimatums."

I opened my mouth to argue, but nothing came out but a harsh, choked noise. That had hit a bit too close to home.

"And if people don't conform to your ideas, you walk away. Just like you did at Thanksgiving. But sometimes you have to hash stuff out. You have to try and understand that the end result isn't all that matters. That sometimes the *reasons* why people do things count for something. You want to know what I really think?"

"Christ, all this has been you pulling punches?" I scowled at the countertop where a few grains of rice clung to the faded tile. Charlie ignored me.

"The truth is, I don't think Vaughn lets you get away with thinking in absolutes and I bet that scares the shit out of you."

"He got someone *reassigned to a different state* because of his last name and his bank account," I reminded her. "After I'd told him to stop manipulating me. That is pretty fucking black, sis. No grays there."

"And *again*, I say, yeah, that might be a factual description of what he did. Sometimes the facts aren't the only important thing. Sometimes the motivation has to count for something. Only you can decide if you think Vaughn's motivation really was to try and…control you, or whatever. Is that who he is?" She shrugged. "Your call. But given that you've spent the time since Thanksgiving looking like you were gonna puke at the idea of not being with him, you probably owe it to both of you to at least think it through. To at least talk to him. Rather than throw him out of Mom and Dad's house and then refuse to ever see him again. Jesus, dramatic move, P.S. At least now I know that nothing I ever do at a family holiday, short of fucking on the kitchen table, will make Mom and Dad think I'm the one with issues."

She smirked. My head was spinning.

"Maybe I'm just trying to keep myself from getting hurt."

"Too late, babe," she said softly, and I slumped back against the counter and didn't look at her for a minute.

"Yeah," I breathed, and knuckled dampness out of my eyes.

"I'm sorry, bro." Charlotte and I reached for each other's hands at the same moment, clasping them over the bowls of food. "You really love him, don't you?"

I nodded and shrugged helplessly.

"Sometimes we have to bend a little bit—compromise what we think we know—for love. It's scary as hell, but what's the alternative? Keep living your black-and-white life and never see Vaughn again."

My eyes flew to her face as I felt panic set in at the thought of never seeing Vaughn again. Never feeling his silken hair twine around my fingers. Never feeling his warmth at my back as he leaned in to whisper something in my ear. Never lying with him and hearing the moment that his breathing changed and he drifted off to sleep, trusting, in my arms.

I couldn't stand it.

"*Or*," Charlie said, leaning in and looking at me intently, "you could go find him, and see if there's a way to make it work. A possibility that you can give up a little bit of this uncompromising version of yourself and still be okay. It *is* okay, you know?"

"What?"

"It's okay to give yourself permission not to be a hundred percent perfect and noble and *correct* all the damn time."

Her voice was fond and exasperated. The voice of some-one who saw me more clearly than I could see myself. And with far more empathy.

There it was: the truth. I *wanted* to forgive Vaughn. Just like I'd wanted to ignore the fact he'd stolen art. But if I let myself do that...if I allowed myself to deviate from the path I'd set out upon...what would that make me? Who the hell was I if I wasn't the one who upheld the law, who followed the rules, who kept everyone—and everything—safe? My head swam and then Charlie's arms were around me and she was squeezing me so tight I could hardly breathe, the way she had when we were kids.

I hugged her back. "I'm still mad you think I'm like Dad," I muttered.

"Dad has his good points, Will. He was a cop and he helped a lot of people, just like you do. You both helped people by following the rules. But hey, take it from me. I make people happy by bringing them light and color and joy, delicious food and perfectly box-pleated table linens." She smiled at me. "And if something doesn't work, I change it until it does."

We pulled apart, and I took a deep breath. "You, uh…you said he's miserable?"

"As a raincloud." She raised her eyebrow and I leaned in before I could stop myself. "He's moping at his place in Jackson Hole. Wyoming. Been there for days and planning to stay until after the holidays."

The idea of Vaughn all alone for Christmas ended me. Charlie and I had planned to spend the day together, but it was obvious she wanted me to go off and retrieve my estranged boyfriend instead. I frowned, something nagging at the tiny part of my brain that wasn't relegated to being sad and conflicted. If Vaughn was at the Jackson Hole property, then Charlie *hadn't* seen him while working on the fundraiser. In which case… "How do you know he's miserable and that I'm not answering his text messages?"

She bit her lip. "Um."

"Has he called you?" I asked, furious all over again. "See, Charlie, that's what I'm talking about! He wants something, so he—"

She didn't let me or my righteous indignation get very far. "Stop, stop, Jesus, no. Natalie told me," she interrupted.

"His assistant? He had his *assistant* call you?" I didn't know if that made me more angry, or less.

"You're doing it again, brother mine," she sighed. "Natalie and I…so, actually, guess what? I'm dating someone, ta da! Natalie. I'm dating Natalie, and she told me. About Vaughn being miserable, and where he's spending the holiday."

Wait, what? "You're—since when?" I blinked.

"Before Thanksgiving. I was gonna tell you, but…" She

shrugged. "Your drama happened."

I scowled, but it made sense. Something had to have been distracting her or she'd have been over here badgering me a lot sooner than the day before Christmas, busy work schedule or no. "Is she—is it serious?"

"It's been like a month," she said dryly. "But I like her a lot. We…" She blushed and cleared her throat. "We, uh. Get along. Anyway, she really likes Vaughn. I do too. I mean, yeah, I get that he fucked up. But Will, he loves you. And if you think about it, it's kinda romantic." She gave me a poignant look. "Besides, don't lie. You're thrilled that Lawson guy's gone. So get off your high horse, cowboy, and go rope your man."

"Go away," I said, drawing her back for a long hug. "Thanks, Charlie."

"You're welcome. You're a good person. A kind and fair person, and I'm not trying to say you should immediately forgive him but…don't miss out on being happy if you can. Life's too short, and all that." She kissed me on the cheek, hugged me one last time, and then left with the remainder of my khao phat.

I sat at my kitchen counter for a long time, then finally broke the cookie in half and read my fortune.

Someone replaced your fortune with this one. Your luck sucks.

For the first time in weeks, I smiled.

Then I went to the bedroom, threw a few things into a backpack, and went to check on flights.

I'd make my own luck, thanks.

CHAPTER 23

Vaughn

ONE NIGHT, YEARS ago, when I couldn't sleep, I'd turned on the television and flipped channels, just looking for something soothing and mindless that might lull me. I didn't know what movie I'd stopped on, just that when I came in, a character was sitting on a bench in Central Park, in the snow, staring moodily at the twinkling lights in the distance, and commenting that Christmas felt ten times more depressing than other days if you had to spend it alone. I'd snorted at the screen and changed the channel, because as someone who was often alone on Christmas, or at an impersonal but obligatory party, I didn't find Christmas to be depressing at all. It was just another day.

Now I knew better. I knew that if you were alone on Christmas when you'd hoped to spend it with the person you loved—with the person you were *in* love with and had disgusted—then it was true. Christmas truly was horribly depressing.

Ever since William had ejected me from his family Thanksgiving, I'd felt the kind of reeling dislocation I'd only ever felt after my parents died. Untethered, freewheeling, vertiginous.

I'd made my way back to D.C. in a daze and I'd called and texted William more times than I could count, needing to believe that it had just been a fight; that after a cooling-off period, he'd forgive me. At first he hadn't answered. Then, when he'd told me he needed time to think, the cold had set in. He didn't tell me how much time he needed, or what my chances were of having my sentence commuted. All I knew was that in the span of one day, I'd gone from making love to William in his childhood bed to worrying that I might never see him again.

So I had done what any man possessed of a fortune, a broken heart, and a lack of familial obligations would do: I ran away and hid in my Jackson Hole chalet for Christmas. And I took the cat.

Ordinarily, when I spent time at the property I had a housekeeper, to have food on hand, prepare the rooms, cook for my guests, and do light cleaning. I'd never been there by myself before, and the last thing I wanted was for my misery to be observed, or—far worse—to have to speak to anyone. I had never had the slightest problem exchanging pleasantries, and I'd never had much by way of misery to hide. But now, I felt like…well, like William, grumbling about how he'd used a self-checkout machine to avoid a social interaction. Only worse. Much, much worse.

No, I'd simply placed an order from the grocery store (and one from the liquor store) to be waiting for me when I arrived, and instructed the property manager to stock up on firewood, make up one of the bedrooms, and turn the heat on. Then I'd gotten on a plane, cat carrier in hand, and done what I had been raised to do: smooth the road of pain by paying for every possible discomfort to be removed. I'd arrived three days ago. Four days before Christmas. Which meant that Christmas was now tomorrow, and I had done nothing for the past seventy-two hours besides drink hot toddies, eat the prepared food I'd found in the refrigerator, stare into the fire, and watch the Home and Garden channel—it soothed me, slightly.

Audrey had prowled around, meowing at the snow and exploring her new surroundings our first night here, and then, as if she'd sensed my mood, had eaten her tins of expensive food, and curled up on whatever piece of furniture I'd been sulking on, suffering herself to be petted whenever I needed soothing.

Today though, walking through the empty rooms of the chalet, I was suddenly angry. Angry not at William, who, I'd admitted to myself, had every right to be hurt by what I'd done. Angry at myself for not doing better risk assessment. For not realizing before it was too late that Will, for better or for worse, saw the world a certain way. And that it was part of what I loved about him.

I'd wanted to make work a place where he could be safe, be himself, be happy. But I had interceded with the powers that ran his world, and no matter what the reason, no matter what my intentions, that was what struck him to his core. I had taken away his ability to trust the thing in his life he most needed to trust. And I'd done it, frankly, with about as much thought as swatting a fly.

And there was fuck-all I could do about it until William decided he was ready to talk. So, here I was. Alone with our cat. At Christmas. In Wyoming. Looking out the window at the snow falling softly on one of the most beautiful views I'd ever seen. And I couldn't appreciate it at all.

I sighed, shut the blinds on the beauty of the sunset over the mountains, and slumped on the couch with the last of the prepared ravioli, which I didn't bother to heat up. I would just sit here, and eat, and drink whiskey, and pet Audrey, and watch the Home and Garden channel Christmas specials, and feel exceedingly sorry for myself until I fell asleep.

I was two whiskeys down and had finished the cold ravioli when I heard the unlikely hum of a car on the long, winding driveway from the main road. Audrey's ears perked up. Whatever wrong turn these holidaymakers had taken, I prayed they were just using the drive to turn around and I wasn't about to end up playing host to a woman going into surprise labor in the snow outside my front door. Of course, perhaps I'd get lucky and it would be a murderer, intent on putting me out of my misery.

But then Audrey bounded to the front door. Trusting her instincts more than my own, I dragged myself upright enough to peer out the window. The car was a white Nissan, totally nondescript, nearly invisible in the snow, and it was… Jesus, it was parking in front of the house. Not quite subtle enough for a robbery. Believe me, I knew. A murder, however…well, I couldn't say.

But the man who emerged from the driver's side door? He had already as good as killed me.

It was William.

My heart started pounding so violently that I had the brief, irritated thought that I was far too young for a heart attack. This was followed by the petty thought that surely, if William were to watch me drop dead of a heart attack through the window, he would regret our fight.

Oh, Vaughn, you are not in a good place.

Will dithered between the car and the stoop, turning to look at the mountains rising behind him, then at the sharp crescent of moon cutting through the starry sky. I could almost feel his reaction to the natural beauty around him, and I wished so badly that I had simply brought him here, for Christmas, to enjoy the snow.

Audrey went up on her hind legs, scrabbling at the windowpane excitedly with her front claws. I didn't have her certainty of reception.

Finally, William took a deep breath and walked to the door. He stomped snow off his boots before he rang the bell. Such a good, midwestern boy. I paused for a moment, taking a deep breath. I had never felt uncertain with William before, and I disliked it immensely.

But the moment I opened the door and saw him looking at me, all uncertainty evaporated in the face of conviction. I *would* make this right again. I *would* have Christmas here with the man I loved. I *would* fix this, no matter what I had to do.

"Umm. Hi," Will said. He was wearing jeans and boots and a heavy winter coat, but carried only a backpack. He looked tired, but his eyes were sharp, taking in everything.

"Come inside, love," I said.

Will swallowed hard and stepped over the threshold. Audrey immediately twined around his ankles, rubbing her face on his jeans, then jumping backward when she got snow on her nose.

"Hi, baby," he cooed to Audrey, crouching to scratch under her chin the way she liked. "Hi, cat. I missed you." She purred loudly.

I'd never been so jealous in my life.

"I—Natalie told Charlie you were here," William blurted.

"I shall have to have a word with Natalie about the propriety of divulging my whereabouts."

"They're dating. Natalie and Charlie. So I guess that's why."

"I'm very happy for them. But I do take my privacy quite seriously." Will stood and I took his backpack from his hand and put it on the side table. "Not that I've ever wanted privacy from you."

He slumped. "We need to talk." My shoulders tightened. "But not now, okay? I'm exhausted and you're..." He regarded me. "You're a mess, aren't you?" He sounded surprised at that.

I did feel rather at loose ends, but I'd thought I had hidden it fairly well.

"You messed me up," I confessed, but confessional wasn't a genre I did very well, and it sounded ironic, quippy, and William glared at me.

"We can talk in the morning," he said.

"Only one bedroom is made up," I told him. I was shooting for flirtatious, but apparently all my calibrations were off tonight.

"I know how to make a bed, Amory," Will said shortly.

But. He had called me Amory, and I saw the moment his words caught up with him and he realized it.

I tried not to feel betrayed and resentful when Audrey slept with William. I failed.

CHAPTER 24

Vaughn

I WOKE WITH a head full of cotton and the distinct sense that I had forgotten to do something important. It was early—out the window, the sun still fell weakly upon the snow—and I should've gone back to sleep. But then, as if we were magnets, I felt Will's presence in the house. I could see him, tucked up in the room at the end of the hall, backpack resting on the chair. Had he even brought pajamas, or had he fled D.C. in a hurry, leaving him naked in my bed? The wrong one of my beds, yes, but it was a vast improvement. He had come here. I could work with that.

As I showered off the week's downward spiral, I gave myself a stern lecture to listen to what he had to say, even if I already knew I'd been wrong. To let him take the lead, since I'd already bungled things so badly.

When I went into the kitchen in the hopes of finding something to make us for breakfast though, William was already there.

"Morning," he said.

In the thin sunlight coming through the windows, I could see lines of stress and exhaustion on his face. I could see pain there, and regret. And, as I stepped closer and he looked up from fiddling with the coffee maker, I thought I saw hope there too.

"I couldn't fall back asleep," he said, gesturing to the appliance as if his lack of a healthy eight hours were what was interfering with his inability to make it function. "I made a fire and fed the cat," he added.

I took over for him, measuring out the espresso, adjusting the levers. But he didn't move far away, and I took a chance that perhaps that meant something. He let me run my palm over his cheek, let me look at him. I ran a thumb over his eyebrow, and pushed his hair back where it fell softly across his forehead.

I could see a hundred thoughts that he wanted to voice, but he closed his eyes and sighed.

"I can't believe you came here," I said.

"You're not the only one who can be impulsive."

Oh, William, bravado even in the midst of exhaustion. I couldn't help but smile.

"Besides," he said, scuffing a wool-socked toe on the wood floor. "Never mind." Then, "It's Christmas," he said, finally.

A chill that I hadn't known I'd carried since Thanksgiving eased off, replaced by the warmth of Will's words. He hadn't wanted to be alone for Christmas; he'd wanted to be with me.

"I didn't want you to be alone," he said. And warmth of a different kind filled me. William wanting me was one thing. William wanting me to have him? That was everything.

"William, I—" The words lodged in my throat like too many people through the same doorway, and I fell silent. I had spoken extemporaneously to international crowds in the thousands, tipsy; I had delivered speeches that would net the foundation hundreds of millions of dollars. I had delivered the eulogies at both my parents' funerals.

But these words, in this conversation, would be the most important ones I'd ever uttered. Because they had the power lose or gain me William Fox.

Will's eyes, skin beneath bruised from lack of sleep, lines around them visible in the morning sun, met mine hesitantly and before I knew what I was doing, I pressed my thumbs to those blue shadows, like I could erase the evidence of every moment of pain I had caused him, every scrap of unrest. I forced my tongue to unstick itself and my lips to part.

"I'm sorry," I said simply. "I'm sorry, and you were right."

William's eyes went wide, and I wondered if he'd not anticipated I could admit when I was wrong.

"I saw a problem—something that was hurting you— and I only thought about how I could fix it. Not because I don't think you can handle yourself. You're the most competent person I've ever met. But because it made me feel good to fix it for you. Because I wanted you to be safe and happy. I didn't think about the part where I didn't ask you what you wanted."

"Or the part where you used your considerable wealth and influence to game the system," Will reminded me hotly.

"Or the part where I used my considerable wealth and influence to subtly influence the system," I echoed. And was that just the hint of a smirk playing at the corners of his mouth?

I poured us both espresso, Will's half-warm milk, and

mine with a spoonful of sugar, and sat down at the kitchen table, setting Will's drink across from me. If we were going to hash this out, we would do it here, face to face and within an arm's length of the coffee maker.

"You get why that's not okay now?" he asked.

"Look, William, you know me. You know my background and how I see the world, and I won't patronize you by trying to tell you that I'm a different person than I was a month ago. This isn't about what is or isn't okay in terms of ethics. We know ours aren't precisely aligned. This is about what we can demand of each other. What we need to trust each other. And I can promise you that I now fully get why what I did was a huge mistake because of what *you* think isn't okay. And I will always respect what you need from me. I won't use my powers for evil where you're concerned again. I promise you."

He did smile a little at that, though he tried to hide it in his espresso. "I, uh, I talked to Charlotte. Who pointed out that I might not have given enough credence to the idea that you really were trying to do something you thought was helpful for me. I get that you wanted to make my problem go away. But I care more about being able to solve my own problems than about them disappearing."

"I understand that now."

"Which isn't to say that, upon reflection, I'm not glad that asshole's gone. I think maybe..." He ran a fingertip along the rim of his cup, and shrugged. "I think I was mad at myself too. Because I *was* glad he was gone and I shouldn't have been. I don't want to be that person. The person who upholds the rules for everyone else but lets himself off the hook. It's not...I can't be that person. And that's why you—"

William locked eyes with me, and the confusion there was painful to see. "You fuck me up, Amory. You fuck me up, and I...I like it. And sometimes I worry that I don't know how to stay me with how *much* I like it."

I reached across the table and took both of his hands in mine. They were trembling.

"You are a deeply ethical person, William Fox. The fact that you can acknowledge conflict in yourself doesn't make you less ethical. It makes you honest and brave. And the fact that you want to make sure you hold yourself to the same— Jesus holy Christ, the same *soaring* standards to which you hold the world?" I shook my head. "You amaze me. Your ethics may not be mine, but I can't express how much I respect you for them."

William flushed red and squeezed my hands, mouth opening and closing a few times before any words came out. "I don't want you to change as a person. I...I love who you are. I just can't be with someone who manipulates me."

"I see that now," I said. "I swear to you."

"Okay," he said, voice small. He didn't quite meet my eyes.

"Okay?"

"Okay, I want us to..." He made a *go on* gesture and rolled his eyes. "Endure."

I couldn't help but laugh. "You want us to *endure*? Like our relationship is torture?"

He turned even redder. "You know what I mean."

"You mean you want to be mine again," I said, voice darkly teasing, "and for me to be yours."

"Yes, if you *must* put it that way. And if we can agree that in the future, all problems will be handled together."

"As a team," I murmured. I liked the sound of that.

"Yeah. Also," Will added, his face the very picture of a man who'd held off saying something for a long time. "Also, just *please* keep your promise about not stealing things, because I don't think you'd do well in prison, and now I know how much being without you sucks."

"Actually, I think I would do quite well in prison."

Will's eyes went huge, just as I'd intended.

"Joking, love." Though, in fact, I *did* believe I was more suited to the psychological mind games inherent in the caste system of prison than most. But that wasn't the point.

William glared.

"Do you want to know why I steal things?" I had never put it so baldly, and William froze. "Stole things, I should say. Not," I clarified, "that I've done it often."

He nodded.

"You're not wearing a wire, are you?"

And, oh, how I had missed his smile while we were apart.

"The thrill of the steal is in changing the terms of the game. Breaking the rule that says what is someone else's cannot be mine. It's covetousness. Not of the object itself, but of the ability to remake the world. A painting hanging on a wall could be removed by anyone, but no one does. Not because of security but because of an acceptance of the rule that they cannot. But I can. I did. And in those moments, the art ceases to be art and becomes proof that the world can always change. That with the willingness to interrogate even the things that seem set in stone, fewer things are fixed than we might realize."

Will was gaping at me like I was talking nonsense.

"I realize that you probably thought it was because

someone who grew up with wealth would only want that which money could not buy, am I right?"

Will nodded reluctantly.

"No." I cupped his face in my palms. "Do you know the other thing that feels like it dismantled all the rules? Feels like it has the power to prove to me that the world can always change?"

He was frozen. He shook his head, but I thought that he did know.

"Love, William. Stealing your heart feels like the greatest theft I have ever perpetrated."

Will was half laughing, half sobbing, and definitely glaring at me in the process. Also smiling. His face couldn't decide what it wanted to do. And I loved all of it.

I loved William Fox like the rip of lightning through a sky I thought would always be dark. Like a shout echoed back to me from a great depth, rounded by distance and time, but still recognizable. Yes, like the most perfect of perfect thefts. The ones I would never admit to, never acknowledge. The ones where something called to me where before there was only silence and emptiness and here, here, here was the thing that would shine on it with beauty.

"You're—I—How do you—What—" Will spluttered. "The things you say should be ridiculous, but I—"

He shook his head and then grabbed me, practically dragging me across the table so he could get at my mouth. When my hipbone hit the edge painfully, I pulled him up.

We kissed in a way we had never kissed before, because now we knew what it was to lose each other.

I craved Will's mouth and his taste with a hunger that was part lust and part relief, and I could feel his echoing desire in the way his hands clutched at my shirt, tangled in my hair. We were trying to fuse ourselves together into a form that couldn't be rent apart.

The living room was warm from the fire, so rather than move to a bedroom, I pushed Will down onto the rug and stripped his sweats off. Audrey was perched on the arm of the chair closest to the fire. She lifted her chin off her paws to glance at us when we entered the room, then ignored us.

"Tell me this isn't really a bearskin rug, because if it is I can't stand the irony of actually fucking here," William said.

"Clearly you know nothing about animals," I said with a bite to his neck. "This is a snow leopard."

Will's head snapped up. "Vaughn!" He sounded horrified. "Aren't those endangered?"

I laughed, and buried my face in his neck again. I had missed this gullible, principled, rigid man so much.

"Oh, you're joking," he huffed.

I kissed him on the mouth, drinking in the taste of him, then moved back to his neck, kissing and biting until he shuddered. He rolled on top of me and pulled my pajamas off, flinging them carelessly, then immediately looking behind him to make sure they hadn't landed too close to the fire. The pants had landed half on Audrey, but she didn't seem to care. When William had ascertained we were safe from living room conflagration, he turned his attention to kindling a conflagration between us. His mouth and hands were everywhere, the ends of his carelessly growing-out hair trailing over my stomach, my thighs, my cock, as he moved over me.

"I need you, love," I said as he kissed the sensitive inside of my thigh. "Show me how it can be between us. Show me we'll be okay."

They weren't words I could have imagined ever saying to another soul. Reassurance wasn't anything I'd ever needed or desired before. But now I wanted to know, beyond the shadow of a doubt, that William was with me. That we could make something together. Love, a life, a future. All of it.

Will nodded, pupils blown, cheeks and chest flushed. "Stay where you are."

"That works better with handcuffs, William." I winked as he flushed even deeper. "And I think the word you're looking for is *freeze*."

"I'm not a cop, Vaughn," he scoffed.

"Does that mean we can't play cops and robbers anymore?"

It was probably too soon to be joking about that, but the teasing words had left my mouth before I realized what I was saying, and I cringed internally, blaming my erection, which had clearly drained all the blood from my brain. I shook my head to dismiss the shadow from between us.

"I didn't mean that," I said.

"I know." Will bit his lip. "It's good it's a joke, maybe. Because it means that's all over now. Stealing and manipulating." His voice was uncertain, and I nodded, wanting to reassure him. "Vaughn," he said, and he sounded scared.

"It is, you're right. I made you a promise. And I intend to honor it."

He nodded.

"Call me by my name," I said softly.

"Amory." It was a whisper in my ear, a kiss to my throat, a warm hand on my erection, the pleasure of the word and his body flaring to life. I moaned at it, and then he was on me, mouth on mine, hands everywhere, grinding our erections together so hard I slid across the rug.

"Can we fuck on this thing?" Will panted. "Not like the one in your apartment?"

I nodded and pulled him closer. "Yes, fuck me, William. Fuck me on this rug—which, for the record, is organic cotton, not fur. Fuck me just like this."

He slicked his cock with his precome, eyelids fluttering at his touch, then he paused. "Do I need a condom?"

"No," I said firmly. "No, of course not."

I could see the relief in his eyes that I hadn't been with anyone else, and I felt my own relief that even if I had, he would have wanted me regardless.

He slid inside me with nothing but spit and precome between us, and we both groaned at the intense friction. But everything about his body around me, inside me, felt right.

"Your hair, god," he muttered as he slid out and thrust back inside me slowly.

He ran shaky fingers through my hair, which had spread out on the rug. As I relaxed around him, he started thrusting harder, and waves of pleasure spread through me. My swollen cock was trapped between us, but I ignored it, focusing on the trails of fire running from my ass to my belly to my erection. William sped up and slowed down, kissing my mouth and running his palms down my ribs, his breath heavy. Then he changed his angle and I seized around him in pleasure. He cried out, and his control snapped.

He grabbed my hips and started a series of deep, long thrusts that had me lust-drunk and breathless. Then he nailed my prostate with quick thrusts and my head went fuzzy, unable to focus on anything but William's hands on my skin and William's cock inside me.

"I love you," I said. "I'll always love you."

He cried out and squeezed his eyes shut. "Oh, god, yes," he panted, and when he looked at me again, his eyes were wet. He leaned down to kiss me, and the friction of his firm stomach on my erection was too much.

"William, please, fuck!"

"I love you so much," he gasped, then he grabbed my cock, his grip almost painful as he jerked my flesh and pumped into me. My orgasm was a blizzard, an avalanche, the crack of a cleaving iceberg. It was a raging fire. Sharp relief and hot pleasure crashed around me, obliterating everything. I came in Will's hand, pulsing hotly between our bellies as every muscle clenched. Will groaned, bit my neck, and came, his peak a rush of heat deep inside me, as if he could blast away everything that wasn't him, that wasn't us.

His hips stuttered and he shuddered in pleasure against me. My skin was humming with the satisfaction of orgasm and of Will's body splayed over mine where he'd collapsed. We lay like that for a few minutes before cleaning up, and sank back down on the sofa, pulling a blanket around us.

"It's Christmas," William said after a while.

I looked around at the house. We had no tree, no lights, no decorations. No food, even, unless you counted things that came in boxes and cans, which I certainly did not. I didn't even have a gift for William. It wasn't how Christmas should be. Especially our first Christmas.

"I'm so sorry, love," I said. "Sorry I don't have anything. I can sort it out though, I promise. I can call the property manager, and order us more groceries, and maybe even get a tree delivered. We can—"

William silenced me with a hand over my mouth.

"First of all, stop it, because you're not calling some poor guy to do your bidding on *Christmas* because he's probably celebrating *Christmas*. Besides, the stores aren't open—seriously, have you ever had to live in the world? Second of all, that's not what I meant. I was actually going to say we should watch *Gremlins* because it's the best Christmas movie."

I quirked a doubtful eyebrow at this evaluation, but Will continued.

"I don't care about any of that stuff, anyway. I just want to be here with you. And the cat. I was...really scared, Amory."

I knew William would never admit to that kind of fear lightly, and I kissed his cheek. "I was too."

We sat together for a while, looking at the fire and the quiet world outside. As new snow began to fall, Audrey tried to bat at it through the window before losing interest and curling up again in front of the fire.

"I don't even have a present for you," I said regretfully. It was hard to get William to accept anything he didn't strictly need, and Christmas would have been one of the few times he might have done so gracefully.

"Me neither," he said. "I was going to get Charlie to help me brainstorm at Thanksgiving, but..."

I made a dismissive noise. "You don't have to get me anything."

Will turned to face me. "I know," he said. "You don't have to get me anything either. You know that isn't how this works, right?"

"What do you mean?"

"I mean that I'm going to take care of you too, Amory. You don't have to be so…alone anymore. Neither of us do."

William's words resounded in my head like an echo chamber.

If he'd asked me to, I'd have found a way to get him everything. I'd have braved the snowy roads into town, tried every store until I found one that would open for me, and returned with my hands full of a Christmas that I could give to him, spread out before him and offer him like it was pieces of myself.

But this was William. That wasn't what he wanted. What he needed. He didn't want to be given anything. He wanted us to share.

"I know what I want for Christmas," I said, my voice cracking in a very un-Vaughn-like way. "What I want for *us* for Christmas."

"What?"

William twined our fingers together on his knee.

I chose my words carefully, not wanting to mess this up with implications he might bristle at. I wanted to make it perfect.

"I want us to be together. To live together. To share everything, to…" How had he put it? "I want us to take care of each other."

Will's eyes widened, then softened, then narrowed in suspicion. God, he was so beautifully, achingly easy to read.

"You're not buying some monstrously expensive mansion for us, so don't think for a second—"

"William, I already *have* a monstrously expensive mansion. And I would love if maybe you might consider that your home too, on the weekends. But I know you need to be near work. I thought we could find an apartment together. In whatever neighborhood you want. Whatever's most convenient."

He bit his lip the way he did when he wanted something he wasn't sure he should want. To eat all the homemade candy on Halloween. To role-play arresting me. To love me.

"Okay, but we *have* to contribute the same amount to rent."

"Well, real estate is such a good investment, and—"

He shook his head. "No. I thought we were taking care of each *other*."

I thought about it. How to express to William how little the money meant to me. But, ah, it meant more to him.

"I think," I said, "that we each bring different things to this partnership. You would let Charlotte plan a party for you, since she enjoys it and has the skills to do so, wouldn't you?"

Will nodded.

"And Charlotte would allow you to investigate a theft that occurred at the party, would she not?"

He nodded again.

"And you wouldn't consider it an unequal partnership. From each according to her ability, to each according to her needs."

He shook his head at me. "Are you seriously quoting Marx to me right now?"

"Marx was an extremely adroit thinker."

"Yes, I'm sure the Vaughn Foundation billions were built on the principles of communism." Will snorted.

"You laugh, my dear, but I make money in order to give

it away. And, all right, to attempt to buy an apartment for myself and my partner, if he'll let me."

Will rolled his eyes, but leaned into me.

"Negotiations over?"

Suddenly serious, Will said, "You know that I would love you if you had nothing, don't you?"

My heart stuttered. I did know, but hearing it filled me with peace. "And you know that I would divest every dime if it meant I could keep you, don't you?"

We kissed, clinging to each other, then broke apart, both nodding.

"Is that a yes?" I asked, at the same time William said, "Okay, let's do it."

We laughed, giddy as children, as the fire cast our joined shadow against the wall.

DEAR READER,

Thank you so much for reading *Heart of the Steal*! We hope you enjoyed Will and Vaughn's story. If you did, consider spreading the word! You can help others find this book by writing reviews, blogging about it, and talking about it on social media. Reviews and shares really help authors keep writing, and we appreciate them so much! The power is in your hands.

Thank you!

Avon Gale & Roan Parrish

Want to get exclusive content and news of future book releases? Sign up for Roan's NEWSLETTER here (bit.ly/1OwuJxu), and Avon's NEWSLETTER here (eepurl.com/bGLSrD)!

ACKNOWLEDGMENTS

We'd like to thank our early readers for offering such helpful feedback on this manuscript, and for your enthusiasm.

Huge thank you to Julia for being a fantastic editor, and for pointing out that using the word "asparagus" in a description of appetizers was not sufficient indication that it was summer, despite Roan's insistence that it was clear because only seasonal vegetables would appear on the menu.

Thanks to the road from New Orleans to Philadelphia, where this project unfolded, with a cat on the middle seat and the weather trying to kill us all. Here's to epic road trips, epically good ideas, and epically bad hardboiled eggs.

Thank you to our wonderful agent, Courtney Miller-Callihan, for supporting all of our endeavors.

And thanks to our readers who were so excited for this story—we hope you enjoy reading it as much as we enjoyed writing it.

ABOUT AVON GALE

Avon Gale was once the mayor on Foursquare of Jazzercise and Lollicup, which should tell you all you need to know about her as a person. She likes road trips, rock concerts, drinking Kentucky bourbon and yelling at hockey. She's a displaced southerner living in a liberal midwestern college town, and she never gets tired of people and their stories—either real or the ones she makes up in her head.

Avon is represented by Courtney Miller-Callihan at Handspun Literary Agency.

Twitter: @avongalewrites
Facebook: facebook.com/avongalewrites
Newsletter: http://eepurl.com/bGLSrD
Instagram: instagram.com/avongale
Website: www.avongalewrites.com

ALSO BY AVON GALE

Let the Wrong Light In
Whiskey Business
Conversation Hearts

The Scoring Chances Series:
Breakaway
Save of the Game
Power Play
Empty Net
Coach's Challenge

ABOUT ROAN PARRISH

Roan Parrish lives in Philadelphia where she is gradually attempting to write love stories in every genre.

When not writing, she can usually be found cutting her friends' hair, meandering through whatever city she's in while listening to torch songs and melodic death metal, or cooking overly elaborate meals. She loves bonfires, winter beaches, minor chord harmonies, and self-tattooing. One time she may or may not have baked a six-layer chocolate cake and then thrown it out the window in a fit of pique.

She is represented by Courtney Miller-Callihan of Handspun Literary Agency.

Newsletter: http://bit.ly/1OwuJxu
Website: www.roanparrish.com
Twitter: http://bit.ly/1QmUcfp
Facebook: http://on.fb.me/1S4vb8G
Instagram: http://bit.ly/1P5AnIH

ALSO BY ROAN PARRISH

The Middle of Somewhere Series:
In the Middle of Somewhere
Out of Nowhere
Where We Left Off

The Small Change Series:
Small Change

Made in the USA
Middletown, DE
12 February 2021